'Twas the Knife Before Christmas

Also available by Jacqueline Frost

Christmas Tree Farm Mysteries

Twelve Slays of Christmas

Kitty Couture Mysteries (writing as Julie Chase)

Cat Got Your Secrets

Cat Got Your Cash

Cat Got Your Diamonds

'Twas the Knife Before Christmas

A CHRISTMAS TREE FARM MYSTERY

Jacqueline Frost

CROOKED LANE

NEW YORK

Copyright © 2018 by The Quick Brown Fox & Company LLC

Published in the United States by Crooked Lane Books, an imprint of The Quick Brown Fox & Company LLC.

Crooked Lane Books and its logo are trademarks of The Quick Brown Fox & Company LLC.

Library of Congress Catalog-in-Publication data available upon request.

ISBN (hardcover): 978-1-68331-803-3
ISBN (ePub): 978-1-68331-804-0
ISBN (ePDF): 978-1-68331-805-7

Cover illustration by Richard Grote
Cover design by Melanie Sun
Book design by Jennifer Canzone

Printed in the United States.

www.crookedlanebooks.com

Crooked Lane Books
34 West 27th St., 10th Floor
New York, NY 10001

First Edition: November 2018

10 9 8 7 6 5 4 3 2 1

To Noah, Andrew and Lily,
my life's greatest gifts

Chapter One

"Less than two weeks until Christmas—can you believe it?" I asked my friends Cookie and Caroline before sinking my teeth into another bite of creamy vanilla cupcake therapy. Their new cupcake shop had fast become my favorite place to unwind after a long day of work at Reindeer Games, my family's Christmas tree farm, and tonight was no exception.

"I can believe it," Cookie said, her blue eyes twinkling behind the counter. "Our cupcakes are going like hotcakes. I think it's because our product makes everyone happy. You can't eat a cupcake and be mad about it."

I peeled back the edge of the blue and white striped liner, then sucked a spot of icing off my thumb. "That's so true."

"In my day, egg creams were all the rage," Cookie said, "but cupcakes are even better."

Cookie was somewhere between sixty-five and eighty, depending on the story she was telling and to whom, and she'd been in my life for as long as I could remember. She'd managed the Holiday Mouse craft shop at Reindeer Games for years before going into business with Caroline, and she'd taught me to love art the way she loved life: voraciously and with spirit. Her real name was Delores Cutter, but her late husband, Theodore, had given her the nickname Cookie because she loved to bake. I just loved the fact that her name was Cookie Cutter.

Her new business partner, and my best friend, Caroline West, shot us a look. Caroline and I had gone to school together as children, but we'd never had much in common then. She'd been raised under a microscope, with a hefty list of rules, while I'd spent my adolescence among the trees, usually with a book. It wasn't until my return to Mistletoe last Christmas that we'd really hit it off, and twelve months later I couldn't imagine my life without her. Caroline had been unusually quiet since I'd arrived. In fact, she'd spent the last fifteen minutes silently unwrapping candy canes and stuffing them into a freezer bag while I polished off a pile of mini cupcakes.

"How about you, Caroline?" I asked brightly. "Are you enjoying the entrepreneurial life as much as your partner?"

Cookie and Caroline had made the decision to go into business together last Christmas, and Caroline's Cupcakes was the blessed confectionary child of their union. The shop had only been open four weeks, but the place was already a town favorite, and even at five bucks a pop, their daily inventory often vanished well before closing time.

"Oh yes," she said, dropping the full bag of candy canes onto her counter and raising a marble rolling pin overhead. "I love making cupcakes. What I don't care for is being forced to attend fancy benefit dinners with obnoxious dates just because my dad's the mayor." She brought the rolling pin down in a sharp arch, connecting solidly with the bag of candy.

Whack!

Cookie flinched.

My jaw slipped open.

Caroline tucked a swath of platinum waves behind one ear, wiped her hand on her apron, and raised the rolling pin again. "It's my job to support my dad, though. I am his only child, after all, so I'd never complain. Even if I've had enough mandatory party attendance and forced merriment to last ten lifetimes, it's important to be a team player." Her sweet voice was at frightening odds with the beating she was giving the poor candy.

"Caroline?" I asked.

She gave the bag another heavy hit, then several more in double time, before stopping to drag a forearm over her perfectly manicured brow.

"What are you doing?" I asked, fearfully eying the candy carnage.

"Making peppermint sprinkles for my holiday icing."

"Don't you normally use a food processor for that?"

"Yep." She smiled sweetly, repositioning the bag.

"Is everything okay?"

Caroline had told me once that her mother didn't think anger was an appropriate emotion for a young lady. I was no psychologist, but it seemed to me that Caroline might need to talk about something.

She nailed the bag again.

I glanced at the empty holder on the counter, where she normally displayed the fancy marble pin. "Aren't you afraid of breaking it?" The pin had been engraved with her initials and made custom by an Italian artisan she'd met in college. She'd

3

had a matching set of knives created last year when she'd taken the leap to quit her job and open Caroline's Cupcakes. I couldn't imagine owning custom marble anything, but Caroline had amazing taste.

"No," she said. "It won't break."

Cookie played with the screen on their new smart refrigerator, and the music to "White Christmas" lifted from the little speakers, followed closely by Frank Sinatra's iconic voice. "I love this refrigerator," Cookie said. "It can do anything. Your mom should get one for the Hearth."

Caroline shook her bag of decimated candy canes and looked my way. "How's the kitchen remodel going?"

I stifled a groan. "Not great." The Hearth was our tree farm's café, and Mom's second home this time of year. She spent most of her waking hours from Halloween until New Year's Day baking coveted treats and serving up heaping helpings of hospitality. She'd been downright giddy about updating the kitchen to make her efforts more efficient, but in reality the remodel had been a total nightmare, and it was over schedule by more than five weeks so far. It was a topic I'd heard enough about today. And most days. So I changed the subject. "Is it possible all this candy abuse is really about the fight you had with your date last night?" I wiped my cupcake crumbs into a tidy pile, smashing them together with my fingertip so I could eat them.

Caroline turned back to the helpless bag and beat it again, her fair skin pinking from the effort. "Has everyone heard about that?"

I suddenly wished I hadn't worn my red and white striped sweater. I pulled my chin back and tried to look less like a candy cane. "Not everyone," I said, and it was true. Anyone who hadn't been present for the argument she'd had with her date or who hadn't watched this morning's news had surely missed it.

She rested the pin on her shoulder like a baseball bat. Her vintage-red lips pursed in determination.

I shot Cookie a pleading look, but she was already moving away.

"Ugh!" Caroline dropped the rolling pin back into its holder. She straightened her cashmere shift dress and untied the apron at her back. "My dad made me go to that benefit dinner with Derek," she said. "I told him that Derek was notoriously smug, pompous, and handsy. Dad told me I was overreacting and that it was just dinner. What really mattered was Derek's father, Judge Waggoner, one of only two judges in Mistletoe, whose favor will carry a lot of weight for my dad's reelection campaign next year. Derek got handsy. I opened my mouth and, lucky me, the whole thing was recorded for the world to see. I've probably ruined Dad's reelection campaign."

"I'm sorry," I said. "I'm sure it's not as bad as you think. Things rarely are."

Cookie inched back in our direction. "Shame the cameraman didn't catch Derek being handsy," she said. "That would've fixed it." She climbed onto the fancy high-backed stool beside mine and let her short legs dangle. "I saw that clip of you telling him off on the news."

I gave Cookie my best cut-it-out look, then smiled at Caroline. "The clip really wasn't that bad."

"No," Cookie agreed, "it was fantastic. I especially loved the part where you said, 'Paw at me like that again and you're going to regret it.'" Cookie giggled. "Theodore was hoping you'd pour a drink in Derek's lap or throw one in his face like they do on television, but I told him that stuff is always staged."

Theodore was a black and gray pygmy goat that Cookie had named after her most recent dead husband and treated like family. She said the resemblance between her goat and her husband had been uncanny, specifically the way they both wore a nice salt and pepper beard.

Caroline hung her head.

"He wasn't judging," Cookie promised. "He's not that kind of goat."

* * *

Caroline stared at the massive whitewashed grandfather clock in the corner of their adorable shop. "We're late." She turned on her high-heeled leather boots and went to hit the light switch. "Let's just go," she said. "I don't want to talk about my dad or Derek anymore, and I don't want to miss the tree lighting ceremony. Plus, I think I could use some fresh air." She threaded thin arms into a pearl-white pea coat and settled a black beret on her head. "Is Sheriff Gray meeting us, Holly?"

I froze momentarily, then took my time tying the belt on my shapeless but warm, puffy coat. Sheriff Evan Gray had saved my life last year when a psychopath had tried to kill me. Then he'd kissed me in front of half the town on Christmas morning. It was all very grand and romantic, but the relationship had gone downhill from there—or if not downhill, then at least out to pasture.

"I think," I said finally. Honestly, I had no idea what Evan was doing tonight. His last text had been cryptic at best. In other words, his usual. "It's just us girls tonight."

Cookie perked at the sound of that. "Oh, I love girls' nights! I don't get nearly enough of them anymore." She packed a jar of hot cocoa mix and a can of whipped cream into her giant quilted handbag. "I'll just take these home for later. I promised Theodore a nightcap, and I don't want to share my special tea."

Probably wise. Cookie's special tea was ten percent Earl Grey and ninety percent schnapps.

"Watching Theodore lick the whipped cream off his nose is a hoot," she went on. "It's what gave me the idea to make the calendars."

"What calendars?" I asked.

Cookie pulled the purse higher on her shoulder and gave a toothy smile. "Twelve Months of Theodore." She swung her arm in a wide arch overhead, as if revealing the grandest idea of all. "What do you think?"

"Cute," I said, though I wasn't sure how she could make one goat interesting for twelve months.

"I saw a woman admiring one of those firemen calendars last month, and the idea just came to me."

Caroline led the way outside with a smile.

The sun had set despite the fact that it was barely dinnertime. A full array of stars twinkled in the cloudless night sky. Around us, downtown Mistletoe bustled with the excitement of another Christmas season underway. Strings of lights lined every rooftop, and pine green wrapped every lamppost. The benches were painted bright Santa red, and crowds had formed along the sidewalks around the square.

Caroline held the door until we passed, then flipped the window sign from "Open" to "Closed," and locked up behind us. "How's the jewelry business going?" she asked.

I puffed a little with pride. My hobby of melting old glass bottles into tiny replica holiday items and sweets, then turning those creations into custom jewelry had grown into a solid second income in the year since I'd come home. "I'm overrun with orders, and I love it." I'd come home last Christmas to recover from a broken heart and help my folks through the busy season, not knowing what I'd do afterward. As it turned out, I'd never been happier, so when they'd invited me to stay for as long as I liked, I'd taken them up on it. Now, I lived in the guesthouse, helped Mom at the Hearth, and made jewelry on the side. Overall, I was having a hard time understanding why I'd ever left.

She smiled proudly in my direction. "Do you need any help catching up? I'm not very crafty, but I can stuff and address envelopes like a champ. Maybe even swing by and pick up the completed orders for you and drop them off at the post office."

"I accept," I said, thankful for the offer. I had plenty of supplies and fun ideas to share. What I didn't have enough of lately was time.

"I'll help too," Cookie said. "It'll be fun."

The big tree ahead of us was surrounded with people, and a red velvet sheet covered a giant glass bowl at its side.

"Oh jeez," Cookie grumbled as we slowed near the back of the thickening crowd. "I'll never be able to see what's going on." She lifted onto her toes, then thumped back to earth. Cookie was reaching for five two on a good day, and tonight she had on flats. "Rip-off," she muttered. "I knew I should've come out here

8

and marked my territory after breakfast. I could've gotten us seats right in front of that big fish tank."

I snorted. "It's supposed to be a candy dish."

The bulbous glass structure had been positioned on the marble basin where a historic fountain spouted water all spring and summer long and then supported a stage and various town centerpieces from October to May. "According to the local historical society, 'Guess How Many Mints' is a fun new twist on an old-fashioned game," I explained.

"What?" Caroline asked.

I made a crazy face. "The bowl is full of candy under that sheet."

"That's dumb," she said. "It was probably my dad's idea."

Cookie pulled a knit cap from the pocket of her bright red coat and tugged it over a cloud of white hair. "I wish they hadn't covered the whole thing with that big blanket. I could start counting now and get a head start."

The cover was enormous, embroidered with golden thread, and the words "Mistletoe, Maine, Home of Holiday Cheer" stretched across the middle. Only the bottom few inches of the dish remained visible. Just enough to tease the crowd.

The crowd quieted as a man I recognized as Caleb France, the historical society president, took the stage. "Hello!" he said. "Welcome to the annual tree lighting! We have lots of fun in store for you tonight. Our preschool choir will sing "Up on the Housetop." Our high school band will join them for a medley of holiday favorites, and if we're all very good, there might even be a visit from the big guy in red!"

The crowd cheered. I smirked. From my vantage there were

at least four men in the crowd dressed as Santa, and experience told me a dozen more were somewhere in town. Mistletoe was a Santa impersonator's paradise this time of year. Many were on staff at local stores or hired to work the various December events, but others just came dressed up for fun.

"But first," he said, "let's light this tree!" Caleb grabbed two giant and obviously fake electrical cords from the stage at his feet and lifted the cartoon-sized prong and outlet in front of him. "Ten!" he began.

"Nine," the crowd continued.

Cookie bounced at my side, desperate for some added height.

I inhaled the blessed scents of hot buttered popcorn and candied pecans from a passing street vendor. "Three," I joined in, unable to fight the spirit. "Two. One!"

The massive tree burst into light, and the crowd erupted in wild applause.

I blinked against the sudden flare, and spots danced through my vision. As my eyes came back into focus, a strange smear of red appeared on the bottom of the massive candy dish, illuminated by the twinkle lights on the neighboring thirty-foot spruce.

I leaned forward, curious. What was the smear?

Were my eyes playing tricks on me? Was it an errant paint smudge from the newly erected stage?

I squinted harder, willing my eyes to make sense of the odd stain. "Do you see that?" I asked no one in particular. I pushed forward without waiting for an answer, forcing my way through the fringe of the crowd, angling closer to the giant dish and its great crimson cover.

Caleb yammered into the microphone as he made his way

across the platform from the tree to the giant bowl, utterly oblivious to the spot I couldn't stop staring at. "Everyone ready?" he asked.

The crowd cheered again.

With one whip of his wrist, the cover was gone, and a truckload of red and white swirled peppermints was revealed.

Along with a very dead Derek Waggoner, Caroline's handsy date, partially buried inside.

Chapter Two

The continuous ebb and flow of ambulance lights added to the creepy ambience as Mistletoe's coroner climbed a ladder and assessed Derek's body.

The crowd had been pushed back, exiled behind a line of flimsy crime scene tape. A few dedicated lookie-lous clung to the insides of shop windows, taking cell phone photos and noshing on treats from lingering street vendors, but most folks had simply dispersed when the sheriff and emergency personnel arrived.

I couldn't bring myself to leave, and thankfully, the sheriff hadn't forced me. Instead, he'd ushered Cookie, Caroline, and me around the back of the stage and allowed us to stay as long as we didn't get in anyone's way. He said he wanted to talk to us when things settled, but I suspected Caroline was the one he was most interested in.

The coroner removed Derek's body with a little help from two men in head-to-toe white coveralls and miner's hats. Then he went to talk with Evan.

His comrades began the daunting process of extracting and examining the candy for evidence.

It was officially the strangest thing I'd seen in Mistletoe, and in a town that celebrated Christmas on a mass scale twelve months a year, *that* was saying something. "Well?" I asked Evan as the coroner moved on to speak with other officials. "What happened to Derek Waggoner? How'd he get in there?"

Evan lifted his gaze, looking past me to Caroline. "I'd like to talk to you about your date with Mr. Waggoner last night."

I slung a protective arm around Caroline's shaking shoulders. "Why?"

"She might have been the last person to see him alive," Evan said.

"Obviously not." I narrowed my eyes. Surely, he wasn't insinuating that Caroline had killed Derek, then dragged his big body up a ladder, and tossed him into the candy dish. Derek was easily six foot two and two hundred pounds. He probably had shoes that weighed more than Caroline.

"Where did you go after the benefit dinner last night?" he asked.

"To my shop," she said. "I spent an hour eating whipped cream and watching *Cupcake Wars*, and then I fell asleep at the counter. Why?"

Evan adjusted his ball cap over his thick dark hair and keen green eyes, the Sheriff's Department logo centered above the bill. "I'm just trying to get an idea of how Mr. Waggoner's night went after that clip that played on the news and before this." He motioned to the coroner's van. "Did he drive you home after dinner?"

"No. He walked out after I made that scene."

Evan nodded. "Why don't you come with me to the station," he suggested. "I can take your official statement there."

I raised a palm, telling him to halt. "Whoa. A trip downtown with you right now will make her look guilty. That's not fair."

Evan fixed me with an impatient stare.

"Caroline!" An unfamiliar voice cut through the evening's white noise, effectively interrupting my conversation with the sheriff.

Cookie grunted. "It's just Scooter," she said. "Should've known he wouldn't be far. He rarely is."

"Who's Scooter?" Evan and I asked in near unison.

"He's that schmoopy guy who's always hanging around the shop," Cookie said. "At first I thought he had a sugar addiction, but then I noticed he only comes in when Caroline is at the counter, and he stays until she leaves."

"He's a nice guy, but I don't want to talk to him right now," Caroline said.

"Nice guy?" Cookie raised her brows. "I think you're mispronouncing *stalker*."

Evan stood straighter. "Stalker?"

Gooseflesh rose on my arms—nothing freaked me out more than the idea of being followed. I shivered.

Caroline rolled her eyes. "He just needs a friend. He's new in town and doesn't know anyone."

I scanned the crowd in search of Caroline's schmoopy stalker. A gangly man in a puffy orange ski coat and Harry Potter glasses waved from the other side of Evan's crime scene tape. "Caroline," he called. "It's me, Scooter."

She groaned, then forced a smile and looked his way. "Hello."

"Can I bring you anything?" he asked, one gloved hand curved beside his mouth for maximum sound projection. "A blanket? Coffee? I've got a space heater in my garage I can bring out here."

"No, thank you," Caroline said. "I'm fine. I'll talk to you tomorrow."

He smiled. Clearly thrilled with her response and unaffected by the body recently removed from a giant candy dish.

Evan scrutinized Scooter. "What's his last name?"

Caroline shrugged. "I've never asked, but I think he could use a friend." A hopeful look crossed her troubled face. "Maybe you could say hello," she suggested to Evan.

"I definitely will," he promised. Though his expression said he wouldn't be looking for a new friend when he did.

A fresh gust of wind whipped hair into my eyes, and I ignored the whiff of gingerbread and cologne that lifted from him in the breeze. "How've you been?" I asked him.

"Good."

"I stopped by to see you last weekend. Missed you again," I said. "It seems like every time you have a day or two off, you're gone." It had been his pattern all year to vanish at every turn. At first, he'd dodged my attempts to get answers about what he was up to. Then he'd just started to dodge *me*. "Maybe you can pencil me into your schedule before Christmas."

"That sounds nice," he said, and he looked as if he meant it.

Evan popped the collar on his jacket, creating a tiny barrier against the wind, then puffed air into his palms and rubbed them together.

"You want a little something to take the chill off?" Cookie asked, pushing her thermos in our direction. "I bought my special tea."

Evan eyeballed the offering. "No, thank you. The last time I had your tea, I needed a designated driver."

Cookie grinned. "You even let me use the lights and siren."

He lifted troubled eyes to mine. "I still don't know how she reached the pedals."

I covered my mouth to stifle a laugh, and turned my attention back to the men at the bowl. Evan and Cookie were hilarious, but this wasn't a time for humor. Handsy or not, Derek Waggoner had lost his life unfairly, and I hated knowing it had happened in our sweet town.

"What are they doing now?" Cookie asked, pouring herself a cup of tea.

"Evidence collection," Evan said. "They'll take the candy to the lab and look for clues about how Derek wound up in there."

I grimaced, trying not to imagine what they might find.

"This is last year all over again," Cookie said.

I pulled my eyes open and fought the nausea swirling in my tummy. "I don't think so," I said, shaking my head no. Sure, someone had been killed last year around this time, but that had happened on my family's property, and afterward the murderer had set his sights on me. "This isn't like that," I insisted. "This is very different." I looked to Evan for reassurance.

He was watching Caroline.

Her ruby lips quivered. "I feel so awful," she whispered.

"Why?" Evan and I spoke in unison again. He gave me a pointed look.

Caroline pressed a wadded-up tissue to her red nose. "The last thing I said to Derek Waggoner was mean. *I'm mean.*"

Cookie slipped a narrow arm around Caroline's back and

tugged her close. "No, honey. He was out of line at the time, and you told him so. There was nothing wrong with that."

Evan shifted his weight, still scrutinizing my best friend. "And you said that was the last time you saw him?"

"Holly!" A familiar voice called my name, and I spun at the sound, a smile immediately budding on my lips.

Ray Griggs, a local reporter and dear friend of mine ducked under the crime scene tape and headed my way. At five foot eight, I was no shorty, but Ray had at least half a foot on me. He was tall and lean, boyishly handsome, and charming in a goofy way that I dearly appreciated. Ray had been a freshman at Mistletoe High School when I was a senior, and he claimed we'd worked on the yearbook staff together, but I had no memory of him. At eighteen, I had been far too mature to notice a freshman. Truthfully, I'd noticed very few men whose names weren't Renoir, Dali, or Van Gogh.

I met Ray with a hug, then turned back to watch Evan chatting with Caroline from a few paces away. "Can you believe this?"

Ray pushed his hands into his coat pockets. "Not at all."

"You heard anything?" I asked, flipping his press badge lanyard with my fingertips. "I know how you hate to miss a story." Ray had been hired at the paper as a photographer, but his heart was in journalism, specifically investigative journalism, and he'd gotten his first front-page headline last Christmas morning. He'd been balancing the photography assignments with his thirst for newsworthy stories ever since.

Ray's eyes sparkled. "Hey, I was only here to cover a tree lighting and the big candy bowl reveal. No one could have seen this coming."

Someone could have, I thought. I took a careful look through the remaining nearby faces. Was one of them the killer?

Ray widened his stance and crossed his arms. "Since I'm here, I figured I'd talk to folks. Find out what they'd heard or seen before the big discovery. I need to prove myself to those senior reporters. They only see me as the guy who takes pictures, but the paper will run this mess as front-page news for days, and I want one of those big bylines like last year."

I didn't like all these references to last year.

"How's Caroline doing?" he asked, watching Evan and Caroline closely. "What's going on with those two? Is the sheriff giving her the business over this?"

"The business?" I smiled.

Evan's face jerked in our direction. "I'm her advocate," he said.

"And there's clearly nothing wrong with your hearing," Ray muttered.

"Don't forget it," Evan said, turning back to Caroline.

I stilled as the men dressed like human marshmallows headed our way with the coroner. One of the men in white carried the equivalent of a giant freezer bag in his hand.

Evan jumped into action, quickly meeting them halfway.

Ray and I followed close on his heels.

"The victim was stabbed," the coroner told him. "Estimated time of death is between midnight and one AM."

The man with the freezer bag offered it to Evan. "We found this in the mints. Looks like blood on the blade and the marble handle. We'll send it to the lab for confirmation and try to match the sample to the victim. We'll run the item for prints while it's there."

Evan lifted the bag into the cone of streetlight, and Caroline made a deep strangling sound behind us. I glanced over one shoulder to find her doubled over and white as a ghost.

The high-end butcher's knife in the evidence bag had a marble handle with two letters etched into the stone: "CW."

Caroline West's butcher knife.

Chapter Three

I woke the next morning to the loving nips of my rescue cat, Cindy Lou Who, who stared into my bleary eyes as I worked to peel them open. Some people might have accused her of biting my nose and fingers, but I recognized the sweet sting for what it was: the gentle encouragement I needed to refill her food and water bowls, which she'd probably overturned in the kitchen. "Morning, Cindy," I croaked.

She leapt onto the floor and strode away.

I pulled a soft, Sherpa-lined robe over flannel pajamas, stuffed my toasty feet into fuzzy slippers, and swiped my phone off the nightstand before padding quietly down the guesthouse hallway, doing my best not to wake Caroline. She'd asked to sleep over, and I hadn't blamed her for not wanting to spend last night alone. We'd picked up some of her things before returning to Reindeer Games and eating our way through three bowls of kettle corn tossed with candied pecans.

The tree farm guesthouse became my home last year when I moved back to Mistletoe following a wrecked engagement. My cheating ex-fiancé, Ben, had dumped me for his yoga instructor a few days before our would-have-been Christmas Eve wedding. Then, in a good show of karma, the yogi dropped him a few weeks later.

I tucked my phone back into my robe pocket and stopped short when Caroline came into view. She stood at the kitchen counter, refilling a mug with coffee. "I hope I didn't wake you," she said as I shuffled into the room.

"Not at all." The delectable scents of blueberries and cream filtered into my fatigued mind, and my tummy growled. "Are you baking?"

"Yeah." The oven timer dinged, and Caroline donned Rudolph-themed mitts to retrieve two big trays of mini muffins from inside. "I helped myself to your pantry. I hope that's okay."

I grabbed a fork and went after one of the little chunks of heaven. "That is always okay. Anytime you want to raid my cupboards and bake, please do." I pressed my hands briefly into prayer pose before shoving a steaming hot bit of muffin between my lips. "Mmm. I usually have to walk all the way to the Hearth for a hot breakfast."

Caroline removed the muffins from the tins with the help of a little spoon, then nestled them in a basket lined with a holiday-print cloth.

I squinted at her perfectly arranged curls and expertly applied makeup. "Did you sleep?"

"A little." She poured a second mug of coffee and extended it in my direction. "I was restless until about four thirty; then I drifted off for a while, but it didn't last." She tipped her head toward the window over the sink in my small galley kitchen. "I heard the construction crew arrive before dawn to begin work on the inn."

Slowly, I registered the faint sounds of morning construction. A hammer. A drill. A compressor motoring on. The muffled voices of workmen carried across the distance outside. "Sorry about that. I guess I've grown immune." I set my fork aside to fill Cindy's dishes, and returned them to the floor.

It had been my dad's lifelong dream to open an inn on the Reindeer Games property, and that was finally coming to fruition. When the place was finished, I would be the innkeeper. I wasn't sure I was up for the job, having never been an innkeeper before, but my parents seemed to think I was the perfect choice, and they were rarely wrong when it came to their farm or me.

"The crew Dad hired to build the inn is really making good time. They had the whole thing under roof in a month. Now they work every day, from dawn to dusk, on the interior and big-picture landscape details. Weather permitting."

Caroline peered wistfully through the window. "Growing up here must've been amazing."

Basically, but I didn't want to brag. Caroline had grown up in town under the heat of a political spotlight, where everyone was watching and her every move mattered. My time in the spotlight had been limited to the holiday season, when I'd helped serve cookies and cocoa at the Hearth and judged our annual Reindeer Games. I'd spent the rest of my formative years reading books under trees and grooming horses. I'd never dreamed I'd still be doing the same holiday things at twenty-seven, but I was learning to let go of my plans and start enjoying life's surprises.

"The inn is beautiful," she said, smiling at the window, admiring the new structure across the field.

I stole another muffin. "The construction noise was an adjustment, but Christopher says they'll be done by Christmas."

"Christopher?" she asked, tucking a second layer of fabric over the steaming muffins in her basket.

"The contractor. He's a really nice guy."

Caroline's shiny red lips quirked to one side. "Is he cute?"

"For someone more than twice our age? Definitely."

She looked a little disappointed. "Christmas is in eleven days. Do you really think they'll be done by then?"

"I think they have to be. His crew has another job up north immediately after this one."

It wouldn't have mattered to us if the inn wasn't finished until spring. Dad was just glad his dream was finally becoming a reality. He was getting an inn, and Mom was finally getting a much-needed kitchen update at the Hearth. They were about as happy as two kids on—well . . . on a Christmas tree farm.

I stirred a little peppermint creamer into my coffee and blew over the tendrils of sweetened steam. "Sorry we have to stand at the counter," I said. The kitchen table was working double-time as my jewelry-making station and office space. "I really need to get those orders filled and out the door."

"Maybe we can work on it tonight," she said. "I'll run the finished products to the post office in the morning. One less thing you'll have to worry about."

I dropped my head back. "I forgot to check my online store's email last night. There are probably more orders." I righted my head and frowned. "I need to set an alarm to remind me to check every day. Between helping Mom at the Hearth and answering all the contractor questions for the inn, I feel like I already have two full-time jobs." I sighed. "It feels a little like I'm running in circles."

"I have an idea." Caroline shoved her palm in my direction, curling and stretching her fingers in the universal signal for "gimme." "Let me see your phone."

I handed it over. "What are you doing?"

She swiped the screen to life and tapped it a few times. "I'm setting up a notification. Anytime you get an order or message from your online store, the phone will tell you. The same way it does when you get a text message." She flipped through a few more screens, then paused. "Oh. My. You have a lot of orders waiting here already. When was the last time you checked?"

I had to think about that. Life on a Christmas tree farm in December was a little busy. "Last week?"

She returned the device to my hand. "We've got a ton of work to do tonight."

The phone applauded, and I laughed. "What was that?"

"You just got another order," she said. "New orders are exciting, so it feels appropriate that you should be applauded each time a new one comes in."

I smiled. "Thanks."

"Don't mention it. You have a ton of things to do. This might make at least one of them a little easier."

My phone dinged now with an incoming text message. "Speaking of things I have to do," I said. "Christopher is starting early with questions." I turned the screen to face Caroline. "So, what do you think?" Christopher was constantly asking for interior design decisions, which I was nearly incapable of making. I

24

knew nothing about the historic Victorian style that my parents had chosen, but they'd delegated me to handle the details since they were slammed between Thanksgiving and Christmas. Had they built a five-thousand-square-foot log cabin, I'd be their girl.

I was ashamed to admit I'd resorted to Eeny, meeny, miny, moe over cabinet pulls for the laundry room.

The current dilemma seemed to be bathroom fixtures. "Should he install this faucet in the main floor half bath," I asked, "or this one?" I flipped between two nearly identical photos while she looked. "I wish Dad hadn't asked me to do this," I said. "I know how important the inn is to him. What if I screw it up?"

Caroline rolled her eyes. "Your dad asked you because he trusts you, and you're about to become their very first innkeeper. This place will be your home. It's kind of exciting, if you think about it."

"I'd be more excited if all these choices weren't so important. It's not like choosing the wrong rug or porch chairs. I can't just switch out the faucets if I change my mind."

Caroline gave an exhausted sigh. "Actually, you can, but I know what you're saying. If I were you, I'd tell the contractor I like the oil-rubbed bronze fixture and the finish, but I'd really like to see the porcelain index buttons included as well. The second photo has the index buttons, but the finish is all wrong, and the look is too colonial. Maybe ask if he can find something like the first photo that also has the porcelain inserts."

I gave her a long blink, then typed everything she said into a response to Christopher. "Thank you." I hit "Send" with a smile. "There. All done. So, what's on the agenda for you today?"

"Well," she said, "I'm thinking of hiding out here until the new year. How about you?"

"I've got to go check on Mom at the Hearth. The kitchen update was supposed to be finished more than a month ago, but everything's still a mess. She's fit to kill her contractor every morning when I get there. What do you say?" I asked. "Want to come save a man's life with me? Help hide a body if we're too late?"

Caroline grimaced.

"Oh, Care," I said, prying the size-nine boot from my mouth. "I am so sorry. I wasn't thinking." The horror of last night's discovery came rushing back to me. "I'm sure Evan has made some progress," I said. "He's great at his job, and he barely sleeps. He was probably up all night chasing leads and pulling threads." Evan had been a homicide detective in Boston before moving to Mistletoe a year and a half ago in search of a break from the darker sides of fighting crime in a big city. Whatever had happened to him in Boston had been enough to inspire a total life change, but that was all he would say on the matter. "We should give him a call after breakfast," I suggested.

Caroline set her mug in the sink and headed for the guest room. "Give me two minutes, and I'll go with you to see your mom. Maybe I can light a fire under the kitchen contractor."

Two minutes? I needed thirty. "I'm going to jump in the shower. I'll meet you back here afterward." I gulped the rest of my coffee and rushed through my morning routine.

Forty-five minutes later, Caroline and I were calf-deep in new fallen snow, taking the basket of blueberry muffins to Mom at the Hearth.

"Miss White!" Christopher and a trio of his men strode in

our direction. "Hello! Good morning," he said with trademark enthusiasm. He'd tucked a red plaid shirt into high-riding black trousers. The pant cuffs disappeared into neatly tied leather boots. His barn coat hung open, and his gray hair fluttered in the wind.

Behind them, the door to the inn stood open while workers streamed in and out with loads of wide wooden planks balanced over their shoulders.

Caroline and I stopped to wait while Christopher and his men caught up.

I lifted a mitten in greeting. "Did you get my message earlier about the faucets?" I asked. If not, the timing was perfect because Caroline could explain what I'd meant.

"Oh yes. Thank you," he said. "I just wanted to give you a general update. Text messages are convenient and quick, but I feel that everything is a little better when people talk face-to-face, don't you?"

"Yes." I smiled. "I completely agree."

"Good." He folded his hands over the curve of his belly. "Thanks to that burst of better weather last week, the back patio has set nicely, and it looks wonderful A few inches of water when the temperature drops, and it will double as a skating rink, just like you asked. A clever idea." He stroked the point of his white beard. "Would you mind if I suggest something similar at other job sites? Giving you full creative credit, of course."

My cheeks heated at the compliment. Being an artist at heart, creative credit felt like something I'd like to have in writing, then framed. "Thank you."

"Of course." He tugged a black knit cap over his thinning

hair and zipped his coat before addressing Caroline with a rosy smile. "Miss West. It's nice to finally meet you."

"Thank you," she said. "You know who I am?"

He chuckled cheerfully. "Of course I do. You make the most delicious cupcakes on the East Coast. Believe me, I've tried them all." He patted his middle and winked. "My sweet tooth is practically legendary."

Caroline cocked a brow. "Really?"

"Cross my heart."

"Everything else is okay?" I asked, eager to get to the Hearth for my morning helping of crepes and cocoa.

"Oh yes." He smiled. "I just wanted to give you the update on the patio and let you know that I'm picking up the sample books for railings and spindles today. There are quite a few to choose from, so you'll want to take a look as soon as you can."

The man on his right shook my hand. A wisp of dark bangs lifted on the breeze. The rest of his head was covered in a red beanie. "I'm Will. This is Bill and Phil." Each man beside him nodded as his name was called. "We're the team handling your railings. If you don't see anything in the book that suits you, or if you see something that sparks inspiration but isn't quite right, let me know. We're happy to create custom pieces. Sky's the limit if you have a special request. *Do you* have any special requests?"

I looked to Caroline. "No?"

She shrugged, attention fixed on the trio of crewmen.

Matching dark hair fell across their brows, the rest neatly tucked into red beanies. They wore dark pants, like Christopher, and sleek green ski coats with the company logo on the breast.

Aside from Christopher, I was the tallest person present.

"While you're considering the options for your balconies and second-floor veranda, don't forget the rooftop widow's walk," Will said. "It's easy to forget the ones that are out of sight. It might help you to walk the space."

"Definitely," I said, having every intention of making my decisions for the veranda and widow's walk from the safety of solid ground.

Christopher's smile brightened. "Well, I think that's all we have for now. Is there anything else you ladies need?"

"Breakfast," I teased. "You're all welcome to join us. Everything Mom makes is delicious."

"No, no," he said. "We have lots to do, but the offer is appreciated."

Caroline gave a small smile and lifted her basket in his direction. "Then at least take my muffins. I made them this morning. They were warm until we walked outside."

Christopher took the basket with an appreciative grin. "We'd be crazy to pass up anything baked by Caroline West." He handed the basket to his crewmen, who quickly dug in. "Is there anything else I can do for you?" he asked.

"Not unless you can stop me from being arrested for murder," she said.

Christopher blanched.

"I'd really like that," she said. "I want to be out of this mess in time for Christmas."

"It's fine," I assured both him and Caroline. "Sheriff Gray will get to the bottom of this. Caroline is *not* being arrested."

"Very well," Christopher said, nodding and tipping his head in a gesture of goodbye. "Have a lovely day."

Caroline watched until they'd gone several yards, before turning back toward the Hearth. "He looks like Santa Claus," she said.

"I know."

"He has to finish the job by Christmas because he has another job to do up north."

"Yep."

"The clothes. The beard," she continued. "The crew of little men."

"They aren't little," I said. "They're all at least five five."

* * *

She gave me a disbelieving look. "I'm just saying. He asked us if there was anything he could do for us. I said I'd like to be out of this mess, and you might've missed a major opportunity."

"I don't believe in Santa Claus," I said.

Caroline guffawed. "How could you grow up on a Christmas tree farm, in a town that *lives* for Christmas, without believing?"

"Probably for all those reasons," I said.

She shook her head sadly.

I bit the insides of my cheeks and cast one last glance in the direction of the inn. It certainly would be nice if getting what I wanted was as simple as asking for it.

Christopher stood at the door, looking our way, and for the first time in years, for my sake and Caroline's, I wished I still believed in Santa.

Chapter Four

I floated into the Hearth on a cloud of anticipation. It was barely eight, and the place wouldn't open for another hour, but scents of warm butter and cocoa already filled the space, pulling me deeper inside.

"Hello, girls," Mom said from behind the counter. I had Mom's brown hair and eyes, but I was six inches taller and twenty-five pounds lighter. Her hair was wavy in all the right places while mine did nothing but reach constantly for the ground, much like the icicles hanging from my porch.

I closed the space between us and gave her a warm hug. "How's it going? Everything looks amazing and smells even better."

I never tired of our tree farm's small café. The Hearth was a trip to another dimension on any day, but dressed for Christmas, it was a wonderland. With its chocolate-bar tables on black-licorice legs and gumdrop chandeliers over candy cane–striped booths, the café's interior looked like the inside of a gingerbread house. Right down to the white eyelet lace lining the windows. For the next month or so, the look would be enhanced with drifts of cotton snow, interspersed with replica snowmen and topped with endless strands of twinkle lights.

The Hearth had been my childhood refuge, and not much had changed.

Mom wiped a paper towel over the glass display case in front of her. "I'd hoped to be further along on my morning baking by now because I've been here since six, but you know." She tipped her head toward the kitchen's swinging door behind her. A loud clatter erupted, and she shut her eyes. "My new oven still isn't hooked up, and my old one only holds so many trays at a time." She forced a tight smile and reopened her eyes. Her rosy cheeks were pink from frustration instead of the usual holiday spirit. "It's fine." She tossed the paper towel into the trash. "It gives me more time to mix all the batters one by one."

Caroline rounded the counter behind me and hugged her. "I can help you," she said. "I'm not opening my shop today. I'm hiding out, and if I can hide *and* bake, then my life is perfect."

A loud crash of metal on metal rattled the wall between the kitchen and us. Mom winced. I nearly swallowed my tongue. "What was that?" I squeaked.

"My bad," a man's voice called. "I'll clean it up."

"Contractor," Mom said as her left eye began to twitch. "Not only is he incapable of *fixing* anything, but he regularly *breaks* the things that were fine before he got here." She pressed a finger to her twitching eyelid. "I should've hired Christopher for this project too. I wish your father had found him before I found this guy."

"Fire him," Caroline suggested.

"Oh," Mom shook her head hard. "I couldn't. Not so close to Christmas."

Caroline considered that. "Do you want me to fire him?"

Mom laughed.

I agreed with Caroline. This guy was hurting, not helping. He'd made a promise to finish the remodel before our busy season began, but a month later he was still disrupting Mom's life and her business in big, negative ways.

Unfortunately, Mom and I also shared a soft personality. We were bleeding hearts, givers of fifteenth chances, and avid avoiders of conflict, at least when the problem only concerned ourselves. Basically, we'd fight black bears with our hands for someone else, then let the bear eat us if we thought he was hungry.

A small swirl of brown powder crept under the swinging door. I wiggled my foot in it, and it dispersed, only to be followed by another, bigger cloud. "Is that cocoa powder?"

Mom gasped. She dropped into a squat and inhaled. Her eyes widened, then narrowed to slits. "Son of a snickerdoodle!" She jerked to her feet and planted her palms against the swinging door. "What happened to my cocoa powder?"

Caroline went back around the counter and took a seat on a lollipop stool. "I'm going to help your mom bake today. This is perfect."

"I was going to make whoopie pies!" Mom hollered in the kitchen. She reappeared a few minutes later with busted plastic containers coated in brown powder. "I was going to make whoopie pies," she repeated.

Caroline patted Mom's hand. "It's no problem. We can start something else for now. We can only do a little at a time anyway, right?"

Hope lifted Mom's brow. "You're really going to stay and help bake?"

"I'd love to," she said. "And I don't mind making trips back and forth to Holly's stove if that helps us catch up faster."

No one looked at me. My culinary skills ended with cold cereal and hot tea, and everyone knew it. I grabbed the newspaper from behind the counter and shook it open.

"Wait!" Mom reached for the paper, but it was too late.

I flopped it out flat in front of me to see if there was anything new about Derek's death or his mysterious appearance in the candy bowl.

A photo of Caroline, red-faced and pointing a finger at Derek's nose, graced the front page. "'Socialite Threatens. Entrepreneur Dies,'" I read.

Caroline guffawed. "I am *not* a socialite."

Mom gave her a sad smile. "Oh, honey. You're so much more than any reporter could sum up in a silly headline."

"Did you read this?" I asked Mom.

She shifted her attention to the floor. "Yes."

Caroline reached for the paper, but Mom slapped a palm on it, rendering it motionless.

"The article is pretty hard on you," she told Caroline. "It sensationalizes the argument you had with Derek and portrays you in an unfavorable light. It asks some rather pointed questions about how Derek's unbecoming behavior might have affected your father's campaign for reelection. A lot of fishing and speculation, but if I were you, I'd skip reading it."

Caroline dropped her hands into her lap.

Mom took the paper and tossed it in the trash bin behind the counter. "I should have done that sooner."

I gave the trash can a long look. "Did the article say Caroline's engraved marble butcher knife was found in the candy with Derek?"

"Heavens, no." Mom's brow slowly puckered. "Why on earth would it?"

I mimed stabbing myself in the chest.

Mom's eyes rounded and she leaned toward us, voice low. "Derek was stabbed?"

I nodded. "Possibly with Caroline's knife. It was found in the candy."

Mom covered her mouth with both hands to collect herself, then quickly recomposed her sweet disposition. "I'm so sorry, sweetie. What can I do?"

Caroline lifted her palms, then dropped them back to the counter with a sigh. "Let me hide from my troubles and help you bake?"

"Done." Mom patted her hand across the counter.

"I wish I knew what really happened to Derek," I said. "Who took the knife from Caroline's Cupcakes? How'd they get it without anyone knowing? Why'd they take it?" To kill Derek? Or for another reason? And was Derek's murder a whim or was it planned out? Did someone want to frame Caroline, or was that an accident too? As usual, I had too many questions and not enough answers. And I was getting that sickly feeling in my stomach, just remembering the horrors that had followed the dead body we'd found last December on our Reindeer Games property.

"Who knows?" Caroline said. "Why would anyone steal anything? Or murder anyone?" She collapsed forward, resting her head on folded arms across the counter.

A few ideas came easily to mind. Greed, for example. Love was a popular motive for all sorts of things. To cover another crime, maybe. Self-defense. The list was actually pretty long, but I didn't want to be negative.

Caroline groaned. "My reputation is doomed. My shop will fail before it's had a chance to become something amazing. My parents will say they told me so. This is awful." She snapped upright, eyes wide. "Not that I'm blaming Derek or that my situation is worse than his. I just mean that I . . . I'm selfish and only care about what happens to me. Oh my goodness. I'm horrible."

"You can't think like that," I said. "You are far from horrible, and your shop will persevere. Dozens of people visit your shop every day. Any one of them could've taken your knife, or anything else they wanted, without being noticed."

Mom nodded. "Sad but true. The only thing locked down around here is the cash register."

"Do you have any idea where Derek might've gone after your dinner?" I asked.

"No. I don't know who his friends are. I don't know where he lived. Nothing like that. He talked about how wealthy and successful he was all the way to dinner." She pretended to gag. "He called himself an investor and said he funded new businesses that needed a boost getting off the ground. They paid him a chunk of their monthly profits in return for his initial backing. He said that now he got multiple checks every month from those investments and spent his time leering at women or looking in a mirror." Her face went tight. "Sorry. That was mean too."

I laughed softly. "It's okay. He was rotten to you. You don't have to be over that just because he's dead."

"He has a crazy ex-girlfriend," she said. "That's all I know about his personal life."

"Who's the ex-girlfriend?" I asked.

"I think her name is Samantha Moss. She was a few years ahead of us in school."

"Doesn't ring a bell," I said. Though it wasn't as if any upperclassmen had known me either, and I still couldn't recall Ray from his freshman year, when I was a senior, despite the fact he seemed to know plenty about me.

Caroline uncrossed her legs, hooking the heels of her boots on the rung of her stool. "Samantha moved back to Mistletoe a few years ago and opened the shop right beside Oh! Fudge. I don't know if she's dangerous, but she's definitely a few notes short of a carol, if you know what I mean."

"Oh!" Mom perked up. "She's a Winer."

"A whiner?" I laughed.

"Yeah." Caroline shot me a look. "That's the name of her monthly tasting club. She owns Wine Around."

"The wine shop?" I loved peeking into that store window. There was a big globe with a changing display of wines from different regions around the earth and culturally dressed dolls like the ones from It's a Small World at Disney World.

Caroline nodded.

Mom smiled. "Her wine club meets monthly for private tastings on new inventory. They do a really nice cheese and

37

appetizer spread from corresponding regions as well. I've heard it's marvelous. I've even thought of joining."

I needed to make a trip to the fudge shop beside Wine Around if I wanted to get Cookie's favorite fudge for Christmas. Maybe while I was in town, I could stop into Samantha Moss's shop and register Mom for the wine club. Knock two more loved ones off my gift list. Maybe get an up-close look at Derek's crazy ex-girlfriend. "Why don't I run into town for more cocoa powder?" I asked. "When I get back, you can make whoopie pies."

Mom straightened. "Really? That would be great. I was just thinking I didn't know when I'd have time to make that trip. The bakery supply shop closes before the Hearth."

"It's no problem," I promised.

First I'd pick up mom's cocoa. Then I'd pay a friendly visit to the wine shop. Register Mom as a Winer and ask Samantha about Derek. When that was done, I'd slip into Oh! Fudge for a pound of chocolate-covered cherry cordial fudge for Cookie, and—voila! Holly White would be getting things done. I imagined checking the items off a giant to-do list.

"Oh, hey!" Caroline hopped to her feet and produced a set of keys from her pocket. "While you're in town, will you stop at my shop and put a sign in the window letting folks know I'm taking a day or two off? I don't want people making extra trips back and forth to see if I've opened."

"Sure." I took her keys with a smile.

"Maybe bring any leftover cupcakes from the display back with you?" she suggested. "I can mix them in the food processor with some icing and make cake pops."

"Got it." I pointed at her and winked.

"Why do you look like you're up to something?" Mom asked.

"What?" I moved another step closer to the door.

Caroline looked thoughtful. "You should probably have the sign say 'I'll be closed the rest of the week,' but make it sound nice, as if I'm mourning and definitely not hiding. Or guilty," she said.

I saluted her. "Be back in awhile."

Mom narrowed her eyes.

She was right. I was acting weird. I wanted to get out of there and talk to Samantha. I didn't know why or what I'd say, but it seemed like a smart thing to do. Who would know a guy better than his ex? Caroline couldn't tell me where Derek lived or who he might've gone out with after the failed dinner date, but I had a feeling Samantha Moss would.

"Don't forget the blind sled challenge," Mom called. "I need you as a judge. Five o'clock sharp!"

I dipped into a low curtsy, and spun on my toes for the door.

My phone applauded.

Someone clapped along behind me. "A new order!" Caroline said. "Today's going to be a great day."

Maybe, I thought, but the only order I was interested in filling was the one that would clear Caroline's name before the inevitable gossip from that news clip and the morning paper could ruin her reputation and tank her business.

She hadn't seen what I'd seen when Evan told her not to leave town last night. He'd added her to his list of suspects.

Chapter Five

I hustled through the snow toward a line of red pickups parked near the main barn. Each truck had a bright red nose tied to its shiny silver grill, a pair of weather-resistant antlers jutting from the window frames, and a Reindeer Games logo painted on the doors. I thumbed my key fob, and the lights on my truck flashed.

"Whoa. Where are you going in such a hurry?"

I heard Dad's voice before I saw him, and turned in the direction of one of my favorite people. "Morning, Daddy."

He stepped outside the big barn, doing his daily impersonation of the guy on the paper towel ads. Plaid flannel shirt, knit cap, and jeans. Dad was as big and strong as anyone I'd ever met. He'd grown up on Reindeer Games just like I had, and a lifetime of rolling logs and cutting timber had kept him fit and happy. He'd taught me to love people, love animals, and tread lightly through life. I'd had a tough time applying that last lesson to more than the forest.

I wrapped him in a big hug and tipped my head back for a look into his kind eyes. "How are you?"

"Excellent," he said. "You?"

"Fine." I released him and smiled.

"How's Caroline?"

I took a moment to choose my words. "She's about as good as expected," I said finally. "Personally unsettled. Worried about her business and reputation. Slightly horrified that someone she knew was murdered."

Dad's jaw tightened. "I know what that feels like. Wasn't that long ago the sheriff had his eye on me for murder."

"That's the thing," I said. "I don't think she realizes that's what Evan's doing. She's more concerned about what the town thinks right now. She stayed with me last night, and she's helping Mom at the Hearth today to keep her mind off things. It hasn't hit her that she might actually be arrested for something she didn't do."

Dad blew out a long breath. "Have you talked to Evan this morning? Asked what he has on the case so far?"

"Not yet. He's been distant for months, so I'm giving him some space before I start bugging him on this."

"Well, that doesn't sound like you."

I laughed. Dad wasn't wrong.

"Have you heard anything about what's been going on with him?"

I raised a brow. Evan wasn't a normal topic of conversation between Dad and me, so I was curious what made Dad bold enough to bring him up.

He shifted his weight, looking slightly uncomfortable.

"Have *you* heard something?" I parroted.

Dad fussed with his knit cap, adjusting it over the tips of his cold red ears.

"Come on," I urged. "Out with it."

"I was down at the pie shop the other day."

I rolled my eyes. Our local pie shop was Mistletoe's unofficial rumor mill headquarters. People went in there, got all sugared up, and spilled their every secret. That place was a high school kid's worst nightmare. And a small-town cop's paradise. "You ran into him?" I guessed.

"No, but I got to talking with Vera while she rang me up, and she mentioned him. She said she'd overheard him on a call that had gotten him so worked up that he'd left half his pie and a steaming cup of coffee. She said he'd answered the phone, "Evan," not "Sheriff Gray," like he usually does, and she wondered if you were on the other end, and the two of you were on the outs. I told her you guys didn't talk much these days."

"Wasn't me on the phone," I said.

Dad shrugged. "You want to talk about the other thing?"

I searched my brain for what he could mean.

"You were at the square last night when they found that guy in the peppermints," he said flatly. "You've had to see two bodies in a year. How are you holding up?"

"I'd feel better if Caroline's knife hadn't been found in there with him."

Shock rolled across Dad's face. "That's not good. Add that to the news clip and this morning's headline . . ."

"Yep. Which is why I'm hoping Evan figures this out fast. Derek's dad is Judge Waggoner, and he'll want swift justice for his son. I don't want to see circumstantial evidence push Caroline into custody."

Dad suddenly crossed his arms. "Caroline's helping your mother, so where are you going right now?"

"Town. I'm going to buy more cocoa. The contractor ruined Mom's supply, and she wants to make whoopie pies later." I spun the truck key around my finger on its ring. "I also told Caroline I'd put a sign in her shop window letting folks know she's closed for a day or two, and I might stop and get Cookie and Mom's Christmas gifts while I'm out. Do you need anything?"

He unfolded his arms and his suspicious expression softened. "I've got everything I need right here." He gave me another hug and kissed my head. "Drive safely and watch out for tourists. I swear half of those folks have never seen snow, let alone driven in it."

"Deal. I'll be back in time for dinner," I said. "Try not to get into any trouble."

Dad turned back for the barn with a laugh. "Back at ya."

I passed a tour bus on my way down the pitted gravel lane leading to and from the farm, before hitting the winding county road with purpose.

The snow-covered forests fell away as I plodded along, exchanged for rolling hills and valleys, then the familiar smattering of homes just outside downtown Mistletoe. The houses popped onto the horizon, one by one at first, then in clusters, puffing smoke from their chimneys and welcoming me back. I smiled at the familiar inflatable snowmen and plastic sleighs parked on rooftops. Some of the displays hadn't changed since I was a child. Others were different every year. Driveways were lined with giant lighted candy canes. Wreaths hung in windows. Big velvet ribbons hugged front doors.

I drove beneath the twisty wrought iron "Welcome to Mistletoe" sign and right into the early morning action. Banners billowed from light posts on Main Street, announcing the Twelve Days of Christmas, a retail celebration. Shop workers dressed as elves handed out flyers announcing daily sales and giveaways. Vendors with brightly colored tents and flashy little carts peddled everything from candied pecans to hot wassail and more. Volunteer Santas made appearances throughout the day, collecting money and unwrapped gifts for local charities.

The town tree stood majestically on the square, wrapped in colorful lights and draped in tinsel. At its base, holiday music piped from speakers dressed as presents. The giant candy bowl previously at its side was long gone. No one arriving in Mistletoe today would have any idea the bowl, mints, or Derek Waggoner had ever existed. I pulled in a deep breath, wishing his death had been nothing more than a bad dream.

I blew out a heavy sigh and hit my blinker, signaling my claim on an open parking spot at the curb, and I waited patiently while the tour bus before me dropped riders at the corner. A couple, standing beneath mistletoe hung from a Main Street lantern, kissed outside my window. Mistletoe was everywhere this time of year. It was pretty, festive, and an excellent pastime for pedestrians waiting on the lights to change.

When the bus finally moved on, I nabbed my parking spot and hopped out. Rich scents of melted peanut butter and caramel warmed the nipping winter air as I hurried past Oh! Fudge toward Wine Around. "I'll be back," I whispered to the drool-worthy window displays of plated cherry cordial delight.

I stopped at Wine Around's door to admire the little histori-cal storefront with its deep purple face and hunter-green trim. The broad black window boxes spilled over with holly, and a fresh pine wreath hung on the door. Unfortunately, the place was closed.

I stepped back in search of posted store hours, and discov-ered a note taped to a "Closed" sign. *Closed for mourning* was scrawled over the paper in thick hasty strikes. A small frown face was drawn in lieu of a period.

"Fudge it is," I muttered, turning on my heels and heading back the way I'd come. I didn't know why I'd expected anything else given the fact Caroline had told me the shop's owner was obsessed with Derek. Maybe even still in love with him.

The door to Oh! Fudge swung open, and a plume of delec-table scents blew out, bringing an excited family with it. "Merry Christmas," I said.

"Merry Christmas," they echoed.

A lengthy checkout line wrapped the display case at the center of the room. A dozen eager faces stared longingly at magical fudge creations beneath the glass. I hurried to the line's end and took my place as temporary caboose. We shuffled forward slowly as each shopper selected and paid for his or her treats at the front.

Tables along the far wall were topped with empty plates and steaming drinks, and women in ugly Christmas sweaters mobbed the nearby buffet. They dipped skewers of brownies, fruit, and marshmallows into a stream of tempting chocolate that bubbled over a three-tiered core. A hand-painted sign on the table explained the delicious trio of chocolate choices.

"Three trips to the buffet for twelve dollars.
One trip for five.
All you care to enjoy for thirty."

"Miss White." A willowy woman I recognized as Jean smiled at me from behind the counter. Jean was part-owner of Oh! Fudge, and one of the chocolatiers that made my wildest dreams come true. "It's always nice to see you."

"Thanks," I said. "You know the feeling's mutual because I can't seem to stay away." I licked my lips and imagined buying one of everything in the curved glass case before me. A box of white chocolate pretzels. A pound of dark chocolate haystacks. Dipped strawberries. Truffles. And *fudge*. I stroked the corners of my mouth, discreetly checking for drool. "A pound of your chocolate-covered cherry cordial, please."

Jean winked. "Cookie's favorite. You must be Christmas shopping." She weighed and packaged the fudge into a small white bakery box. "How's business at the tree farm?"

"Busy."

She smoothed a golden sticker over the box's edge, sealing the deliciousness inside. "A good problem to have." She smiled. "Are you taking photos with the reindeer again this year?" she asked. "My great-niece says all her little school friends had one taken last year, and she missed out. I promised I'd get her over there this year."

I tilted my head and formed what I hoped was an apologetic smile. "I'm glad to hear those photos were a hit, but sadly for us, Mr. Fleece and the reindeer now live next door on Paula Beech's maple tree farm." He'd found true love, and we'd lost the reindeer and their keeper.

"That's right," she said. "I completely forgot that he and Paula got married."

Jean's business partner, Millie, handed a package to the man in a bolero next to me, then turned to smile at me. "They had a beautiful wedding. I saw the photos online."

"A destination event in Bermuda," I said. "Dad hired a Santa to replace Mr. Fleece, but I'm going to miss the reindeer."

Jean set my package on the counter and fixed a red bow on top. "There's your gift for Cookie. Now, what can I get for you?"

I gave her a contemplative look. The mention of Fleece and Paula, two of my main suspects in last year's murder, had ignited my curiosity about Mistletoe's most recent tragedy. "Nothing for me," I said. "I'm strictly Christmas shopping today. It's a shame the shop next door is closed, though. I'd hoped to get Mom a membership to the wine club while I was out."

Millie shot Jean a cryptic look.

"Do you belong to the wine club?" I asked the women.

Millie shook her head no and took the next customer's order.

Jean leaned over the counter conspiratorially. "Samantha is very upset. We heard her ranting alone in her shop this morning when we came to open up. There were sounds of breaking glass and quite a bit of her muffled yelling. It was a little worrisome, to be honest."

"Who was she yelling at?" I asked. *And why?*

Jean ran a palm over her sleek silver bob. "Who knows? We only heard her voice, and we didn't see anyone leave with her."

"Maybe she was on the phone," I suggested.

Jean lifted her palms, then let them fall onto the counter between us.

"Do you know Samantha Moss?" I asked. "What's she like when she's not so upset."

Jean relaxed her stance. "Honey, that woman is always upset."

Millie slid her eyes toward Jean as she handed the next customer his change. "She's intense."

Interesting.

The next customer made a sour face as she moved around me to Millie's register.

"Sorry," I mouthed as she stared.

I turned back to Jean, knowing I was holding up the line and pressing my luck with shoppers' patience, but not quite done prodding. "Did you know Derek Waggoner?" I asked.

She shook her head in the negative. "I only know that he and Samantha had an on-again, off-again relationship for years. The off-again part tore her up every time, but their most recent breakup left her in the worst condition I've ever seen."

"How so?" I asked.

"Well, for starters, she hasn't stopped crying since it happened. I'm sure his death is part of the reason for her tears now, but Samantha had already been crying over Derek when news of his murder came out."

"How recent was their last breakup?"

Jean puzzled for a minute. "Thursday afternoon, I believe. I was arranging the lights on the fence posts. That morning's wind had them all catawampus." She pointed toward the shop window. "She and Derek were right out there on the sidewalk. I heard the whole thing."

Millie snorted. "Half the town heard the whole thing."

"Samantha was mad as a snake about Derek attending some benefit dinner the next night with Caroline," Jean continued. "He must've been all kinds of dumb because he looked as if her reaction was utterly shocking. I mean, really, how did he think *his girlfriend* would react to him taking another woman to dinner?"

The fine hairs along my arms and the back of my neck stood at attention. "Are you telling me Derek and Samantha fought and broke up the day before he died? And it was because he was taking Caroline to the benefit dinner?"

Jean gave a slow nod. "That Friday morning news clip of Caroline telling him to keep his hands off her sent Samantha into a tailspin."

"I don't blame her," Millie said, motioning the next customer to her register. "She'd probably cried herself to sleep after their break-up, but he was already getting handsy with the date he'd sworn meant nothing."

I handed Jean some cash and collected Cookie's boxed fudge. Derek had broken up with an obsessive girlfriend one day before his murder, and it was because of his upcoming dinner date with Caroline. If Evan didn't know that, he needed to. "Well," I told Jean, "I'd better get going. I've held up your line too long already." I glanced over my shoulder at the number of folks who'd gathered behind me. A man in a Santa suit turned away when we made eye contact. A drip of chocolate from the fountain plopped onto the furry white trim of his costume, and he set one palm over the mess. I pretended not to notice. "Merry Christmas," I told both chocolatiers as I headed for the door. "And thank you!"

I hurried back into the cold, shamelessly happy to know Caroline wasn't the only one to have argued with Derek so soon before his death.

Three hours later, it was just after one, and I'd purchased something for nearly everyone on my list and had literally bought the baking supply shop out of cocoa powder. My feet and fingers were frozen. My nose was runny, and my hair had been whipped into a series of knots by the blustery wind as I'd hurried store-to-store. I was due for a hot coffee, and I still needed to make a trip to Caroline's Cupcakes before going home.

I crossed the street a few blocks away from where I'd parked and hustled up the sidewalk with my packages. My breath caught in my throat as I passed the Sweet Scents candle shop and something large moved in the bushes. It took my brain several long beats to recognize the man crouched there with a high-end camera pressed to one cheek. *"Ray?"*

Ray poked his head free of the holly branches. "Oh, hey." He stretched upright and let the camera hang from the broad strap around his neck. "What's up, Holly?"

"Shopping," I said, lifting my haul. "Why were you in the bushes?"

He shoved his hands into his pockets and moseyed over to join me on the sidewalk. His cheeks were red, but it seemed as if the cause might be more embarrassment than the chilly temperature.

I turned in a slow circle, searching for the possible subject of his covert photography. A familiar woman in a plaid ski coat and blue boots caught my eye. Her mouth was open in a wide smile. "Is that your mom?"

Ray leapt for me, and I jumped back.

"Shh." He caught me by my arm and pressed a finger to his lips. "I don't want her to know I'm over here." He angled his back to her and ducked his head.

"Why?"

Ray and his mom were close. She'd moved in with him a few years ago after his dad had died. The farm where he'd grown up had been too much for his mother to handle on her own, so she'd sold it, and they'd become roommates. They were great together. At least, I thought they were. "Why are you following her? With a camera?"

The man to her left removed a cell phone from his shoulder and tucked it into the pocket of his wool coat. Then he took her hands in his and planted a kiss on her cheek.

"Oh," I said, beginning to get the picture.

The man lifted his eyes pointedly at the mistletoe swinging from the lamppost overhead, and she rose onto her toes to kiss him on the lips.

Ray groaned beside me, then mimed being sick.

"Your mom has a boyfriend."

"Please don't call him that," he said. "Don't. It's too much. I can't handle it, and it's making me crazy. I'm waiting up when she goes out. Asking her judgmental questions when she comes home. I'm like the most overprotective parent ever, and I know I should trust her, but all I really want is a thorough background check on this guy." He hung his head in shame for a long moment and then raised his face to me with excitement in his eyes. "You can ask Sheriff Gray to check him out for me!" He pulled a piece of paper from his pocket and scratched two words on it with a tiny pencil: *Pierce Lakemore.*

I took the paper and stuffed it into my purse. "I'm not asking Evan to do that."

Ray's expression fell. "Please?"

"Ray." I stepped closer, then ran my arms around his middle and squeezed. My packages bumped and jostled together behind him. "You're not the parent. She is."

He reluctantly squeezed me back.

"Trust your mom." I stepped away and smiled. "She knows what she's doing."

Evan's cruiser swung into view and parked outside the pie shop across the street.

Ray pointed. "That is cosmic timing. It's fate. Destiny is telling you to talk to him for me."

I gave the cruiser a skeptical look. It wasn't destiny. It was Mistletoe, and the pie shop was everyone's favorite hangout. If I stood there long enough, I was guaranteed to see him and half the town before dinner.

Ray folded his hands and shook them at me. "Please. Please. Please."

"No. You need to respect your mother. Her decisions. Her opinions. Her privacy." I put a heavy emphasis on the last part, but he kept giving me the look of desperation. "Besides, I need to talk to Evan about something else, and I don't want to go in with too many requests."

Ray frowned. "What's your request?"

"I don't want him to waste time looking at Caroline for Derek's murder. I don't care how much the early evidence seems to point in her direction—it's false. A misdirect. Smoke and mirrors. Time is precious right now, and I don't want him losing the real killer's trail because he's chasing his tail over the butcher knife situation. Caroline didn't do this."

Ray pursed his lips. "It doesn't look good."

"I know it doesn't." I rattled my shopping bags between us. "And she doesn't even seem to understand she's a suspect."

"Maybe she isn't."

"Of course she is. That's why he told her not to leave town. Evan always follows the evidence, and the only evidence he has so far points right at her."

"Maybe he has more," Ray suggested. "When was the last time you talked to him about it?"

Evan climbed out of his cruiser, checked the scene around him, and walked into the pie shop without giving Ray and me a second look.

Ray peeked at his watch. "I'd go with you to talk to him, but I've got to get moving. I'm meeting Cookie at the Hearth in thirty minutes."

"My Cookie?"

"Yeah. I'm the official photographer for Theodore's calendar."

A laugh bubbled out of me. "Of course you are." I shook my head and laughed a little more. "Well, you'd better get going. Cookie's pretty excited about the calendar."

Ray gave me a smug look and twisted his first two fingers

together. "She and I are pretty tight now. Kinda makes her *my* Cookie."

I rolled my eyes. "Fine. I'll share."

Ray did a fist pump. "Our Cookie."

"Goof."

My phone broke into applause, and I peeked at the screen. An order for lady gingerbread earrings. Nice. I turned back to Ray. "I'll be there soon. I'm going to see a man about a pie first."

I threaded my way through knots and clusters of shoppers on the narrow sidewalk. I needed to be quick when I spoke to Evan. If I got home in time, I could hide or even wrap my newly purchased gifts before heading over to judge the blind sledding challenge.

I made it as far as the giant red nose strapped to my grill before a small red gift box on the hood caught my eye. I looked for signs of the giver, but no one seemed to be around.

I moved to the driver's side and slid the gift off my hood. There wasn't a tag. How did I know it was meant for me? Could someone have simply set it down a moment while they arranged their packages from a long day of shopping and walked off without it? Was it, perhaps, meant for another employee who drives one of our company trucks? I gave the area another look. Who was I kidding? The trucks were available if needed, but it was almost always Dad or me who drove them. Curiosity gripped me, and I tossed my packages into the truck so I could slide the lid off the little box.

A handful of red and white mints lay inside with a note printed on festive holiday paper.

'Twas the Knife Before Christmas

My heart stuttered at the sight of the mints. They were exactly like the ones in the bowl where Derek Waggoner had been found. The little message had just six words.

Leave it alone. Or you're next.

Chapter Six

I tucked the little threat-present under my arm and headed to the pie shop with my heart pounding painfully in my chest. *This isn't like last year,* I told myself. *It's* not *happening again. I'm fine. I'm safe. Evan will handle this.*

I stopped to catch my breath at the crosswalk, still scanning the faces around me for someone who looked guilty of delivering a threat in broad daylight.

The door to Wine Around opened, and a woman stumbled out. She was dressed in black, from the fantastic Jackie O scarf covering her hair to the coordinating swing coat, tights, and boots. She gave the pie shop a long look before arranging a pair of large black glasses over puffy red eyes and starting in my direction. Was this Derek's ex? I'd never met her before, but she certainly fit the description of a woman in mourning. The box of mints weighed heavy in my hands, and my throat tightened. If this was Samantha Moss, she would have been right by my truck. Could know how close I am to Caroline. Could have somehow heard me asking about her at the fudge shop next door.

I skittered into the road the second the little red hand

vanished on the pedestrian signal and dashed around a slow-moving crowd. My fellow pedestrians were worn down by a long morning of shopping and sightseeing, encumbered by strollers in slush and weighted with packages, but I was fueled by panic and adrenaline as I jumped onto the curb outside the pie shop and darted inside.

A warm burst of air blew over my shoulders as I rushed past the hostess sign.

I spotted Evan in his usual booth and bounced onto the red vinyl bench across from him, setting the threat-present on the table between us and swinging my gaze out the front windows to watch the lady in black make her way through the crowd. "Hello, Evan. How are you today?"

He raised his brows. "What are you up to?"

I pulled my gaze back to him. "What do you mean? Can't a friend drop by unannounced to join another friend for coffee?" I asked.

"Maybe. But why does this feel like it's an ambush?"

My eyes slid back to the window, visually tracking the woman as she slogged impatiently behind the crowd crossing the street.

Evan looked outside just as she opened the pie shop door and entered.

I felt my muscles stiffen at her nearness, but I forced a smiled. "How's the coffee?"

He narrowed his eyes on me. "Hot."

"Great." I tapped my thumbs on the table's edge, trying to ignore the threat-present until I could emotionally deal with it, and wondering manically if the woman at the counter was the one who'd delivered it. My phone applauded inside my handbag, but I ignored it, pretending purse applause was a completely normal thing.

"What was that?"

"Just my phone." I looked beyond him to the shop's entrance.

The woman in black shifted impatiently under the "Carry Out" sign.

Evan followed my gaze again, this time lifting a lazy wave at the subject of my interest.

She lowered her sunglasses to the tip of her nose and waved back before turning away with a hearty sniff.

"Isn't that Derek Waggoner's ex-girlfriend, Samantha Moss?" I whispered.

"Yes."

"I heard that she and Derek had a major fight the day before he died. They broke up over it. I guess it was pretty bad." I rubbed my palms against my coat sleeves, trying to rid myself of the goosebumps crawling all over me.

Evan's expression went sour. "Are you following her? Is that the real reason you came in here? You're trying to find a way to talk with her."

"I got here first. How could *I* be following *her*?" My gaze jumped to the window, afraid he'd see the lie on my face. "What about you? Have you spoken with her yet?"

Evan tapped a finger to the shiny sheriff's star on his chest. "Kind of my job."

"Well? What did she say?"

He turned that same finger on me. "Not your job."

I slumped in the booth, and my traitorous eyes fixed on the awful red box between us.

"What's in the box?"

I swallowed hard, having avoided the thing as long as possible. I pushed it across the table to him.

"For me?" Curiosity turned his brows up.

"No. I think it's for me."

Evan scrutinized my heating face.

"I found it on my truck before I came in here."

He pulled the lid off with a frown, peeked inside, and swore. "Is this what you were talking to Ray about outside?"

"No. Ray left before I found it."

A waitress arrived at the table. "What can I get ya?" she asked, snapping her gum, clueless to the tension filling our booth.

"Coffee," I said, more from habit than intention. I doubted I'd be able to eat or drink anything until the blizzard of nerves settled in my stomach.

"Coming right up." She turned and disappeared into the busy kitchen.

Evan snapped photos of the box and its contents with his cell phone. "I'm going to keep this."

"Okay."

"You're going to go home and stay there," he said.

I bristled. I didn't like being bossed around, but I also had no intention to argue.

"Why are you poking around in my investigation?" he asked. "And before you pretend you're innocent, remember that I have evidence suggesting you've already ticked off another killer.

Unless this note and these peppermints have some other unde-termined meaning." He made a show of looking at his watch, his faint Boston accent growing thick with frustration. "Hasn't been sixteen hours since the body was found, and you've already been told you're next. This has to be some kind of a record."

"Please don't tease me. I'm freaking out."

He shifted in his seat, sharp green eyes flashing. "Talk."

"I asked a couple people about Derek and Samantha, and then this showed up."

He pursed his lips and laced his fingers together on the tabletop. "See, you think what you're doing is no big deal because you only spoke to people you assume aren't killers. The problem with this kind of thinking is that, first off, you don't know who the killer is. It's not like the perp is out there wearing an "I Did It" T-shirt. Secondly, it doesn't matter who you spoke with. It matters who *heard* you, and I've been to a store or two myself this week. You can't sneeze in any of them without getting two dozen bless-you's in response. People are everywhere. And they hear everything. You have no idea who was listening to your conversations, and that scares the hell out of me."

I opened my mouth to say that no one had been paying attention to my private discussions, but he interrupted me by pointing at the box.

"Listen," he said, scrubbing a hand over his mouth, "I've had my hands full all year, and Derek's murder is putting me over my limit for time and patience. I can't keep you safe if you go poking a bear again. So do me a favor and stay away from this. Let me handle it. Give me one less person to worry about right now before I lose my mind." The plea in his eyes nearly got me.

"You're worried about someone else," I asked. "Who? Does this person live somewhere else? Is it the same place you keep disappearing to for a couple of days at a time? Is it Boston?"

He relaxed his shoulders, letting them roll forward as he leaned against the table. "I don't disappear. Even the sheriff gets two days off every week."

"And you go to Boston?" I guessed.

He narrowed his eyes.

I accepted his silence as confirmation. "Do you want to talk about it?"

"When I can, I will," he said, shocking me to my toes. "Not today."

My eyes widened. "Why not?"

"It's not my story to tell."

My heart beat erratically, both at his confession and at the renewed realization that I'd upset someone willing to threaten me with peppermints.

What kind of person leaves their victim in a giant bowl of candy? Aren't killers supposed to be ashamed of themselves and hide the bodies? What's next? Stringing someone up with twinkle lights? Stringing me *up with twinkle lights?* "I have to go." I scooted out of the booth as our waitress arrived.

She looked a little shocked by the announcement. "I'm sorry it took me so long. There was a long line at the register, and I helped out."

"Not your fault," I said with a forced smile. "I just have to go." I dug a wad of ones and store receipts from my pocket and picked the cash out for her. "Merry Christmas."

I brushed past throngs of people on my way to Caroline's

Cupcakes, moving unnecessarily fast and burning up wicked amounts of energy. I had too much on my mind and needed to get back to Reindeer Games for the blind sled challenge. I pulled my scarf over my chin to protect myself from the ever-falling temperatures as I powered ahead.

Caroline's Cupcakes was two blocks up on Main Street and alight with twinkle lights.

The front door had been whitewashed to match the reclaimed wooden sign in the little patch of snow-covered grass by the sidewalk, a preview of things to come. Caroline's key slid smoothly into the lock, and I stepped into the heavenly scents of spun sugar and frosting.

The door popped open behind me before I could flip the deadbolt back into place.

A thin hand appeared around the door's edge. Security lighting reflected off polished black fingernails. A heartbeat later, Samantha Moss's face came into view. "Are you open?" she asked, peeping her head inside.

"No." I said, checking to be sure no one else was on the steps waiting to come in.

I shut the door but couldn't bring myself to turn the deadbolt and lock her inside with me.

Samantha strode to the counter and set her big black designer bag on top.

"I'm sorry, but the shop is closed," I said.

Samantha extracted a wad of cash from her wallet and fanned it over the counter. "How much for the cupcakes?" She pointed to the leftovers inside the display.

I had instructions to bring those back with me so Caroline

could make cake pops, but I also hated to miss an opportunity for a sale. I slid little plastic gloves over my hands and plastered on a pleasant smile. "Which ones would you like?" I asked, planning to take my sweet time loading her choices into a pastry box.

"I'd like them all," she said. "How much?"

I gave the leftovers another look. There were eleven cupcakes in the display. All normally five dollars apiece, but they were officially a day old. I split the difference. "Thirty-three bucks?" The woman was in mourning after all, and I really wanted to talk to her.

She dropped a ten, a twenty, and three ones on the counter and then turned her big dark shades on me. "Pack them up."

I hopped into action, folding a new box into existence and lining it with Caroline's coordinated paper. "Eleven cupcakes? Special occasion?" I asked, unsure of how to get the conversation I wanted started, and also desperate to get her out the door in case she had been the one who'd threatened me.

Samantha's bottom lip quivered. "Yes." Tears began to drip from beneath the dark lenses of her sunglasses. "The love of my life died last night," she cried. "We were soul mates."

I opened the display case and began loading up cupcakes. "Are you talking about the man found on the square?"

"Derek Waggoner," she moaned, removing her glasses and wiping her eyes. "And he didn't deserve to die in some gargantuan, commercialized mint pit."

I set the box before her, struggling to close the lid properly. "I'm very sorry for your loss."

"Thank you."

Samantha pulled the box from my bumbling fingers. "Don't

worry about the lid. I'll be opening it again the minute I walk outside anyway."

I nodded. "I hope they find whoever did this to your friend," I said. "You both deserve justice."

"Derek was my soul mate," she corrected. "All I can do now is wait."

"Did you talk to the sheriff?" I asked.

She choked out a humorless laugh. "Fat lot of good it did. I told the sheriff about Derek's archnemesis, but that guy's still walking free, and the sheriff is across the square eating pie."

I glanced through the window at the cruiser still parked outside the pie shop. "He really likes pie."

Samantha squinted now, looking closely at me for the first time. "Hey. Weren't you just over there with him?"

"Yeah." No sense in lying. She had seen me. "Did you say Derek had an archnemesis?" Did people really have those?

"His name is Brian Ford, and he's awful. Derek and Brian have hated each other since they were kids. They can't spend five minutes in the same room without arguing." She cocked her head. "What did the sheriff say to you about Derek? Does he know who did it?"

"He wouldn't tell me anything," I said. "He never does."

"Men." Samantha shoved a white handkerchief under the bottom of her glasses to dry the tears. "I heard they pulled something out of those mints that linked Derek's death to Caroline West. Do you know her? You must, if you're here," she said. "What do you think of her? Is she a killer?"

"No." I shook my head hard. "Caroline is gentle and kind. She would never hurt anyone."

Samantha set her mouth into a hard line. "I wouldn't put anything past her. She's too perfect, and it's always the ones who seem to have it together who are actually crazy," she said.

"Disagree," I said. "I've known Caroline a long time. She's pretty close to perfect, and she's not crazy."

Samantha's top lip curled back in a sneer as she moved toward the door with her purchase. "Tell your perfect friend that if I find out she had anything to do with Derek's murder, she'll be sorry."

My jaw dropped. I was suddenly glad to be behind the counter and out of Samantha's reach.

I craned my neck to watch her walk down the steps. Then I ran over and flipped the deadbolt before she got any ideas about coming back. Jean from Oh! Fudge hadn't been exaggerating when she'd said Samantha Moss was intense.

I ran shaky fingers through my ratty hair, then turned in search of sign-making supplies behind the counter. Time to do what I'd been asked to do and get back to the farm. I picked through a mug filled with writing utensils until I found a nice, thick marker to do the job. Then I selected a plain white sheet of copy paper and folded it in half.

Now, what was I supposed to write? Caroline wanted people to know she would be closed for the rest of the week, but she didn't want the note to make her sound guilty. I tapped the marker against the paper, wishing I'd asked her to be more specific.

Thunk!

I froze as the front window rattled, having taken a solid hit.

Thud!

Thud!

Thunk!

What on earth?

I dropped my marker and made a run for the front window. Dark shadows marred the formerly crystal-clear glass. "What's going on?" I demanded, yanking the door open and staring at the group of people on the sidewalk outside.

Samantha glared up at me, a cupcake in her throwing hand, the box clutched protectively to her chest. She laughed evilly, then threw the little vanilla treat against the window, where it stuck for several seconds before sliding down the glass, leaving a wide blue frosting trail in its wake.

"Stop!" I yelled. "You can't do that."

She threw another.

I freed my cell phone from my pocket. "I'm calling Sheriff Gray," I said hotly. "You're going to have to clean this up."

The next cupcake flew past my head, sticking briefly on the door behind me.

"Hey!" I'd barely dodged the delicious treat, and now there was frosting in my hair.

My phone applauded as the call connected. Three new orders before I'd left town. I would never sleep again at this rate.

"Holly?" Evan answered.

"Evan!" I cried. When I explained the situation, he agreed to come immediately.

Samantha stilled for a long moment, listening as I spoke. When we disconnected, she broke into a sprint, tossing the empty box aside and tearing down the sidewalk.

I waved apologetically to the circle of people who'd witnessed the whole thing, then went inside to get a bucket of water, my mind reeling. She'd bought out all the cupcakes just to throw them at the store. Right after asking me to pass on a threat to Caroline for her.

How long had Samantha been at her shop this morning? Had she been there when I'd tried the door? Had she known I'd been looking for her? I'd seen her leaving just minutes after I'd found the threat-present. Could she have slipped out and left the box on my truck while I was shopping? Was she the one who wanted me to stop asking questions?

My heart raced painfully as I watched Evan jog across the street in my direction.

Had I just been alone in a closed shop with a killer?

Chapter Seven

I arrived at Reindeer Games in time to leave most of my packages in the truck and race to the field outside the Hearth for the blind sled challenge. I took Mom's cocoa powder with me.

She met me at the sign-up table, where visitors were already pressing name tags to their coats and choosing their sleds. "I thought you forgot about us," Mom said.

"Never." I hoisted four handled shopping bags onto the table. "I was hunting cocoa, and I bought every last pinch in town."

She clapped. "That's magnificent!" Mom strained to lean her short body across the table for a hug. I met her halfway, and she hugged my head. "You saved my whoopie pies."

I straightened with a laugh. "Were you able to get more baking done with Caroline's help?"

"We did as much as can be expected," she said, her chipper voice going low. "The contractor left at eleven and said he won't be back until after New Year's Day. He wants to spend the holidays with his family."

"What?" I squeaked. "So you're stuck working in an unfinished kitchen at a café on a Christmas tree farm at Christmas? Is that even possible? Can he just walk out like that?" I looked around for a lawyer and wished I'd gone to law school so I'd know Mom's rights. "That's awful!"

"Yeah, but at the moment I need to get this cocoa into the kitchen and start mixing dough. Caroline's in there finishing up another round of thumbprint cookies." Mom handed me a wireless microphone and swiveled the volume control on my old karaoke machine. "See you in a bit," she whispered.

I turned to the expectant group, paired up by twos, an old fashioned wooden sled between them. My personal problems were my own and not something to bring down the spirits of all those smiling faces. Time to put on the charm.

"Hello, sledders!" I called as brightly as I could. "This event is called the blind sledding challenge for a reason. One of you on each team will be blindfolded." I reached behind the table and collected Mom's bag of blindfolds and giant plastic candy canes. I passed one blindfold to each team as I walked toward the field. "One of you will be the sled-rider, and one will be the sled-puller."

The teams began to giggle and make choices as I sunk candy canes into the snow, hooked side up.

"Once you've decided who's who, please move behind the blue line painted on the snow." I smiled and pointed. They obeyed.

I set the final candy cane and returned to the table. "On my whistle, the sled-pullers are going to put on their blindfolds and pull the sled. The sled-riders are going to try to collect as many candy canes as possible while shouting directions for the puller to get them close enough to reach the targets. Riders must stay aboard the sleds. Pullers must remain blindfolded. Any questions?"

A group "no" returned to me.

Onlookers trickled over, forming an audience behind the teams.

"The team with the most candy canes at the end of five minutes gets free hot cider and apple streusel from the Hearth. Who's ready?"

Everyone cheered.

"On your marks," I called.

The sled-pullers lifted their blindfolds, ready to tie.

"Get set." I readied my phone to countdown from five minutes, then blew long and hard into the whistle.

Sledders burst away from the starting line, racing into the field as the riders directed the pullers toward the nearest candy canes. They ran them over more often than they passed within their rider's reach. Pullers collided and fell over. Riders toppled off from the impact.

The crowd went wild.

I puffed hot breath against my frigid mittens, then rubbed both hands up and down my coat sleeves for friction. I was chilled by more than the temperature. Try as I might, I couldn't shake the creepy box of peppermints from my mind.

Someone in town had overheard me asking about Derek's death, and they didn't like it. I hadn't mentioned it to Evan, but in reality, my morning shopping had been eye-opening. The body in the Guess How Many Mints bowl had been a topic of conversation nearly everywhere I'd gone. Most older and male folks seemed to think Derek was a delight, but women between twenty and forty weren't so quick to praise. In fact, they said very little, exchanging looks with their friends instead of voicing their opinions. They were holding their tongues, I'd realized, trying to be polite. If they'd had something nice to say about him, they would have freely done so.

I'd heard it said that death makes us all saints, but that didn't ring true today about Derek Waggoner, with the women of Mistletoe. He'd treated them or someone they knew the way he'd treated Caroline.

Could one of them have had enough of his misogynistic behavior? Perhaps lashed out in a fit of anger and done something she could never take back?

The timer on my phone went off, and I called the sledders to a halt.

Sled pullers removed their blindfolds, wiping tears of laughter from their eyes. Riders raised empty hands and rolled off the sleds into the snow, if they weren't already there, still cracking up.

"Looks like a tie," I announced, "so I have cider and streusel vouchers for everyone!"

I handed out the vouchers, wondering if one of the folks accepting my offer was actually an angry killer keeping an eye on me. Thanks to Evan's warning that the person who'd threatened me could be anyone, my tongue was officially stuck to the roof of my mouth, and my heart was racing again. I hadn't intended to upset a killer—I blamed my insatiable curiosity. An inquiring mind was the thing that had driven me to test every hiking trail on the farm when I was young, skate on questionable ice when I got a little older, and taste-test leftovers in my fridge that weren't properly dated last weekend. I liked knowing things, and each time I'd heard folks talking about how Derek could've ended up in that candy bowl, I was drawn to the conversation like a magnet. Watching. Listening. Though, sadly, I hadn't learned anything new, and I'd put a spotlight on my back for nothing.

When the last voucher was distributed, I went to see if Mom needed help serving sweets inside the Hearth. A warm rush of chocolate-scented air swept over me as I crossed the threshold, kicking tufts of snow off my boots and onto the giant welcome mat just inside the door.

The space was packed with smiling folks sporting whipped-cream mustaches and munching headless gingerbread men.

On my way to the counter, I passed Cookie and Ray pushing papers back and forth across the table between them. Mom stood near the register, spraying cones of whipped cream into a row of steaming mugs. Caroline followed her with a sugar shaker, dusting the tops with shimmery red and green crystals.

I took the last seat at the counter and admired the teamwork. "That looks amazing," I said.

Mom beamed. "It's your favorite. Peppermint mocha cocoa." She arranged a plate of brightly colored cookies at the tray's center. "Plus a few homemade cutouts and Nana's nummy icing."

My tummy growled. "I love Nana's nummy icing."

"I know. You used to eat it right out of the bowl. More than a few angels and Santa silhouettes have gone naked because of you."

Caroline tucked the sugar shakers into her apron pocket and laughed. "How was town?" she asked, her mood looking much lighter than it had when I'd left her. "Did you have any trouble at the shop?"

I considered lying but knew my face wouldn't cooperate, so I stuck with offering as little information about the trip as possible. "I left a sign in the window that said, 'Caroline's Cupcakes has had a Cupcake Emergency, but 'Don't worry! We'll be back in time for Christmas!'"

Caroline considered this a moment. "What's a cupcake emergency?"

"I don't know," I said. "Probably no one else will either."

She waited a long beat before bobbing her head, satisfied. "Okay. Thanks for doing that for me."

"No problem." I'd given my official statement about Samantha Moss's vandalism when Evan had arrived, and he'd been on his way to have a chat with her when I'd left.

Mom stared at me as if she could see I had more to tell.

I squirmed. "Do you need any help back there? I can deliver orders. Clear tables."

"Nope," Mom said, wiping her hands on her apron. "I believe we've got this." She hefted a stack of books from behind the counter and set them in front of me. "But Christopher could use your help. He stopped by with these and said he needs you to look them over and make some choices this week. His guy, Will, said you should stop at the inn and look at the railing choices in person when you have time. There are photos in one of these catalogues, but he thought seeing them in person would be better."

I eyeballed the stack before me. Each three-ring binder of options was at least three inches thick, and there were twelve of them. Twelve. Making a full yard of homework. Their spines had words like *baseboards* and *molding, custom built-ins, kitchens and baths, subway tile,* and *knobs and pulls.*

My eyes crossed.

"Your father and I really appreciate this," Mom said. "We're both so busy, we can barely keep our heads above water this month. We know you're swamped too, but making all these decisions has really lifted a burden, and we appreciate you very much."

I dragged the perilous stack of binders a little closer. "Glad to help." Maybe I could flip through the binders in my jammies with Cindy Lou Who at my side. If Mom threw in some peppermint mocha cocoa and Nana's nummy icing, it wouldn't be a bad gig. "I'll work on this tonight."

My phone applauded, and I dropped my head. Another order. My fourth since Caroline had set the notification sound on our way to breakfast. Never mind the fact she'd said there was already a bunch of orders waiting. "Any chance you've got the makings for a grilled cheese back there? I missed lunch."

Mom reached over the counter and pinched my cheek. "Anything for my sweet baby girl. How does smoked gouda on sourdough sound?"

I preferred American on white, but I wasn't going to be picky. "Perfect."

Caroline turned toward the kitchen. "I've got this." She looked at Mom and smiled. "We haven't had time to eat yet either. How about I make three?"

Mom put a hand over her heart.

Caroline winked, then disappeared into the back.

74

Mom lifted the tray of cookies and cocoas and ferried them away. "Be back in a jiff."

When she'd gone, the lady on the lollipop stool beside me cleared her throat. "You know the owners here?" she asked, arching her pencil-thin eyebrows. A cropped silver pixie cut showcased beautiful mini-ornament earrings and pretty green eyes. Her cardigan was embroidered with the words "Merry Christmas Ya Filthy Animal."

"I do." I smiled. "This is my family's farm."

"Really?"

"Yep. Four generations now. That was my mom and my best friend I was talking to."

She leaned back and smacked the counter. "Well, you're just the person I want to talk to then because this is the most fun I've had in years, and your family needs to know."

"Wow. Thank you." I smiled brighter. "We love hearing that."

"You certainly deserve the praise. The girls and I came in with a tour group from Ocala, and we had high expectations, but this place surpasses them all. We've been at the farm all day, and we can't wait until that inn is finished. We saw the crew working and the "Coming Soon" sign out front, and we're planning to come back next Christmas just so we can stay there. When will it be open?"

"We're planning an official grand opening early next fall, but the inn could be finished as soon as Christmas."

The ladies on the other side leaned around their friend to look at me, broad smiles on their faces.

"Will you be staying around to play some of the Reindeer Games?" I asked.

"Maybe," the lady at my side said. "We watched the blind sledding and nearly wet our pants."

The woman on the opposite side of her reached a hand toward me, gathering my attention. "That was worth braving the New England cold. Hilarious."

"Build a Big Frosty is tomorrow," I told them. "That's always a lot of fun, or if you prefer to stay inside and keep warm, we have bingo night," I said, ticking off on my fingers, "holiday trivia night, Bling that Gingerbread, and Gingerbread Goes to Hollywood." I grabbed a flyer with the daily itinerary from the stack by the register. "There." I pressed it to the counter between us and smiled.

The woman next to me worked a pair of frameless glasses onto the end of her nose and grinned. "Oh my! Thank you!" She swiveled on her lollipop stool and showed her friends, who oohed and aahed along with her.

I waved goodbye and went to see Cookie and Ray while my grilled cheese was cooking.

Cookie looked up when my shadow fell over the stacks of photos on the table. "Well hello," she said, scooting down to make room for me on the padded bench beside her. "How was town?"

"Crowded."

"And?" she popped a gumdrop into her mouth from an open bag on the table.

"Dangerous," I mumbled.

Ray stared. "What do you mean, *dangerous*?" he asked.

I looked around for prying ears before leaning in to whisper.

"I found a present on my truck that was filled with mints, and there was a note inside that said to leave it alone or I'd be next."

Ray's face went red.

Cookie's went white.

Ray leaned over the table toward me, our faces uncustomarily close. "Leave what alone?"

"Derek's death, I guess," I said. I was still a little shocked that I'd been watched while I'd been shopping this morning. "I asked the ladies at Oh! Fudge about his ex-girlfriend, who happens to run the shop beside theirs."

"You told Evan," Ray said. His tone implied the words were more a demand than a question.

"Yeah, and I gave him the box."

Cookie set her hand on my arm, a hint of fear in her blue eyes. "No one tried to hurt you, though?" Worry rose in her voice. "You're okay?"

"I'm fine. No one tried to hurt me," I answered quickly but then reconsidered. "Well, Samantha Moss threw a cupcake at my head, but she missed, and it probably wouldn't have hurt anyway."

Cookie's mouth fell open.

"That reminds me," I said as the incident and Samantha's strange words came back to mind. "Do either of you have an archnemesis?"

"No," Ray answered in timely confliction with Cookie's firm "Yes."

We looked at Cookie.

She popped another gumdrop into her mouth, then rolled

the bag shut and stuffed it into her purse. "I'd better lay off these, or they'll be gone before I get them home to Theodore."

"You have a nemesis?" I asked, certain she'd misunderstood the question.

"Sure, back in Vegas. I was a cigarette girl, and there was a bunny from the nightclub next door who'd always come around shaking her tail near my first husband, Casey. He wasn't my husband at the time, but. boy. did she get on my nerves. We had a cold war going for years. A few decades later, after I'd been in Maine for most of my life, I thought I was finally rid of her, but Mark Zuckerberg went and created Facebook. For five years I had to watch her brag about everything from her yoga routine to her thousand-dollar crowns." She showed her teeth and tapped one with her finger. "So, I'd brag back, then she'd try to top it. Eventually she died, which was sad, but I suppose that means I won." Cookie puzzled. "I need to change my original answer. I guess I don't have a nemesis anymore."

I did a slow blink.

"I want to know why Samantha threw a cupcake at your head," Ray said. "Are you sure you weren't hurt?"

A plate clattered onto the table in front of me.

Caroline stepped closer, now wide-eyed. to my side. "That really happened?" she asked. "What is wrong with her?"

"She's mourning," I said, "according to the sign in her shop window."

Caroline collapsed on the bench next to Ray. Her eyes flicked up and caught my gaze. "Where did she get the cupcakes?"

My cheeks flamed hot. "She bought what was left in your

display case from last night. I figured I'd ask her about Derek while I packed them up."

Caroline deflated against the seatback. "Did you learn anything?"

"She said Derek had an archnemesis who might've had reason to hurt him. The guy's name is Brian Ford, but I've never heard of him."

"What did you think of Samantha?" Caroline asked.

I pointed a finger at my temple, then circled it around my ear.

Ray snorted. "I hope you told Evan about the vandalism too."

"I did. He wasn't happy."

Cookie reached for my grilled cheese. "Are you going to eat that or watch it get cold?"

I pulled the plate to my chest. "I'm going to eat it."

"Then eat it," she said.

I took a salty, gooey bite, stuffing half of the grilled cheese into my mouth at once. My eyelids fluttered. When I opened them, Cookie was staring.

I handed her the other half of my sandwich.

"Thanks!" She nibbled the corner and hummed a cheery tune. "I know Brian Ford's wife," she said suddenly. "Did I say that already?"

I gawked. "You definitely didn't. Who is she? How do you know her?"

"Nadia Ford." Cookie turned her half of my sandwich around and started on the other side. "She's in my gardening club."

"You're in a gardening club?" I asked, unsure why anything about Cookie surprised me anymore.

"Sure. I'm in all the clubs," she said. "At my age, I can't afford to miss out on things."

"Are you a Winer?" I asked.

Cookie gave me a disbelieving look. "Free wine and finger foods once a month? Do I look like a fool?" She finished the grilled cheese and wiped her mouth on a checkered cloth napkin. "Are you thinking of joining?"

"No. I'm trying to find out about Samantha Moss." I clamped a hand over my mouth and felt my eyes go wide. I was doing it again. Asking questions that were relative to Derek's murder but completely irrelevant to my life.

"Samantha's a lot of fun," Cookie said. "Very passionate. You've got to get out of her way when she gets mad, though."

"Because she throws stuff," I deadpanned.

Cookie pointed to her nose.

Ray waved from his side of the table. "I think we need to focus here. You were threatened with more than a flying cupcake today," he said. "Who could have left that box of peppermints for you?"

"What mints?" Caroline asked.

Ray filled her in on the threat-present.

I blew out a long breath. "I have no idea who could have done it. There were scads of people in town, and I didn't ask a single question about Derek's death. I'd only asked Jean and Millie at Oh! Fudge about Samantha and listened in on a bunch of other gossip while I'd shopped. Until I found the box, I had no idea anyone was upset or following me."

I gave Cookie a careful look. "Do you think there's a chance Samantha could've killed Derek?"

"Oh sure." Cookie nodded. "She's got a legendary temper.

Nice thing is she's not afraid to apologize, and she usually gets over her fits pretty quick."

Yeah, I thought, *after she brains her offender with whatever is within her reach.* I remembered Jean and Millie saying they'd heard Samantha yelling and breaking things in her shop. Behavior like that wasn't exactly a hallmark of stability. Samantha would definitely be at the top of my suspect list, if I had one, of course. "What is Nadia Ford like?"

"Quiet," Cookie said. "Young. Adorable. Her green thumb is unparalleled. She's the envy of the garden club. We all think she should've married a farmer or a florist instead of that leather worker. He's too old for her, and he's a big bore."

"You know Brian Ford?" I asked, twisting in my seat to see her more clearly. "Why didn't you tell me?"

"I don't know him." Cookie wrinkled her nose.

"You said he's a bore."

"He's a leather worker." She closed her eyes and pretended to snore.

I rubbed my forehead.

Caroline shoved her sandwich toward me. "Would you like this? I'm not hungry anymore. Honestly, I was only half sure I could eat anything in the first place. Knowing that this mess has put you in some lunatic's crosshairs again is making me nauseous. I'm so sorry you got dragged into this."

"I wasn't dragged," I said. "All I've done is hung a sign in your shop window and jumped in on some town gossip. That's it. Hardly capital crimes."

She pressed a palm to her middle. "Maybe I should go lie down."

81

I pushed the sandwich into the table's center for Ray and Cookie to share and tried not to comment on the dozen or more photos scattered across the polished wood—all of Theodore in various outfits from Easter bunny ears to swim goggles and an inner tube. "I'm going to walk Caroline to the guesthouse," I said. "I've got a ton of research to do on local historic Victorian homes so I can deal with my homework." I pointed to the mountain of binders on the countertop.

Mom stood in the kitchen doorway with half a sandwich in one hand. Her other palm rested on Dad's chest. He had the other half of her grilled cheese and a big smile as he tugged her close. I hadn't heard him come in, but I wasn't going to interrupt their moment.

My chest tightened at the fantasy of having what those two had one day.

"Sounds good." Caroline stood, and I snapped back to reality. "I'll just grab my coat," she said.

Ray trained his steady blue eyes on me. "Be careful, Holly. Remember last year."

"This isn't last year," I said. "I'm fine, and I'm not meddling." I raised both palms in innocence, then drew an X over my heart with one finger. "From now on, I will watch everything I say and do."

"Good." He sank his teeth into the sandwich with a deeply satisfied moan. "This is unreal."

"Ready?" Caroline returned a few minutes later with a handled bag. "I made you another sandwich and ladled some tomato soup into a container for dipping."

I stared at the bag. "Bless you."

She smiled. "Anytime. Now, don't forget your homework." She tipped her head toward the stack of binders.

I dragged myself to the counter and loaded my arms up to my chin. I said my goodbyes, then followed Caroline into the cold.

The wind had picked up since the blind sled challenge, and I shrank deeper inside my coat, wiggling the soft material of my scarf over my mouth and nose. Barely past dinnertime, and the moon was already high in the winter sky.

"Are you sure you don't want me to carry a few of those?" Caroline asked.

"I'm fine," I lied. The binders made a nice windbreaker, but my arms were burning with fatigue before we'd made it halfway to the guesthouse.

Caroline kicked one boot through the snow every few feet, a distant look in her eyes.

"This will pass," I said. "We can wait it out together."

"Okay." She pinned me with a pitiful smile. "Do you mind if I stay with you one more night?"

"Not at all. In fact, I'd actually appreciate it. The threat-present really freaked me out. Plus, I could use your help making sense of all these inn choices."

She scrutinized the binders. "Don't forget your jewelry orders."

I closed my eyes for a long beat, feeling sorry for my lack of available time.

Caroline glanced my way again. "Do you think Cindy Lou Who will mind having company for a second night?" she asked. "I try to be nice to her, but I'm not sure she likes me."

"I'm not sure she likes *me*," I said, laughing because it was true. "Cindy Lou Who is slow to warm up, but she's great company as long as you don't talk to her or try to touch her."

Caroline laughed.

I pressed my frozen chin against the stack of binders, stabilizing them so I could reposition my hands. "Cindy has to initiate the cuddling," I explained, "or she bites. And don't look directly at her for too long. She hates that. She'll hiss. Oh, and if you ever see her bowls are empty or upside down, you should right and fill them, or she'll be mad."

Caroline nodded calmly as I spoke. "Follow all the unspoken rules or be hated for insolence. Got it. It's like living with my mother all over again."

The wind picked up, whipping snow and ice into the air that pelted my face. "We should build a fire, spike the cocoa, and stay inside until the storm passes." I meant that both figuratively and literally.

Caroline smiled. "It's like you're reading my mind."

In the hours since breakfast, I'd been accosted with a cupcake, threatened with peppermints, loaded down with binders, and overrun with jewelry orders.

I wanted nothing more than to build that fire, spike my cocoa, and stay inside until the work was done and the danger had passed.

What I needed was for someone to stick a fork in me because I was so done.

Chapter Eight

I t felt good to be home, lounging with Caroline and Cindy Lou Who and wearing flannel pajamas, with nowhere to go. Mom's friends had volunteered to help at the Hearth until close, so she'd called to suggest Caroline and I spend the rest of the night inside. We hadn't argued. Unfortunately, comfortable as I was, there was still plenty of work to be done.

I balanced my laptop on my legs and printed all the orders in need of being filled. The printer rocked to life in the corner, precariously balanced on a narrow stand. I'd tried to free up the kitchen table by moving my "office" into the living room, and had succeeded in swapping one cluttered room for another. The order sheets plummeted overboard as they were expelled from the machine. I watched helplessly as they swept across the floorboards and disappeared beneath the couch. "Shoot."

Caroline propped her slippered feet on the coffee table and swiped a binder off the stack. "Aren't you glad you'll be living at the inn soon? You'll have an actual office where you can keep your business things. All your files and supplies will have homes, and your living room won't look like you just moved in." Her blue eyes shifted to indicate a line of boxes I'd stacked against my front wall last year and meant to put into storage but hadn't. Currently they doubled as miniature snow-covered mountains for decoration. I'd tossed a sheet over them and set my light-up Christmas village on top.

It might be nice to have an office, but I was comfortable right where I was, and not in any hurry to move again. "I'm still getting used to the idea that the inn is really being built." Dad had talked about having an inn at Reindeer Games all my life, but I'd assumed long ago that it would never happen. Then, a few months ago, Dad found Christopher and struck a deal, and Christopher's crew hit the ground running. Part of me was still shocked every morning I walked outside and saw a home there. "What if I'm a terrible innkeeper?"

Caroline dropped the binder against her thighs and turned to me in an astonished huff. "Are you kidding me? People love you, and you love them. Innkeeping will be your dream job. I'll bet every room is booked before you even open. I heard people talking about it all day at the Hearth. They can't wait."

I levered myself off the couch and went to collect my fallen orders from beneath it, then arranged them in a grid on the floor, by the date they were placed. "Innkeepers usually cook. I can't cook."

"Nice try," she said. "Your mom already told me guests will receive their meals at the Hearth. All you have to do is keep the pantry and refrigerator stocked with things to set out between meals, like fruits or cheese and crackers. Maybe nuts and mints, or chocolates at night." She pulled a stack of sticky notes from an open office supply box beside her and pasted one onto the binder page. "You just don't like change."

"I don't *mind* change. There's just been a whole lot of it this year. I'm finally comfortable again, and things are really good." I fished through my tackle box–turned–jewelry box for various pieces to fill the orders. Once I'd matched up as many as I could, I lined the completed orders against my hearth and slid a bubble mailer underneath each one. "Okay, these piles are complete but still need to be stuffed, addressed, and mailed."

Caroline turned the page in her binder and peeled another sticky note from the stack. "What about all those?" she asked, nodding to the dozen or so papers still sitting alone on the floor.

"I don't have the things those people ordered in stock, so I have to make them."

"Yikes." She gave the pages another look. "They each ordered only one item?"

I shook my head. "No."

Caroline cringed. "How long does it usually take you to make a piece of jewelry?"

"Depends on what I'm making. Depends on how involved it is. Depends on if I already have the supplies I need." Which reminded me, I'd already melted down every discarded bottle, votive holder, and glass bowl in the county. If the orders kept coming faster than I could acquire glass, I'd have to start ordering materials off the internet. Which would drive my jewelry prices up and possibly push my order numbers down. I rubbed a palm against the ache in my chest. Maybe fewer orders would be a good thing. It wasn't as if I had enough time to complete the orders I already had.

Anxiety leapt and whirled in my stomach at the thought of all the work to be done, but according to my dad, anything could be accomplished. One step at a time. I collected the remaining order sheets into a neat stack and set them on the coffee table. I'd simply start at the top and keep going until I hit the bottom.

Caroline and I worked in companionable silence for a long while: she, flagging pages in the binder with things she liked for the inn; and me, turning wire and bits of old glass bottles into tiny replica holiday sweets for charms on necklaces, bracelets, and earrings.

The wind howled against my windowpanes, rattling them soundly and consistently for hours on end. The fire in my fireplace flickered briefly, but it kept up its job as well, strong and steady.

"Holly?" Caroline asked after she'd put her seventh binder aside. "Who do you think could have left that box for you?"

My hands stilled on the miniature lollipop pendant I'd been stringing onto a thin silver chain. "I don't know." The question had been on my mind all afternoon as well, and no amount of jewelry making had removed it. "What do you know about Brian Ford?" I asked. "Samantha says he was Derek's nemesis, but is he capable of murder?"

"I don't know Brian," she said. "He's older than us. Older than Derek too. He has a shop where he makes those expensive handbags with the scripted letter *F* on the buckle and button clasp. I'm sure you've seen ladies carrying them."

"Is his store inside the old tack shop out on Mill Road?"

"That's the one," she said. "Brian's got to be in his mid-thirties, but I hear he married a younger woman. Met her on a business trip down South, I think. I didn't pay much attention to the story, so I don't know the details. I never dreamed a stranger's personal life would be relevant to me."

"It's not," I assured her. "Whatever happened to Derek has less than nothing to do with you. The timing is unfortunate—coincidental at best. I'm guessing a lot of people yelled at him that day."

"I hate that I yelled at him," she said, a heartbreaking look on her face. "I made a big scene. Got us on the news. What if those were the last words anyone ever said to him?"

"Caroline," I started.

She raised a finger to stop me. "I should have held my tongue, gotten my coat, called a cab, and left with my dignity. I can't control someone else's behavior. Snapping at him didn't change anything. The only person I can control is myself, and I did a really horrible job."

I set the necklace aside and scooted onto the cushion beside her. "No one who knows you would believe you hurt Derek, even if they saw that news clip a hundred times."

She set her head on my shoulder. "And how about after they learn my knife was found with him in those candies?"

I opened my mouth to speak, but words didn't come.

Caroline shoved onto her feet with a sigh. "I'm going to spike my cocoa now. What time is it?"

"Time for Caroline's special cocoa," I said wryly as she marched into the kitchen, mug in hand.

* * *

I woke early the next morning to the makings of a panic attack. The weight on my chest and cheek forced my blurry eyes open, but I couldn't breathe. It was as if someone was suffocating me with a warm, fuzzy pillow. I tried to sit up, roll over, flee. "Help!" I croaked, sucking in a mouthful of calico fur.

Cindy Lou Who looked over her shoulder at my desperate face and stared, seemingly irritated that I'd disrupted her rest. On my face.

My heart raced erratically as I worked myself off the ledge. I was fine. No one wanted to kill me. My cat was kind of a pain, but at least she wasn't demanding I fill her bowls. Why wasn't she demanding I fill her bowls?

"Ugh." I shoved her off me, onto the pillow at my side. "Good grief, Cindy. If I hadn't died from lack of oxygen, you could've given me a heart attack."

She rolled onto her side and flopped her head down, uninterested in my complaints.

I climbed out of bed and followed the delicious aroma of warm apple pie to my kitchen.

Caroline was at the counter, wearing skinny jeans and a pale pink cashmere sweater. Cindy's bowls were righted on the little rubber placemat near the window, and fresh water sparkled in one dish.

"Morning," Caroline said. Her blonde waves were tucked neatly behind her ears, held in place with rhinestone-studded bobby pins. "I fed the cat and did some yoga before getting ready for the day. I was feeling a little better about everything until the newspaper arrived."

Uh-oh. I shuffled closer, drawn by the heavenly scents of black coffee, and apples and cinnamon. "What was in the paper?" I asked, rubbing my tired eyes and begging my brain to focus.

"A grenade," she grouched.

"What?"

Caroline caught a tear sneaking from the corner of one eye. She swept it delicately away with the pad of one thumb. "I left it on the table for you to read before I throw it in the fire."

I turned the paper around to face me, then read the headline. "A Mistletoe Murderess? Cupcake Baker's Butcher Knife Linked to Local Death." Caroline had known this would happen—we'd talked about it last night. "Does the article accuse you?" I asked.

"Not directly," she said, roughly tapping the screen of her cell phone. "My dad has been texting all morning. The fact I'm even peripherally involved in a murder is a PR nightmare for him. He wants me to come home and be debriefed by his lawyers, then work with a strategist to put a positive spin on me being accused as a murderess." Her phone buzzed in her fingers, and she growled at it.

"I'm so sorry." I poured a mug of coffee and began sipping myself awake. "Someone must've leaked the information about your knife." I skimmed the article, which was mostly details about Caroline's life that everyone already knew and a recap of Derek's appearance in the giant candy dish. "At least the sheriff's department had no comment. None of the information is confirmed."

"No one will care about that. It's front-page news, and lies don't make the front page. Plus, it's not a lie." She gritted her teeth. "My knife *was* involved in the crime."

"The article never uses the word *involved*," I said weakly, "and the headline only says 'linked.'"

"Well the knife sure looked involved to me when I watched those crime scene guys fish it out of the mints."

She had me there. "But you aren't a murderer," I reminded her. "That's the important part."

Caroline expelled an exasperated sigh. "I've spent my whole life trying to be Mistletoe's sweetheart. First, for my dad's sake and then because I liked how it felt. Now I've let people down."

"You haven't let me down," I said, wrapping an arm around her shoulders. "Not my folks or Cookie, not Ray or his family, or anyone else who matters. Besides, people will realize this article is nothing more than hype when they ask themselves why you aren't in jail. I mean, if you're a cold-blooded killer, then why are you here with me, baking the best muffins on planet Earth?"

She studied her boots. "Sheriff Gray doesn't have any reason to arrest me."

"Exactly." I gave her shoulders a squeeze, and hoped desperately that was true, then released her in favor of more coffee. "I think I'm going to get dressed and do some errands," I said. "I don't have to be at the Hearth until this afternoon, so I'm going to make a run into town. Feel free to stay here as long as you want. Hide out alone. Hang with Mom. Whatever gives you a little peace."

I sucked the dregs of steaming black coffee into my mouth and dropped a few muffins into a paper bag for later. A hasty—and probably stupid—plan was solidifying in my mind. I didn't want to keep asking questions about Derek's death, but the gloves had come off the moment I'd read that obnoxious headline.

Caroline pinched the top off a muffin and stuffed the bit between her petal-pink lips. "I'll be right here when you get back, assuming Sheriff Gray hasn't hauled me away in cuffs."

"That's not going to happen," I said. "I won't let it."

* * *

Two hours later, I was in the parking lot outside the old tack shop. The previous night's storm had added two inches of snow to the eight we'd already accumulated, leaving road conditions questionable and the department of transportation working overtime to clear and salt everything.

When I'd arrived at the line of Reindeer Games pickups, my truck had looked less like Rudolph and more like the Abominable Snowman. I'd spent an infuriating amount of time removing the white powder to get inside and start the engine, and even after fifteen minutes on the road, the heater struggled to make a dent in the interior temperature.

A neon "Open" sign glowed in the window of the tack shop, beside an array of beautiful handbags and accessories, all with matching script *F*s on the zippers and button closures. Strings of women and a handful of couples wandered in and out while I debated the merits of my plan. "This is the place," I told myself. So, why wasn't I getting out?

Well, for starters, I thought, *it's freezing cold out there, and also I've been warned to let this go.*

But photographs of Caroline's knife had been on the front page this morning. The implications were unfair and unthinkable. Caroline was a mess. Evan might really arrest her if he didn't find another suspect soon, and all I wanted was a look at the guy Derek called a nemesis. Could Brian Ford have killed Derek? Would I know by looking at him? I hadn't recognized last year's killer until it was too late, but maybe I'd gained something from the horrific experience. A sixth sense of some kind.

There was really only one way to find out. I'd take a peek at Brian Ford, see if some new form of intuition kicked in, and then I'd go look for Evan and listen to what he had to say about this morning's unfair headline.

Decision made, I climbed down from the cab and locked the truck door behind me.

Biting wind cut through my soft blue jeans and battered my puffy black coat. I zipped up to my frozen eyeballs and tied my scarf in a knot over my nose. The lot was full of holiday shoppers and vehicles moving in every direction. I ducked inside after a couple in matching pea coats, then blinked the snow from my eyes.

Displays of purses, wallets, and key chains reached for the arched, shiplap-lined ceiling. Belts hung from hooks along the walls. A saddle served as the room's centerpiece, homage to the store this had once been, or a chance to show off Ford's leatherwork via two elaborately detailed saddlebags—I wasn't sure. What I did know was that I'd never seen so much leather in one place. I lowered my scarf to take it all in. The scent was both nostalgic and overwhelming. It was the scent of childhood riding lessons. It was my dad's steady hand guiding me and my pony around the ring for hours.

I stroked the pebbled pink side of a distinctly feminine handbag, admiring the elegant silk and lace bow drooping from its strap. The soft material slid gracefully through my fingertips.

My phone applauded, pulling me from the moment of grand appreciation. I could almost understand why so many were willing to shell out a week's salary for one of these bags.

A woman giggled nearby, and I turned to find a pretty girl smiling behind the counter. She looked at my phone. "We get plenty of compliments, but applause is a first."

I silenced my notifications and smiled back. "Sorry. That was just my phone."

"Can I help you with something?" she asked, swinging a mass of long dark hair over one shoulder, the magazine-worthy waves landing on her name tag. Her cheery freckled face and fitted holiday shirt suggested she was barely out of college. The material of her top hugged her narrow frame and proclaimed, "Dear Santa, I can explain."

I approached slowly, unsure what to say. I didn't want to ask any questions about Derek Waggoner or Brian Ford, but here I was, faced with someone who worked with Derek's nemesis, and she wanted to know if she could help me. I snagged a maroon wallet off the checkout display, buying time to think. "My friend loves wallets," I said. "Can you tell me about this one?"

"Sure." She lit with enthusiasm as she explained in painful detail how the zipper and credit card slots worked. Lastly, she tapped one pretty red fingernail on the script *F*. "This shows your wallet was handcrafted by Brian Ford himself. It says other things too."

"Like?" I asked, admiring a beautiful dove tattoo on her wrist. The image of two twined ropes extended from the bird's spread wings as if it were a smooth velvet bracelet instead of incredibly detailed body art.

"Like you've got a discerning eye for quality and fashion."

"Ah." I tried not to look down at my ten-year-old outfit and slightly older hobo bag. Was I the only person on the planet who never thought about brands, labels, or what either said about me? "I had no idea a little *F* said all that," I admitted. "Brian Ford sounds like a local celebrity."

"I guess he kind of is," she said with a smile.

"Do you ever get to talk with him? Does he come into the store?" Maybe Brian produced the pieces elsewhere, and maybe I'd been wrong about finding him here. That would make sense. There were a whole lot of handbags around me, and each one took time to create. I could barely keep up with making necklaces. How could he be both creator and salesman?

The young woman's smile widened, and she pointed her finger toward a crowd near the back wall. "Yes, he does, and I get to talk with him every day."

The man at the center of the excitement wasn't what I'd expected. He looked like a gym rat with too much product in his spiky hair. "That's him? In the V-neck sweater and skinny jeans?"

"Would you like me to introduce you?"

"No." I shook my head hard.

The bell over the front door rang, and I nearly jumped out of my skin.

A Santa walked inside.

"Be right with you," the young woman called.

I gave Brian Ford another look. It was silly that I'd come just to see his face. Now that I had, I just wanted to forget it. My gaze fell on the morning paper lying beside the cash register. Was it coincidence or cosmic timing that I noticed it just as I was preparing to run?

She followed my gaze to the paper, then snatched it up.

"I read that story this morning," I said. "Awful, wasn't it?"

She rolled the paper up tight and clutched it to her chest. "I don't know anything about what happened."

Had I asked her if she knew what happened?

A creeping sensation spread over my skin, raising gooseflesh on my arms. "Do you know the woman they're talking about?" I asked. "The cupcake lady?"

"No." Her gaze jumped to the spiky-haired man in the back.

The itchy feeling reached higher up my neck and into my hair. "Did you know the man who died?"

Her cheeks flamed red.

My intuition screamed. "You did," I said. "How?" Was this woman another of Derek's groping victims? Worse?

"Nadia?" The spike-haired man moved swiftly in our direction. "Everything okay?"

Nadia? I flicked my eyes between the man and woman. "Nadia Ford?" I asked. "You're his *wife*?"

She swung the hair off her shoulder, revealing the previously hidden name tag and confirming my guess.

"How old are you?" I asked, unable to stop myself.

"Twenty."

I felt my eyes narrow on Brian. He had to be thirty-five. How long had they been married? Better yet, when had they started dating? Was it a whirlwind romance that began no more than two years ago, or was their courtship grounds for an arrest?

Brian moved to her side and squared his shoulders, probably surveying the tension between his young wife and myself, a scowling customer. "What's going on?" he asked, a fake smile plastered over his lips.

She mumbled something about the maroon wallet, but his gaze fell to the paper, rolled and wrinkled in her grasp.

His smile drooped. He jerked the paper from her hands and yanked open a drawer between them, stuffing the paper inside. A sheet of writing paper, like the one found in my threat-present, poked stubbornly out of the hastily closed drawer. Little snowflakes and Santas floated around the edges. My heart rammed into my throat.

Brian turned heated eyes on me. "I'd be happy to help you with the wallet. I'm Brian Ford. You look familiar. Have we met?"

I shook my head, paralyzingly intimidated by his broad shoulders and ugly scowl. "No. I'm just shopping for a . . . uh . . . friend. Christmas shopping. I'll just take the wallet," I said, sliding it over the counter to him.

* * *

Brian pulled his shoulders back and wedged his hands over his hips. "I know you." His eyes widened exponentially. "You're always with the blonde lady who's in the newspaper. The one who killed my friend."

"Friend?" I squeaked in shock and disbelief.

Nadia's eyebrows shot into her hairline. She clearly didn't agree with that description of Brian and Derek's relationship either.

"Caroline didn't kill Derek," I said. "The entire theory is ridiculous."

Brian leaned in my direction, looking impossibly more frustrated. "Is that why you're here?" he asked. "Trying to find someone else to pin his murder on?"

Kind of.

"No!" I gasped, then dared a look at the near-silent store around us. Everyone had gone still to eavesdrop, including the Santa. I turned back to the unhappy couple, wondering desperately what Nadia was mad about and why Brian seemed borderline belligerent.

"Get out," he said, meeting my face halfway across the counter. "And don't come back in here, or I'll report you for harassment."

Nadia's wide eyes welled with tears. She cupped both hands over her mouth and ran away.

I stared after her.

"Go." Brian's face was red, and his pulse was beating visibly at his temple. "Get. Out."

Panic jerked my feet into motion. I'd done the exact thing I'd promised myself I wouldn't do. I'd poked a bear.

I dropped the fancy wallet on the counter, turned on my toes, and broke into a graceless sprint for the door. I'd barely gotten a foot on the sidewalk when I plowed headlong into a wall of muscle. Strong hands gripped my biceps, holding me in place, and the familiar scent of gingerbread and cologne nearly stopped my heart. Wild relief washed over me and raised a lump in my throat. *Evan.*

I stepped back for a peek into his face and found stern green eyes focused over my head and into the store.

The expression on his face said I had some explaining to do.

Chapter Nine

"What are you doing here?" Evan asked, slowly releasing me from his grip.

I grimaced against the wind and tugged my scarf higher. "Shopping."

He frowned. "For a four-hundred-dollar purse?"

He had me there.

Evan locked strong fingers around my elbow and tugged me into the parking lot.

"Where are we going?" I asked, fumbling through the slush, stalling and mentally flailing. Experience told me Evan knew darn well what I'd been doing in there, and I was busted.

Evan stopped at the passenger side of his cruiser and wrenched the door open. "Get in."

I stared at a pile of delicious-smelling takeout food bags on the seat.

He rounded the hood to climb behind the steering wheel. Inside, he gathered the bags together and arranged them closer to him. "Get in," he repeated.

I took a seat and pulled the door shut behind me. "You're being bossy, and it's rude, you know."

He reached across his dash and pointed the vents at my face.

Warm air blew across my cheeks in steady streams, thawing my icy-cold skin. I warmed a little inside too at his caring gesture. "Thanks."

Evan stared, blank faced and silent.

My tummy groaned at the spicy scents of General Tso chicken and salty fried rice. "Is that Chinese takeout? For breakfast?"

Evan tied the bags' plastic handles into knots. "What are you really doing here?" he asked again, his voice softer this time. "You told me you weren't going to meddle this time. You promised."

"I'm not trying to meddle. I'm curious. I can't help it, and this is scary. It could really screw up Caroline's life."

Evan's serious gaze traveled through the lot, making its way across his rearview mirror and my face, then back to the store before us. "We talked about this. You know I can't babysit you and do my job. It's too much, and my life is already—" He broke off, letting his eyes shut briefly before reopening them and saying, "complicated. I nearly lost you over something like this last year. I don't want to go through that again."

I wasn't interested in going through it again either. "Sorry," I said. "I know it looks bad, but I didn't come here to cause trouble. I was only curious and worried about Caroline." My stomach made a frightening sound, and I gave the takeout bags another look until the number of foam containers slowly registered.

"That's enough for two. You have lunch plans with someone." My silly heart clenched, and I reached for the door handle, my cheeks aflame with senseless humility. Evan and I weren't a couple. We were barely friends these days. "I should go. Don't let your food get cold on my account. We can talk later. I won't get into trouble again before then."

The power locks snapped down.

"Hey." I swung my face around to frown at him. "Let me out."

"Not until you tell me what you're doing here. You said you came because you're curious. I want to know what you were curious about."

I fidgeted with my coat sleeve. "I came to see Brian Ford's face. Happy?"

"Do I look happy?"

I rolled my eyes. "No, but you're apparently hungry. Who's the takeout for?"

"Me."

"And?"

"Why did you want to see Brian's face?"

I looked at the shop. Customers filed in and out. Even Santa. From the looks of it, the Santa business was good. He climbed into a slick black sports car and motored away while Evan and I sat inside the cruiser, getting nowhere. Evan's jaw popped and locked. "Holly."

"I came because Samantha Moss said Brian was Derek's archnemesis, and it got my attention. I wanted to see what a grown man's nemesis looked like."

"Did you see him?" he asked, brows furrowing deep. "Did he say something to you? Threaten you? Is that why you ran out?"

"He told me to go away and not come back or he'd get a restraining order."

Humor lit in Evan's eyes. His jaw relaxed. "Smart man."

"Ha ha," I said humorlessly, finally fully unwinding. "Did you read the morning's headline? Now everyone knows Caroline's knife was found with Derek's body. People are going to look at her differently, maybe boycott her store. She thinks you're going to arrest her."

"I'm still waiting for prints," he said. "Could be as long as another day or two, but I'm hoping to hear something today."

"Why is it taking so long? It's not like there are any other crimes for the lab to process. Are there?"

Evan looked exhausted. His eyes were a little puffy, lined in red and underscored in purple. He'd told me once that he wasn't much of a sleeper, but he'd never looked like this.

"Are you okay?" I asked. "You don't look so good."

He pinched the bridge of his nose. "The problem with the fingerprints is that Mistletoe's forensics team consists of one guy named Dirk McDoogle, and according to the crime lab, Dirk took a few days off to put up two miles of Christmas lights out by the old covered bridge."

"Oh, I love McDoogle's lights," I said. A thousand childhood memories rose quickly to the surface. "Have you seen them?"

"No."

"Once he's back in the office, we can get this all cleared up," I said. "It's all circumstantial anyway. Everyone will see that, and Caroline's dad can insist the paper write an article formally exonerating her of any lingering suspicions."

Evan forced his troubled gaze to meet mine. "We found Derek's car last night. Parked behind Caroline's house. There were trace amounts of his blood inside, along with Caroline's hair."

"So? They rode together to dinner that night. Everyone knows that. Of course her hair was in there. Do you know how much hair that woman has?"

"And the blood?" he asked.

"Someone stabbed him. I'm sure he lost lots of blood."

Evan nodded slowly. "And why was his car at her house?"

"Maybe he went there after dinner to apologize," I suggested. "She wasn't there because she's already told you that she slept at the cupcake shop." Caroline and I had gone to her house when we left the square that night, but it had been dark, and we didn't stay long or look out back before we left. Still, Evan had a good question. *Why was Derek's car there?*

"Add her custom-made knife in the mints with our vic, and the case against her is getting uncomfortably strong," Evan said.

I pulled my chin back. "You wouldn't arrest her."

"I don't want to have to," he said, "but the truth is that everyone has a breaking point, and we know Derek Waggoner was harassing her that night."

"Unlock the door."

"What?"

I grabbed the handle. "Let me out."

Evan obeyed, and I opened the door. A cold gust of wind smashed into my face.

"Holly, wait."

I looked back, wanting him to say any one of a dozen different things. "What?"

He stared. Maybe sending some sort of message with the dip of his brow or those suddenly brooding eyes.

My heart softened.

Wind fluttered the bags at his side, pulling my attention back to my recently unanswered question. "Who are you having lunch with?"

He pursed his lips, and I climbed out of the cruiser. My eyes stung as I hustled across the lot to my truck, probably a result of the relentless wind. "Goodbye, Evan," I whispered, if only to myself as I pulled past his cruiser a moment later.

Evan sat motionless behind the wheel.

I drove back to Reindeer Games at half the posted speed limit, my heart squeezing painfully in my chest, energy zapped.

My phone buzzed with an incoming text before I'd reached the halfway home mark, and I pulled onto the shoulder, hoping ridiculously that Evan had sent an apology for suggesting there was a world where Caroline was a killer or for refusing to tell me who was meeting him for lunch. Why all the secrets? What was the point? Because from where I was sitting, his silence felt like a big push out of his life.

The message was a string of lowercase letters from Caroline: *this was on the porch.*

Beneath the message was a photo of a small red gift box like the one I'd found on my truck.

* * *

I drove to the newly created parking area outside the inn and jammed my pickup into park, then made a run for the guesthouse. "Caroline!" I called, jogging up the steps. "Caroline!"

She threw the door open before I could reach the knob. "Get in here."

I jumped inside and locked the door behind me. "Are you okay? When did the gift come? Did anything else happen?"

"No. Nothing. I texted you as soon as I saw it out there."

"Where is it now?"

She pointed to the little offender, seated on my hearth. "I locked myself in the bathroom after that and waited for you to get back. What should we do now?"

I stared at the thing. It seemed silly for two grown women to fear a small red box, but neither of us moved toward it. "I forwarded your text to Evan," I said. "He's on his way. Did you open it yet?"

Caroline shook her head, eyes wide, one fist pressed to her lips. "No way. It's for you."

"There's no tag," I countered. "Maybe this one is for you."

Her head kept wagging left to right.

I took a step forward. Then another.

"Should we wait for Evan?" she asked.

"Probably." But I was mad at him, and he was having Chinese food with a secret friend. I crouched before the fire and reached for the little box.

Caroline's shadow stretched over me as I gripped the lid in both hands and ripped it off like a bandage.

The box rocked slightly, but didn't spill.

Caroline and I leaned forward, peering warily inside.

Once again, red and white swirled peppermints filled the small container, and they were topped with another small rectangle of festive paper. Another message scrawled angrily across the center.

Keep looking for trouble, and
trouble is going to find you.

I jammed the lid back on and took Caroline's hand. "Let's wait for Evan at the Hearth."

She grabbed her coat, and we made a run for the truck. I texted Evan to meet us at the Hearth, then drove back to the busiest part of the farm, sailing past folks in every color coat and hat. Visitors dotted the snowy field outside the café, competing in the annual Build a Big Frosty competition. Dad stood atop a ladder, shouting encouragement from a bullhorn. Festive music piped through overhead speakers. Competitors laughed, poking carrots and sticks into their giant snowfolk's faces and sides.

It was hard to believe a killer could lurk here where there was so much silliness and joy.

We parked and hurried toward the Hearth, my creepy candy threat tucked safely under one bent arm.

"Caroline!" A man's voice stopped us outside the door.

I craned my neck for a look at the source. A man in a bright orange ski coat came into view.

Caroline sighed, then forced a tight smile. "Scooter. What are you doing here?"

"Oh, you know," he said, smiling, "enjoying the festivities." Scooter opened his arms, then dropped them to his sides. His nose and cheeks were red from the cold, and his hat had a collection of snow on the top.

How long had he been outside?

I ushered them toward the café, eager to get inside for multiple reasons. "Which festivities have you been enjoying so far?" I asked, pulling the door open for them to pass.

Scooter's cheeks darkened. "Just checking things out, I guess."

An unsettling feeling coiled in my middle. Had he been here long enough to have delivered the peppermint threat? Had he killed Derek for putting his hands on Caroline?

Evan's cruiser appeared on the long gravel drive before I could follow Caroline and Scooter inside.

"I'll be right there," I called after them. "Save me a seat?"

Caroline nodded politely.

Scooter looked as if he'd hit the lottery.

I met Evan in the lot and climbed into his cruiser. "Here," I said, handing him the box and ignoring the heady scent of takeout clinging to his car's interior.

Evan looked it over, peeked inside, then secured it in a big plastic bag marked "Evidence." "How are you?" he asked, a mix of fear and anger brewing in his eyes. "Are you okay?"

"Yeah."

He looked me over, pausing at my hands where I'd folded them on my lap, but he made no move to reach for me. The air between us was thick with unspoken burdens.

"Come inside for cocoa," I said. "Or maybe something sweet? Mom's been baking, and Caroline's in there. Plus, Christmas Karaoke is starting soon."

"I can't," he said. "I have to go, but I'll be back to get a formal statement from Caroline about the threat's arrival."

"Where are you going?" I asked, utterly shocked at his refusal. Sure, he'd been pulling away for a while, but it wasn't like Evan to leave without dusting the whole farm for prints and personally examining every building, tree, and snowflake for evidence.

He turned a blank cop stare on me. "McDoogle called. I need to meet him at the lab."

"What did he say?"

The screen of Evan's phone lit. He raised the device from his cup holder and grimaced. "Sorry, Holly. I hate to do this, but I really need to move."

"Fine." I climbed out and watched him go.

When I turned back, Cookie stood at the Hearth's door, holding it open for me. She had a cup of tea in her free hand. "I thought you could use this."

I tossed the steaming contents into my mouth and swallowed in a heavy gulp. Peppermint schnapps and Earl Grey for the win.

Cookie's eyes went wide. "You're supposed to sip it. It clears your sinuses and warms your belly."

My belly growled.

"Better follow that tea with some whoopie pies," she said.

I followed her to a booth, where Caroline sat awkwardly across from Scooter, sipping on what smelled like peppermint tea.

A moment later, Mom appeared with a tray of warm whoopie pies and four cups of hot cocoa. "We're about to start the

Christmas Karaoke," she said. "Would you all like a spot on the lineup?"

Caroline, Scooter, and I shook our heads in the negative.

Cookie charged the makeshift stage with a big "You betcha!"

Dad had built a mobile stage years ago that fit snugly into a four-by-six-foot section of the Hearth. Two tables had been moved this morning to make room for the unit, and farm hands had hauled the stage inside. A pint-sized disco ball had been hung from the ceiling above the unit, and a projector was positioned on the counter, shining a carousel of festive colors onto the shiny, mirrored ball.

For a small cover charge, Mom's hot cocoa and select treats were an all-you-care-to-eat option, at least until the karaoke ended.

I shoved a whoopie pie into my mouth while Cookie chose her song.

She pushed a button on my old karaoke machine, and the introductory notes to "Jingle Bell Rock" began.

Mom dimmed the lights slightly, and the Hearth erupted into applause as patrons turned their chairs to face the stage.

Cookie danced in a small circle until her back faced the room, donned a felt hat with elf ears from a pile of available costume choices, then spun back in dramatic Cookie fashion. "Jingle bell, jingle bell, jingle bell rock . . ."

I sucked cream filling off my thumb, wishing for another cup of special tea but knowing better than to have it. I lowered my forehead to the cool tabletop and groaned.

Scooter shifted on the bench across from me. "See?" he said. "You can find anything about anyone online."

Caroline made a few disgusted noises.

I tried to concentrate on Cookie's grand, high-kicking finale and ignore the conversation happening beside me. Scooter gave me the creeps, and I wasn't feeling patient or cordial enough to get to know someone new.

"I can't believe it," Caroline whispered. "Look at all these women. I know I shouldn't be shocked, but I totally am. Where are their clothes?"

I straightened up and peeked over her shoulder. "What are you looking at?"

Caroline angled her phone screen toward me. "Derek's social media profiles. Look at all these photos of him with random women," she said. "Most of them are in itty-bitty bikinis."

"He can't possibly know that many ladies," Scooter said.

I blinked at Caroline's schmoopy stalker, recalling his sudden appearance tonight. "How did you know Caroline was here?" I asked. I was hoping to sound genuinely intrigued and not half as suspicious or cranky as I felt.

He shrugged one shoulder. "You're her best friend. She hasn't been home, so . . ." He left the sentence hanging for a long beat.

I waited, not releasing eye contact.

"It didn't take a professional investigator to guess she was here with you," he said.

I swallowed hard, trying not to read too much into his words. "How do you know she hasn't been home?" I asked.

"Mail." Scooter unzipped his coat with a proud grin and reached inside before retrieving a stack of envelopes. He turned his smile on Caroline. "Once I realized you were avoiding your place, I thought you might want your mail. It is Christmas, after all. Maybe the sight of all these holiday cards will cheer you up."

"Thank you," she said, sounding genuinely thrilled as she fanned out the stack of brightly colored envelopes.

I lacked her enthusiasm. "Did you check the mailbox at the cupcake shop too?"

"Nah," he said with a regretful tip of his head. "Her business uses a post office box."

Caroline stopped shuffling through her cards and raised her eyes slowly to mine.

There. Now we were on the same page. Creepy.

I swung my attention back to the phone she'd set on the table when she picked up the Christmas cards. "Hey," I said, reaching for the device. "Can I take a look?"

"Sure," she said.

I studied the group photo on the screen. The couples were on a boat, wearing swimsuits like Caroline had said. The time stamp in the corner indicated the photo had been taken six months ago.

I increased the photo size until only the center couple was visible, then dragged my fingertip over the screen, pulling the picture along until I reached the couple on the end, their bodies wrapped greedily around each other in a passionate embrace.

"Gross," Caroline said, refocused on the phone. "Who posts photos of their public make-out sessions on the internet?"

"Derek Waggoner," I said.

"Of course," Caroline scoffed. "Who's that poor baby he's mauling with his grabby hands and suffocating with his mouth?"

I stared at the young woman's partially visible but highly freckled face; her thick, flowing dark hair; and the familiar tattoo of a dove on the wrist, where her fingers were curled knuckle deep in Derek's hair. "Oh my goodness. That's Nadia Ford!"

I didn't know about Nadia, but I thought that if she'd cheated on her husband, and Derek had posted the evidence online, she'd definitely want to kill him for it.

Chapter Ten

I yanked my phone from my pocket as a new karaoke duo took the stage. Two white-haired women had selected oversized black sideburns from the costume box and pasted them to their cheeks. They began an enthusiastic impersonation of Elvis as the track to "Blue Christmas" began.

Caroline gaped at me while I fumbled with my phone. "Are you calling Sheriff Gray?"

My thumb stilled above the screen. My eyebrows crowded so tightly together, I could feel the permanent crease forming. I looked at Caroline. Evan needed to know that the murder victim was kissing his nemesis's wife just a few months ago, and the photographic evidence was online, but I'd promised to stay out of this.

"What?" she asked, waving one hand toward my phone in encouragement.

"If I tell him I was snooping, he'll yell at me."

"He shouldn't yell at you," Scooter said.

I started, caught off guard again by the man I kept forgetting was there.

"No one should ever yell at you," he said.

I had to admit I agreed. I looked closely at him for the first time. Scooter had thick dark hair and brows, and brilliant blue eyes behind Harry Potter glasses. From the neck up, he looked like a cover model for one of those computer magazines. He'd sloughed his orange ski coat onto the seat beside him, revealing a puckered thermal shirt that clung to his lean muscled frame, giving the rest of him an altogether different appearance. Bundled up, I'd mistaken him for tall and lanky. Now, I could see he was fit and lean. Maybe even strong enough to dump Derek Waggoner into a big vat of mints. "You're new to Mistletoe," I said.

"I moved here in September," he said. "My family visited every year when I was a kid, and I always said I'd live here one day."

"Where are you from?" I asked. *And did you kill Caroline's date and dump him in a giant candy bowl?*

"Massachusetts." Scooter grinned, looking suddenly young and bashful. "I bounced around in the service, then landed back there for college. After that, I asked for a military transfer to Kettering, Maine, and here I am. It's a bit of a commute, but I don't mind."

Caroline tilted her head, curiosity narrowing her eyes. "You *just* finished college? How old are you?"

"Twenty-eight."

She wrinkled her nose. "Did you start late? Take some time off after high school?"

"Nah, but I could only take classes part-time while I was in the service, and only when I wasn't deployed. It was a slow process, but it was worth it." He smiled back at her. "Where did you go to college?"

"Yale."

Scooter sat back with a grin. "Impressive."

Caroline smiled. "Well, Dad is an alumnus. They practically had to take me."

"What was your major?" he asked.

"Business with a minor in political science. I learned to bake to handle the stress."

"Well, that worked out well for you," he said, cheeks ruddy, hands fidgety.

He was nervous. Why? The conversation seemed innocent enough. "Where did you go to college?" I asked. "What was your major?" Navy or not, ten years seemed excessive. Was he delayed for some reason other than the ones he'd named? A jail stint for homicidal tendencies perhaps?

Scooter fiddled with his napkin, eyes on Caroline. "I had a few majors."

"Where do you work?" she asked. "What do you do?"

"Department of Defense. It's classified."

I leaned back in my seat, putting a few more inches between myself and Scooter. Was the geeky look for real? Or a way of making himself seem harmless? I imagined Scooter doing a fatal military attack on Derek Waggoner for upsetting Caroline.

Scooter rubbed the skin beneath his glasses. "It's none of my business, but I meant what I said earlier. Your friend shouldn't yell at you. Doesn't matter if he's the sheriff or the president."

"I agree," Caroline said.

I looked at my phone. "Did I tell you he bought Chinese food for two earlier and refused to tell me who he was eating with? He's been secretive and distant for months, and now he's just acting outright squirrelly."

Caroline flashed a mischievous all-teeth smile. "Maybe you should check his social media."

I laughed. "Believe me. I've looked." The minute he'd started accusing my dad and his staff of murder last Christmas, I'd lost sleep trying to find out who the new sheriff really was. "He doesn't even have a Facebook account."

"Bummer," Caroline said. "My granny has a Facebook account."

We watched a dozen more people sing and dance along to Christmas classics like "Frosty the Snowman" and "Rockin' Around the Christmas Tree," hopped up on holiday spirit, caffeine, and sugar. Scooter stayed until our cocoas and whoopie pies were gone, then said his goodbyes and promised he'd see Caroline again soon. I couldn't help wondering if she'd know it when he did.

I pinched the bridge of my nose and forced back the paranoia. My suspect list was up to four people in two days. Caroline's schmoopy stalker; Derek's crazy ex-girlfriend; his nemesis, Brian Ford; and that guy's cheating wife, Nadia. And those were just the people I knew had motive.

Eventually karaoke ended, and there was a mass exodus from the Hearth.

I still hadn't texted Evan to tell him about Derek and Nadia, but I needed to.

Caroline slipped her coat on. "I have an idea," she said. "If we can't find out what Evan's up to by looking online, maybe we can learn something about him the old-fashioned way."

"You want to go talk to him?"

She nudged me out of the booth. "Noooo." She dragged the word out for several syllables. "We're going to spy on him. Just like in high school. We'll drive past the pie shop. If he's not there, we'll try his home, count how many cars are in the driveway. See if we recognize them. If the curtains are open, we might see what's happening inside."

She pushed me again, and I nearly fell out of the booth.

"That isn't something I did in high school." Or ever. "What if he sees us?"

"Then we'll tell him about Nadia and Derek. We have a reason to be looking for him, remember?"

I put my coat on.

Half an hour later we turned onto Evan's street. No sign of him at the pie shop, but the lights were all on at his house, and the sun was low in the sky, thanks to daylight savings time. There were no vehicles in his driveway. I idled my truck along the curb and marveled. "Do you think he'd leave all those lights on just for the cat?"

"I don't know." Caroline watched the home from her car window. "Some people really love their cats."

I leaned across the bench, staring through the fading sunlight, idly wondering if Cindy Lou Who would like me to leave more lights on, or maybe the television.

"Where did he say he was going when you saw him at the farm tonight?"

I thought back to the moment I'd spent in his car. "He said he'd been in contact with McDoogle at the crime lab and couldn't stay for cocoa. Then he got a text message and rushed off."

"Ooh." Caroline smiled. "I love McDoogle's lights. We should drive by the covered bridge while we're out."

A shadow fell over the front window, and someone pulled back the curtain. The television flickered in the background, and a slender silhouette stood stock-still for a long beat.

I jerked myself upright and gripped the wheel. "Time to go."

"What? Why?" Caroline turned to look at Evan's house.

Someone opened the door before I could answer. The figure marched onto the porch and something flashed.

"Who was that?" she asked as I motored away.

I pressed the gas pedal with a little more purpose, and the figure shrank steadily in my rearview mirror.

"That wasn't Evan," I said, hating the lump in my throat. No, the person who'd marched onto Evan's porch was distinctly female. She was petite and redheaded, with curves everywhere, and I thought she'd been wearing one of Evan's Boston Red Sox T-shirts.

Caroline turned wide eyes on me. "I'm so sorry. This was a stupid idea."

"It's fine," I said, forcing back the truth. *I was hurt and had no right.* I took another left and headed through downtown toward the covered bridge. McDoogle's lights would surely cheer me up.

The square came into view, and my gaze caught on something broad and glowing. "Is that a fire?"

"Whoa." Caroline leaned forward, squinting at the freestanding white cross that had been erected in place of the giant candy dish. The words "Derek Waggoner" were painted on it, along with two years, the current one and another I presumed was his birth year. The base of the cross was surrounded by cards, flowers and candles in jars—even a few stuffed animals.

Samantha Moss sat on a pop-up chair beside a trash barrel with a fire going. She too was surrounded by flowers, candles, mementos, and photographs of Derek Waggoner. She'd embedded her chair into the mix as if she was one of the offerings, or maybe the guardian of his memory. There was a three-foot fir tree on her right. It had a star on top, and she had a box of colorful bulbs on her lap.

I slowed to a crawl so I could gawk as we passed.

"That's so sad," Caroline whispered. "She looks like a hobo sitting in the cold with that fire. Maybe we should try to help her. That kind of grief isn't normal."

Samantha took notice of my truck a moment later and did a double take. "You!"

I read her lips through the glass.

She hopped to her feet and slid her gaze to Caroline at my side. Her face went crimson. "And you!" She ripped an ornament from her box and chucked it at my truck.

Smash! The silver ball connected with the window beside my face and exploded into a million shards of glass, or whatever ornaments were made from.

I screamed.

Caroline jumped. "Did she just throw one of those at us?"

"Yes," I said. I accelerated, hurrying to catch up with the traffic ahead of me and get out of range.

Smash! Another bulb crashed against my truck's door and exploded. Then another.

I watched impatiently as crowds filled the crosswalks, some

of them staring, and cars stopped repeatedly to allow jaywalking pedestrians to pass. "Come on," I murmured, impatient to get out of there.

Samantha stalked my way.

Smash!

"Hey!" I lowered my window and glared. "Knock it off."

Smash!

"What should we do?" Caroline asked.

"I don't know!" I scanned the area in search of an escape. An alleyway came into view.

Smash!

I yanked the wheel and stepped on the gas, jumping out of traffic and into the desolate alley on our right. My truck bounced and rocked over the pitted narrow road as I pulled it to a stop behind the resale shop, then looked both ways. "I think we should visit McDoogle's lights another night," I said. "Let's just go back to the guesthouse. Samantha's a lunatic, and Evan has some redhead staying with him. I've got a ton of work I'm avoiding at home. I don't need this drama tonight."

Caroline rubbed my shoulder. "Okay. Sorry—this wasn't the night I'd imagined when I suggested it."

I shot her a half smile. "We should definitely refer to it as an adventure in our retellings."

She laughed. "Deal. Now, let's get out of here before she finds us."

* * *

My truck flew over the rolling hills back to Reindeer Games. My mind raced with details I had for Evan, along with several questions. I crested a hill, then maneuvered around a curve and back down the other side, checking my rear view periodically for signs Samantha Moss had acquired a vehicle and was coming for us.

Several minutes later, a set of headlights appeared in the distance, and my muscles went rigid. My grip on the wheel began to hurt as I squeezed tight enough to make a dent.

Emergency flashers flicked to life behind me, circling on top of the assailing vehicle.

Caroline sucked air. "Are we being pulled over?"

"Looks like it," I said. I checked my speed, then slowed gradually to see if the cruiser would fly past, on his way somewhere else.

No luck.

"But we didn't do anything wrong," she said.

I eased to a stop along the roadside. "I might've been speeding a little."

She frowned. "Do you think mentioning you're a good friend of Sheriff Gray's will get you out of the ticket?"

I powered my window down, watching the uniformed man approach in my side-view mirror. "Nope."

Evan stopped at my side and peeked around me to Caroline. "Ladies."

We waved.

"Any idea why I'm pulling you over?"

We shook our heads no.

His lips ticked up on one side, but he squelched the smile before it appeared. "You ran a stop sign leaving downtown."

"I did?" I racked my brain trying to think of which sign I'd missed. "I don't think so," I said.

"You did," he assured me. "I saw you. I also saw Samantha Moss throwing Christmas bulbs, so I stopped to talk with her before coming after you."

"Are you going to give me a ticket?" I asked. I'd never had a ticket. I had a long list of things I wanted to accomplish in life—being ticketed for breaking a traffic law wasn't on it.

Evan tented his brows. "No. I wanted to check on you. See if you were okay after Samantha went after you with those bulbs. I know she's hurting, but she's going to have to learn to control her temper before someone gets hurt."

I hiked a brow. "Like Derek Waggoner?"

His lids slipped shut, and he pressed a thumb and forefinger against them. "Are you okay?" he asked, looking back at me with resolve. "Was the truck damaged? Do you want to press charges?"

"No. Of course not," I said. Being an unstable person seemed like trouble enough for her.

Evan lifted one finger, then pulled his phone from his pocket and looked at it. He returned his gaze to mine, shock written all over it. "What were you doing in town tonight?"

"Um." I looked at Caroline.

Evan cocked a hip. "Did you go anywhere specific?" he asked. "Do anything unusual?"

"No," I lied and felt my face protesting. My forehead wrinkled. My nose twitched. My lips pressed tight.

Evan stepped closer. "Happen to take a spin past my house?"

I made a thinking face and looked at Caroline again. She shook her head innocently. "I don't think so," I said. "Why do you ask?"

He turned his phone screen to face me. A photograph of the

back end of my truck pulling away from his curb centered the screen. The photo had been texted from someone named Libby.

I stared dumbly at the big red truck with reindeer antlers and my license plate number.

"Why were you at my house?" he said. "Is something wrong? Did something happen?"

I tried to think of a good excuse for being a peeping Holly. Then I remembered. "Yes!" I cleared my throat. "Yes. We were looking through Derek Waggoner's social media accounts and saw a photo of him kissing Nadia Ford a few months ago. Since Nadia's husband is Derek's nemesis, we thought you might want to know about this. It gives Brian Ford additional motive."

A vein pulsed in Evan's forehead. "Why were you looking at Derek's social media?"

Caroline leaned across the bench toward me and Evan. "That was me," she said. "Scooter and I were going through Derek's photos to make sure there weren't any of me on there. I was hoping not to be forever linked to him via the internet. Turns out I wasn't, so no worries." She shifted back to her side of the truck muttering, "Thank goodness."

Evan evaluated me.

"Who's Libby?" I asked.

"Huh?"

"I saw who texted that photo of my truck," I explained. "Is she the secret you've been keeping from me? Because you really don't need to do that. You and I are friends, and I'm not judging you or whatever you think I might be doing that is causing you to push me away. I don't care if you have a girlfriend who eats Chinese food with you for breakfast and wears your T-shirts. It's fine. In fact, I'd love to meet her." I lifted my chin, hoping to look more confident than I felt.

Evan crossed his arms and leaned on my open window ledge. "You wouldn't care if I had a girlfriend? You'd want to meet her?"

I nodded.

He looked like I'd shoved a lemon in his mouth. "Libby's my little sister," he said. "She's staying with me while I help her through a mess back in Boston, but that's not my story to tell." He groaned and turned his phone over when it lit in his palm. "Hang on," he said. "I've got to take this, but we're going to talk about that other thing."

My heart rate picked up.

Caroline pushed me gently. "The woman he's been hiding is his little sister," she whispered. "He's been helping her with something this whole time, and he's only being secretive to protect her." She pressed both hands to her chest and beamed.

I smiled. "That seems nice of him."

"So I guess our peeping wasn't a total bust. It forced the truth out of him. Now, maybe things will get better between you two. Like, maybe this moment is the turning point from a very bad week to a very good one."

I squeezed her hand on the seat between us for a quick beat. She was right. Everything about the moment felt like a turning point. And it was great to have some hope again. About Evan. About Derek's killer. About everything.

"Caroline?" Evan said, poking his face back through my window. "I'm going to need you to get out of the truck."

"What?" Caroline said at the same moment I asked, "Why?"

Night had fallen as we'd sat there. The county road was dark save for the occasional set of headlights going or coming. Above us a universe of stars twinkled down.

Evan was illuminated in the beams of his headlights, and he kept a steady gaze on Caroline as he spoke. "McDoogle confirmed the knife as Derek Waggoner's murder weapon, and your prints are the only ones on it. His car was found parked behind your home with traces of blood inside. You were seen in a heated argument with him a few hours before his death."

"But—" she said, stopping short as tears and panic filled her eyes.

"Caroline West," Evan continued, "I'm taking you into custody for the murder of Derek Waggoner."

I powered my window up and locked the door. I gripped the wheel, debating how far I could get before he caught us. According to my gas tank, the answer was *not very*.

Caroline tapped her phone screen frantically, tears falling onto the glass.

Evan rapped a knuckle against my window. "Roll it down, Holly."

I shook my head.

"Come on out, Caroline," he said. "It's better if you do it on your own."

"I'm calling my dad," she said loudly, projecting her cracking voice through the glass. "I want his lawyer to meet me at the station."

I lowered the window by an inch and tipped my mouth toward the opening. "This is ridiculous. You know she didn't kill him."

"I'm following the evidence," he said. "There are procedures." His sharp eyes pleaded for me to understand his position.

I couldn't. The only thing I understood at the moment was the sheer terror coming off my best friend in waves. "I'll drive her," I said. "She doesn't need to be seen riding in your cruiser. We'll meet you at the station. I'll park out back and text you when we get there."

Evan watched me, visibly torn.

"What?" I said. "It's not as if she's actually a killer and you're letting her get away. She's not going to flee. She's going to take a minute, collect herself, then sneak in through the back. It's the least you can do to help the innocent friend you are wrongfully accusing."

He lifted both palms, relenting his position. "You have an hour."

"Thank you," I said, tears brimming in my eyes.

He patted the roof of my truck and walked away, pressing his cell phone to his ear.

I turned to Caroline and pulled her into a hug. "I'll figure this out," I promised.

And I intended to do exactly that.

Chapter Eleven

I arrived at the Hearth on Mom's heels the next morning. She was just turning on the kitchen lights as I came through the front door. The festive café was quiet as a mouse, and I lingered, taking it in. The still. The peaceful moment. *Hopefully not the calm before the storm,* I thought. Unless the storm portion would involve saving Caroline. I took a full deep breath to anchor myself in the moment, but that turned into a yawn.

I'd been up all night, plagued with a busy mind and restless energy. I couldn't stop remembering the expression on Caroline's face when I'd dropped her off at the sheriff's department. I'd walked her in, passed her over to her family's attorney, then stayed behind as she was escorted out of sight. A door had shut between us, and my heart had deflated.

Caroline was the embodiment of positivity, hope, and goodness. And she was in jail.

I slogged my way toward the front, pushed my bursting backpack onto the counter, and collapsed onto a lollipop. Mom hadn't baked a thing yet, but the sweet scents of cinnamon, sugar, and vanilla had long ago embedded themselves in the walls, curtains, and floor.

"Holly?" The swinging door flipped open, and Mom appeared with her usual ready smile. "Hey there, sweetheart. How are you doing this morning?"

Awful. "I'm okay. How are you managing back there with a half-finished kitchen?"

She groaned. "I broke down and fired the guy. I didn't trust him to come back after his two-week break, and even if he did show up, how could I believe he'd ever really finish what he started? He's five weeks past the completion date, the job is half-done, and he skipped out for Christmas. I'm not sure where I go from here, but it's time I took back control of my kitchen."

"Good," I said. It was time I started taking control of the things that were important in my life too.

Mom studied me closely. "You look half-asleep. How about I make you the first cup of coffee?"

"Yes, please."

The coffee machine grunted to life, puffing bitter steam into the air and filling the pot with liquid enthusiasm. I needed all of it. I would've stuck my head under the drip if it wouldn't have violated multiple health codes.

Mom poked my book bag with one finger. "What's all that? Looks like it's ready to pop."

I levered myself upright and unzipped the bag. "That's one of the reasons I'm here so early."

I hadn't slept, but I had gone through all of the contractor's binders for the inn and chosen my favorites from the selections that Caroline had flagged. I'd also found a massive archive of historically correct details on the Mistletoe Historical Society website. I used the information to best match the new to the old and uphold the traditions of our historic town.

Pulling the binders from my bag, I pushed them toward Mom. "I made all the choices for the inn."

She stretched her eyes wide. "All of them?"

"Not the railings and spindles, but everything in those." I pointed to the binders.

"Heavens," Mom said. She poured me a mug of coffee and patted my hand. "Have I thanked you lately for all you do around here? I don't know how we got along all those years while you were away, first at college and then making a life on your own."

I tried to smile, but I needed more coffee for that. "Thanks."

"What's on your agenda for today?" she asked. "Going to catch up on some sleep, I hope? Maybe make some more adorable jewelry?"

My phone applauded on cue. "I caught up with my jewelry orders around dawn, and I've only had a few more since then. I thought I'd help you if you need me. Maybe wrap the rest of my Christmas gifts or check on Caroline."

"Will they allow her visitors?" Mom asked. "Maybe I should call her parents and ask how she's doing? Let them know your father and I are here if they need anything."

"That sounds nice," I said. I was also hoping to run into Evan. Maybe then I could get some answers about anyone else he was looking at as a suspect. I had four solid options if he needed them. I paused with the mug halfway to my lips, tummy clenched. "Do you think Evan stopped looking for other suspects when he took Caroline into custody?"

Mom rested her elbows on the counter, a penguin-shaped mug held between her palms. "I think you need to talk to Evan."

Mom was right. I needed answers about Caroline, and Evan had them. The other answers I wanted, I'd have to get on my own. "I'm really frightened for her," I admitted. "What if she has to spend Christmas in jail? If Evan doesn't find the real killer in the next nine days, it will be too late."

"Evan knows Caroline's not a killer," Mom said. "I'm sure he's still looking."

"He says we're all capable of losing control under the right circumstances," I told her, "and that all the evidence points to Caroline."

Mom frowned. "Well, that might all be true, but it doesn't mean he believes Caroline did this or that he's stopped looking for the real killer. You know what else? If there's a season for miracles, this is it, so you've got to keep the faith, and don't give up on Evan. He won't give up on her either."

I concentrated on believing everything would turn out okay, and then another idea popped into mind. Maybe it was the coffee kicking in, but it seemed like high time I visited Caroline's Cupcakes for some reconnaissance. I still had the key, but I was more interested in how someone had gotten inside. How had they stolen her butcher knife? This sort of investigating should have been a lawman thing, but today it was a jewelry maker, café waitress, and best friend thing. "Okay," I told Mom. "I'll have faith that Caroline will be cleared of this mess before Christmas." And I'll do all I can to help faith along.

"Atta girl." Mom clinked her mug against mine.

The Hearth door swung open, and a blast of icy wind blew up my shirttail.

Cookie stomped snow from her boots and did a whole-body shiver. "It's cold out there," she said, pulling her scarf and knit cap free. "I would have stayed home in my PJs if I didn't have such great news."

Great news? I didn't see Caroline running free behind her, so Cookie must not have heard about the arrest. She looked too pumped to know her friend and business partner was in jail for murder.

"What's your news?" Mom asked, setting a new mug of coffee next to mine.

Cookie climbed onto the stool beside me and lifted the cup, eyes twinkling with delight. "Ray and I have all the pictures we need to make Theodore's calendar. We're calling it a Goat for All Seasons, and it can even go to print today—I could have copies in time for Christmas. That's a much faster turnaround than I'd expected. Originally, I'd only wanted to have them in time for fall fundraising, but now . . ." She kneaded her hands together. "Now, they can be Christmas gifts and give folks a little taste of what's to come. Then I can do a second calendar next year, and customers will be lining up to give me their money. With all those donations, I can really make a difference somewhere," she said, "and Theodore can be the celebrity he's always wanted to be."

"That's great," I told her. "You and Theodore deserve this."

"Darn skippy," she said, hauling a stack of photos from her handbag. "Ray was a hoot to work with, and he has the patience of a saint." She paused. "I'm not sure why you aren't dating him."

"Hey." I made a face at her. "What's that supposed to mean?"

"He can't say enough nice things about you. He's handsome and smart. Fun-loving. Good to his mama. Those are all excellent qualities in a mate."

"I like having Ray as a friend," I said. "And I'm not looking for a mate." That sounded more like something she should find Theodore. Besides, I wasn't great with relationships. Friendships, on the other hand, were where I did my best work. "Once two people date and break up, things get strange between them, even under the best of circumstances," I said. "Friendship is better."

Mom shuffled through the photos. "I don't know. All the best marriages I know are built on strong friendships. Look at your dad and me. Love and friendship aren't mutually exclusive."

"Like Theodore and me," Cookie added, wrinkling her nose. "My husband, not the goat."

I smiled, perusing Theodore the goat's photos one by one as Mom passed them my way. "How about I leave my love life up to destiny?"

"Destiny's a real biscuit," Cookie said. "What do you think of the pictures? Great, right?"

Theodore had more accessories than me, and a beard any man would envy. Who wouldn't want a Goat for All Seasons calendar?

"Where's Caroline?" Cookie asked, swiveling on her chair. "Did she sleep in?"

I swallowed an instant lump of emotion. "No." I chugged my coffee, shoring up the gumption to say the awful thing aloud. "Evan took her in last night for Derek's murder. Her knife was confirmed as the murder weapon, and the only prints they found on it were hers."

Cookie climbed off her seat. "Well, what are we waiting for?" she said. "Let's go bail her out."

"Her family attorney was at the station last night when I dropped her off," I said. "I'm sure he's handling it."

Cookie looked from the door to me, seemingly undecided on which way to go. "Have you spoken to her?"

"No." I tapped my mug, asking Mom silently for a refill. She obliged.

"We should go see her."

Mom nodded. "I'm going to give her parents a call in a bit."

I let the warmth of Mom's coffee curl through me. I could almost feel my limbs pepping up and my eyes growing wider. "I'm going to stop by the cupcake shop again. Make sure Samantha Moss hasn't taken another run at the windows or done anything else mean to the store."

Cookie grabbed her bag and the photos from the counter. "Good idea. I'm coming with you."

"Whoa," Mom said. "You've got first shift at the Holiday Mouse craft shop, remember? And you're helping me with Bling that Gingerbread this afternoon."

Bling that Gingerbread was a Hearth tradition, and it was part of the Twelve Days of Reindeer Games. Players were blind-folded and given a tray with a preassembled gingerbread house and piles of frosting and embellishments. Everyone had five minutes to apply the frosting, gumdrops, sugar sprinkles, and other sweets to their house before Mom blew a whistle. The winner got free holiday hot cider and Saint snickerdoodles. It was always a tight competition.

Cookie sat down dutifully. She looked at me. "If they let you see Caroline, tell her we'll fix this," she said. "I don't know how yet, but make sure she knows she's got a squad out here working to spring her."

"I will."

My phone rang, and Evan's face appeared on the screen. "Hang on," I told Mom and Cookie as I stepped away from the counter to answer. "Hello?"

"Good," Evan said. "I was hoping to catch you. Can we talk?"

"Sure."

There was a long pause. "Can I make you dinner tonight? My place?"

"Your place?" I looked at Mom and Cookie. Both were smiling. "Tonight?" I couldn't help wondering where his secret sister would be. "Are you sure? What about your sister?"

"You said you wanted to meet her, right?"

"Yes. Are you sure you're ready for me to meet her?"

"Yes."

Huh. I rubbed the remaining sleep from my eyes. "I can't promise not to ask questions," I said, "and I'm still mad that you arrested my friend."

"We can talk about anything you want tonight. Libby will be here to field the questions involving her, and I will say as much as I can about Caroline's case. Will you come?"

I gave Mom and Cookie another look. They both appeared to have stopped breathing in favor of eavesdropping. "If I come down to the station today, can I see Caroline?" I asked Evan.

There was a long beat of silence before he answered. "I don't think so."

"You don't think so?" I parroted back, hackles up. "Everyone is allowed visitors," I snapped.

"Not when they're in isolation."

"What?" I screeched. "What is wrong with you?"

"It's not me," he growled. "Her dad insisted. He says it's for her protection."

Fire drained from my veins as I realized what was happening. In Mayor West's world, nothing was more important than public opinion, not even his daughter's happiness. "He's making sure as few people as possible find out she's there."

"Probably," Evan admitted.

"Okay. I'll come for dinner," I said. "See you tonight."

* * *

I parked in front of Caroline's Cupcakes and breathed easier knowing Samantha Moss hadn't been back to throw anything at the front window. I let myself in and made a quick loop through the shop.

A note on the counter caught my attention immediately. For one terrifying moment, I feared it was another threat, but the border on the paper wasn't made of Santas and snowmen—it was a parade of tiny feather dusters and brooms.

I eased closer and recognized the Merry Maids logo anchoring the note's bottom right corner. The message was signed with a cursive *G* and filled with praise for Caroline's willingness to stand up to Derek.

I couldn't help but wonder if the note was a general

statement for all women being treated poorly by a man or if this member of the Merry Maid staff had a problem with Derek too. I dialed the number from the logo on my cell and waited.

"Merry Maids," a whiny voice answered.

"Hello," I began, floundering for a game plan. "This is Caroline West. One of your crews cleaned my shop this week, Caroline's Cupcakes."

"Of course, Miss West, what can we do for you?"

"Well, I think one of the maids left her . . . hat here, and I wanted to return it to her. Can you tell me who was here?" I listened to the sounds of fingernails on a keyboard for several long seconds.

"Looks like your usual crew. The hat wasn't reported as lost. You can probably just leave it somewhere visible before their next visit, and the owner can reclaim it then."

"I don't know," I said. "It's pretty cold outside. Maybe I should bring it to her. There seems to be a letter *G* on the tag inside."

"Gina."

"Right! Is Gina working today?"

"She is."

I listened again to the swift click-clack of a busy keyboard.

"What are the odds," the woman said. "She's cleaning Derek Waggoner's home now. I can't give you the address, but I'm sure you have it. She should be there for another hour or two."

"Thank you!"

"Miss West?" the voice pressed. "I'm sorry about what's happening to you. No one believes the rumors or the ridiculous headlines."

"Thank you," I said. "That means more than you know."

We disconnected, and I googled Derek's address. When that didn't work, I scrolled through his social media profile until I found a photo with him outside a house holding keys and a "Sold" sign.

The homes in Derek's neighborhood were oversized and overpriced. It was the kind of place where people with four-car attached garages parked outside all summer just to show off their vehicles and further inflate their already out-of-control egos.

I parked my muddy pickup along the curb and double-checked my GPS. Derek's driveway was occupied by an unmarked white minivan. Hopefully, the van's driver was Gina from Merry Maids.

I climbed out and my phone applauded. My lids fell shut for a long beat before reopening. There was no way I could fill any more orders without restocking my glass reserves. I'd used the last of my supplies around dawn.

I knocked on Derek's door, then added the recycle station to my mental tally of things I needed to do today.

The door opened a minute later, and a middle-aged woman in khaki pants and a polo shirt smiled at me. Her name tag had four little letters: *G-i-n-a*. "Can I help you?"

"I'm Holly White," I said. "I came to ask about Derek Waggoner."

Her mouth turned down on the sides. "Are you a reporter?"

"No. Just someone who wants to be sure he gets justice for what happened to him."

She looked over my shoulder toward the street. "Were you one of his, you know, *women*?"

The way she said *women* made my skin crawl. "No! I didn't even know the guy. My best friend did."

"Is she in trouble?" She lowered her gaze to my stomach and hiked a brow.

I wrapped my arms around my middle, heebie-jeebies racing all over me. "No. The police think my friend killed him, and I know she didn't. I want to know who did so I can save her in time for Christmas."

"Your friend is Caroline. The cupcake lady from the news." Her expression softened. "I clean for her too. She's a wonderful tipper, and she always leaves boxes of her cupcakes for me and my crew."

I nodded. "That's her. Can you tell me anything about Derek that might help me prove she didn't hurt him?"

"I didn't know Mr. Waggoner personally," she said. "We spoke briefly each week when I arrived to clean. Sometimes he was alone. Sometimes he had company." She made a sour face at that.

I could only assume she was referring to the parade of women I'd seen on his social media. Which reminded me. "Did you ever see Brian Ford or his wife, Nadia, here?"

She shook her head. "He didn't introduce me to his friends. I'm just the maid." She lifted a feather duster between us as evidence. "I watched that clip of Caroline telling him off at least ten times. It made me proud. It takes a strong woman to stick up for herself like that."

"Did you ever see Derek arguing with anyone while you were here?" I asked. If he pretended she wasn't here while she cleaned, he might have let his guard down. "Maybe someone in the days leading up to his death?"

"No, I've never seen it, but I've heard him yelling at his business partner on the phone plenty of times. I bet he can help you. He's one of the most charming men I've ever met. A little too young for me, I suppose, but a lady can dream, right? Have you spoken with him yet?"

"I will. Thank you." I got Mr. Charming's name from Gina, wished her a Merry Christmas and headed out.

According to Gina, I needed to talk to Greg Pressey at 1919 Mill Street.

I wasn't familiar with the address, and Gina warned me that it was a bit of a drive, but I had all day before I needed to be at Evan's house, and I planned to make the most of it.

Chapter Twelve

I pulled into a crowded parking lot on Mill Street, surprised, but not completely shocked by Derek's office headquarters. An etched glass sign wrapped in thick metal bore the words "Ironman Training Facility." A smaller, more understated marble sign sat beside the first. This one had been engraved with the words "Tranquility Day Spa."

I left my truck at the back of the lot and followed a group of women with duffel bags and yoga mats onto one of many cobblestone paths. We wound through the snowy landscape, past a fountain at the property's center that was ringed with benches and ornamental statues. The water, however, was frozen.

A series of weathered-looking buildings dotted the immediate area, all facing the pond. Most had walls of floor to ceiling windows and patios stretching away from them. Whatever furniture had sat there all summer had long ago been put away. The buildings resembled some historic sites I'd seen online, clustered together near the water like a port or fishing town. Except, these were clearly modern builds, and someone had taken great care to add an abundance of pine green and white twinkle lights to everything in sight. Even the replica lampposts had red bows tied to them. The overall aesthetic was stunningly gorgeous.

The women swept through a set of double doors at the third building on our left and flashed their badges at a scanner that let them into the locker room. I stopped to take in the soft, calming music and faux waterfall. The double doors might as well have been a gateway to another land. Everything smelled of patchouli, and the staff wore white clinical scrubs. I smiled at a woman ambling silently across the high-polished floor.

"Excuse me," I said. "Can you help me?"

She set a stack of thick white towels on the nearest counter, turned to face me and bowed. "How can I help you?"

I was dumbstruck, unsure if it was custom that I return the bow, or if my bow would cause her to bow again, and then we'd be stuck in a goofy Chevy Chase sequence. "I'm looking for Greg Pressey," I said, deciding to skip the bow and hoping not to offend. "Do you know where I can find him?"

"Of course." She moved to the exterior doors and held one open for me.

I followed her as she cut across the courtyard to a large, serious-looking building with a weight room visible through the rear window wall. She opened the door for me again and ushered me inside.

This building was nothing like the last. It was loud and bright, no waterfall. Just lots of male grunting and the sharp clanging of metal when behemoth-sized men dropped their dumbbells after each deadlift. Instead of the mystical wooden flute music, classic rock pumped through overhead speakers, and it didn't smell like patchouli. It smelled like sweat. No clinical white scrubs either. Everyone here seemed to be wearing black bicycle shorts with ripped tank tops.

"Right this way," she said, swinging her sleek black ponytail behind her.

She led me to a welcome desk and left me with a beefed-up woman in an Ironman Training Facility tank top. "Welcome," she said, giving me a full once-over. "Are you here for CrossFit?" Her voice was husky and rough. I couldn't have replicated it if I tried. It was the smoky voice of a jazz singer on three packs a day, but I doubted she smoked if she worked here. She was in amazing physical shape, and I envied that. The whole place reminded me of a muscle factory where everyone ate a strict diet of raw eggs and protein powder. I kind of wanted to go back to the yoga studio.

"No. I'm not here to exercise," I told her. "I'm looking for Derek Waggoner's business partner. Do you know how I can reach him?"

"Maybe," she said. "You mean Greg or Rick?"

There was a Rick? "Greg Pressey," I clarified. "I didn't realize there was a third partner."

She shrugged. "Neither did we until we did."

"I don't know what that means," I said. And I wondered if I should add Rick to my interview list.

A door swung open nearby, and a man in his late thirties, khaki pants, and an Ironman Training Facility shirt entered. When the door closed behind him, it was marked Staff. The man smiled when he saw me. "Have we met?" he asked, extending his hand as he approached.

"Well," the lady behind the desk said, "there you go." She grabbed her water bottle and walked away.

I concentrated on the man. The name tag on his polo confirmed him as Greg Pressey, Owner/Operator and President. "Hi, I'm Holly White," I said. "Do you mind if I ask you a few questions about Derek Waggoner?"

His smile fell a bit. "Sorry. I'm not giving any interviews."

"I'm not a reporter," I said. "I'm just a friend."

His brows crowded over narrowed eyes. "You don't look like a friend of Derek's."

Someone dropped a dumbbell behind me, and I nearly jumped onto the ceiling. "I'm not. I'm just looking for answers about what happened to him."

"Like I said, I'm not doing interviews. Unless you came here to work out, I have things I need to do." He brushed past me.

"Wait!" I touched his elbow, and he stilled. "How much for a day pass?" I asked. I wasn't above bribery if it garnered me the information I needed. Caroline was worth an hour at the gym. Besides, after this I could check "Exercise more" off last year's resolution list. "If I stay, will you be my coach?"

His lips curled into a sinister smile, and I could practically see the dollar signs popping up. "Thirty bucks for the pass, and you can't work out in street clothes. You'll have to buy gear from the Sweat Shop."

"Okay," I nodded. "I haven't worked out in a while, but I did yoga twice a week for years before I moved back to Mistletoe. You'll talk while we work?"

He crossed thick, muscled arms over a broad chest and stared.

I took that as a "yes," and ponied up the cash. I hurried into the Sweat Shop and bought their most modest workout gear. Ten minutes later, I'd stuffed my clothes into a pint-sized locker and dressed in black stretch pants and a baggy logoed T-shirt. The pants didn't reach my ankles, they had rips like claw marks on both thighs and the shirt hung off one shoulder because nothing in the Sweat Shop had a collar or enough stitching to properly hold it together. I was sure the idea was to look hardcore, but I just looked like a street urchin. "Ready," I said, pulling my wind-battered brown hair into a ponytail. I took a step back when Greg reappeared near the counter.

He'd changed into bicycle shorts and a stretched-out tank top that said "COACH" in all capital letters. His ensemble showcased his extremely muscled physique. Greg must've been nearing forty, but I suspected he could bench-press two twenty-year-olds at least fifty times without breaking a sweat. "Here." He handed me a rope so thick I needed two hands to hold on to it, then he stepped onto the concrete floor. "Give me ten," he said.

"Ten what?"

He turned to lift the unmanned rope lying on the ground beside me and whipped it up and down a few times. "Ten."

"Oh. Okay." I firmed up my grip and attempted to shake the rough material like he had. It didn't budge. "Can you think of anyone who might've had reason to want to hurt Derek?" I asked.

He pointed to the rope. "Ten."

"I'm trying."

"Try harder."

I put Caroline's sad face in my mind's eye and yanked the rope with everything I had. I broke into a sweat immediately. By the tenth rep, I checked the floor to see if my arms had fallen off when I released the rope. "Well?" I huffed. "Do you have any idea who might've hurt Derek?"

"Maybe," he said. "Let me think." He moved across the room while I bent at the waist to catch my breath.

"Heads up," someone bellowed.

I looked up in time to see a tire taller than my mother headed right for me. I screamed and jumped out of the way, pasting my sweaty back to the wall. The tire crashed a few inches away, bounced off the painted cinder blocks, then circled to a stop on its side. "What are you doing—trying to kill me?" I croaked. This "gym" wasn't a place to get fit. It was a place to dodge death.

Greg looked disappointed. Maybe because he'd missed me with the tire. "Pick it up," he said. "Roll it back. If you can't stand it up, you've gotta drag it over here."

"Are you kidding me?" I moved to the big tire and kicked it with my new sixty-dollar gym shoes. It didn't budge. I nearly gave myself a hernia trying to set it back up. "No go," I said.

"Come on."

I shot him an angry face. "Fine, but you have to answer me while I bring this to you."

"Sure thing," he agreed. "Use your legs, not your back."

I curled my fingers around the edge of the massive tire. The rubber beast stood knee-high to me, even while on its side. I tugged. It didn't move. I widened my stance, planted my feet, and leaned back. Nothing. "I can't move it. I'm not heavy enough."

"You mean you aren't *strong* enough," he said, moving forward several feet. "Okay, just move it to me here. You don't have to go all the way to the other side of the mat."

I tried again and my legs burned. My arms shook. My stomach ached. The tire shifted an inch. "Did you see that?"

"Yeah." He nodded. "And I saw Derek fighting with someone the night he died," Greg said. "Keep working and I'll tell you more about it."

The tire didn't move again, so Greg put me on a stair machine for ten minutes that might as well have had me mashing concrete with my feet. Then he told me to plank. After forty minutes in his hands, I was done. I rolled out of my plank and stared at the ceiling. Sweat stung my eyes and trailed over my temples into my hair. I wasn't sure I could get up if I tried.

Greg crouched over me. "Wasn't that great?" he asked. "You can't get a workout like that at some frou-frou yoga palace, doing some high kicks and lifting five-pound weights fifty times. To build muscle, you've really got to get into it. Push yourself. Rip those muscles apart so they can build themselves back up stronger." He made a fist and his eyes gleamed with passion for his topic.

"For sure," I moaned, pretty sure he'd ripped every muscle in my body apart in under an hour.

"When can I expect you back?"

"You never answered any of my questions," I panted. He'd just kept putting me off and baiting me into harder tasks until my body felt like cooked spaghetti. "I'm trying to find out what happened to your partner. Don't you want to help?"

"I saw him arguing with that blonde on the news," he said.

"And Derek wasn't my partner," he mumbled, jaw clenched, teeth grinding. "Derek Waggoner had no partners. He only had time and interest for one person, and that was himself." He straightened to his full height and looked down at me. "See you tomorrow?"

I rolled over and pressed my steaming cheek against the mat. "Never."

Eventually, the woman I'd met at the desk came and helped me up. "Who's Rick?" I asked her as she wound my arm over her shoulders. It had been one of the questions I'd wanted Greg to answer, but he wasn't talking.

"Rick's another investor," she said. "I heard what Greg said earlier about Derek not having partners, and he's probably right. Derek was self-absorbed, but he was also a genius at investing money and growing businesses. This place was only one building when Derek came along and expanded it. Now look. We've got a whole complex with something for everyone. The lot's always full, and there's never a shortage of clients. It won't be the same without him."

I showed myself to the locker room, shoved my nice clothes into the shopping bag, and pulled my coat on over the sweaty, ripped-up outfit I hated. I didn't think I could pilot my limbs well enough to change clothes yet, and I didn't want to find out I was right halfway through. At the moment, I was just hoping I could drive.

On the way out, I groaned at a marketing poster of Greg Pressey in a Santa suit with an Ironman Training Center shirt visible beneath an unbuttoned coat. "Let Ironman Training Center fulfill your fitness wishes for a stronger you in the new year." I shoved the door open and tried to imagine a life where my Christmas wishes were fitness related instead of about hoping to collect enough evidence to get my best friend out of jail without getting myself killed in the process.

I pulled up to the light at Main and Vine, dreaming of a hot bath and plotting a pit stop at Mistletoe's recycling center when I spotted Ray in the bushes again. "Hey." I powered my window down and leaned against the door. "What are you doing?"

Ray waved. "Hey, hang on," he called, climbing off the pile of snow he'd been using as a chair. He was dressed in white from head to toe, and his face was almost as pale. His nose, cheeks, and chin, however, looked a little frostbitten.

Someone honked when the light turned green, but Ray was headed my way, so I waited while he climbed inside. I lifted a hand to thank the guy behind me for his patience, and winced from the effort. I needed more than a hot bath. I needed someone to carry me around until I could feel my limbs again.

Ray pointed all the vents at himself and cranked up my heat. "Mom went into that restaurant with her boyfriend more than two hours ago. What do you think they're doing in there? And why didn't they get a window seat? It's a beautiful day. What are they hiding?"

"Maybe they wanted a little privacy," I said, "and to answer your other question, it's a restaurant. They're eating and talking. It's called dating."

"For two hours?" He shook his head. "I don't like it."

"You and I have stayed up until dawn watching old movies and playing board games. More than once," I said. "Just because they're spending time together doesn't mean they're doing anything wrong."

Ray scoffed. "And just because I'm a gentleman doesn't mean that guy is too."

I slowed behind a trolley picking up a new load of shoppers. The headsign at the top of its windshield gave the destination as "Reindeer Games."

"No, but it means your mama raised you right, and since it's your mama that you're worried about, give her a little credit. She's not going to put up with anything less than gentlemanly behavior from a man she's dating if she wouldn't tolerate it in you." I slid my eyes his way. "What did you mean you were a gentleman? Are you talking about the nights we've spent together? Because those weren't dates—we were just hanging out, so I don't know how else they could've gone."

He grinned. "Things could've been different. I could've used my moves on you."

"You have moves?" I asked, my curiosity climbing. "What kind of moves?"

He smiled. "I think we'd better concentrate on our major problem right now. How are we going to save Caroline?"

I motored ahead, following the trolley as far as Main Street. "Who told you about Caroline?" I asked. "Evan let us in through the back door last night so no one would know. Does the press know?"

"Cookie called." He gave me a sad look. "I wish you would have. I know how hard that must've been for you. I could've stayed with you afterward or gone with you to say goodbye."

"It's not goodbye," I said, feeling uselessly emotional again. "We're going to get her out. I just have to figure out who the real killer is first."

Ray's expression went hard. "That didn't go so well for you last year."

"It's different now," I said.

"Why?"

"Because it has to be," I snapped.

I covered my mouth with one hand, embarrassed by the outburst. "Sorry."

Ray rubbed my shoulder. "Why don't you tell me about the next step in your investigation, and I'll do it for you instead? I'll report back. You can go take a nap or see a doctor or something. Don't take this the wrong way, but you look wrecked."

I frowned. "I don't have another plan yet. Everything hurts, so I'm going home for a long soak in the tub. Assuming I can get my clothes off."

Ray smiled again. He looked me over with a shake of his head. "What happened to you, anyway? Have you been crying? What's wrong with your pants?"

I looked at my forty-dollar ripped spandex. "I went to see Derek's business partner, who turned out to be a big jerk like Derek. He made me work out at his gym to earn information, but then he didn't tell me anything."

Ray's smile grew.

"It's not funny," I said. "I want to go back as soon as I can walk again. That guy knows something, and I want to know what it is." How had Gina from Merry Maids thought Greg Pressey was charming? Clearly, she'd been confused by all his muscles.

"I'll go with you next time," Ray said. "For now, would you mind dropping me at my pickup? I parked in customer parking outside Caroline's Cupcakes so my mom wouldn't spot my truck."

I took Ray to his car, and he gave me a long look before climbing out. "You sure you're okay to drive?"

I tried to lift my arm to shoo him, but I whimpered instead. "Yes."

"Do yourself a favor," he said. "Avoid mirrors until after your shower."

I finished the short trek to the recycling center with visions of bath bombs dancing in my head.

The place was closed, so I parked and forced myself out of the truck to check the hours. "Shoot," I muttered when I saw the day's schedule. The recycling center wouldn't open until two o'clock, but I couldn't wait that long today to replenish my glass stock for my jewelry. I didn't have the energy to busy myself with shopping, and I didn't want to make a second trip into town, but I had orders to fill at home and a hot date with my bathtub as soon as humanly possible.

I didn't like my options.

It was after noon. Maybe someone was inside, getting ready for the day, and would let me make a quick purchase. Mom was always at the Hearth hours before it opened.

I shuffled closer to the window and pressed my forehead against it. I didn't see anyone, so I tried every window along the front with the same result. I probably looked like a potential burglar.

Across the street, a Santa watched.

"Hello," I said as cheerfully as possible. "Merry Christmas."
He moved on.

I went to look through the fence out back, but when I leaned against the gate, it swung open. I let myself inside and pulled some ones from my coat pocket, then levered the clipboard and pencil off the nail by the door. I scratched three words on the back of one sheet of paper and signed my name.

Needed glass bottles—Holly White.

I left the note on top so that it could be easily found, then stuck the dollars under the clip.

Inside, the recycling center was a bit of a museum or kiddie science center with information on the importance and process of recycling. Outside, it was a bit of a junkyard. I picked my way down rows of deposited steel to the glass barn, a massive pole barn where the incoming recycles were collected.

I didn't see a light switch, and the light inside the barn wasn't great, so I propped the door open and helped myself to a sturdy-looking box. With any luck, I wouldn't see a mouse because I couldn't run if I did. I'd just have to stand and scream until it left or until the place opened at two, whichever came first. I chose a few heavy wine bottles and set them into the box. My arm drooped and ached immediately. I considered leaving with just those bottles, before I couldn't lift the box anymore.

Something rumbled against the barn's metal roof, but I didn't see anyone through the open door. *Falling pinecones?* I wondered. The sound came again and I started. The rumble was louder this time.

"Hello?" I called, lowering my box onto a stack of other boxes. The metal roof thundered, loud enough to rattle my teeth, with the sound of bottles, cans, and stones bouncing over my head. My heart jerked into a sprint, and I yelped. I yanked the box back into my arms and headed for the door, deeply regretting my decision to let myself in through the back gate where no one was around. *People are only safe in broad daylight, when there are witnesses,* I told myself. At the moment, I had none. Worse, I'd told Ray I was on my way home, so no one knew where I was.

No one.

I jogged painfully toward the open door, slowing as it swung shut in my face with a grinding *thunk*! My heart stopped. My chest burned. My world was dark. I watched the strip of light flow beneath the door and willed my lungs to take in air. A shadow passed through the light, and a peel of dark laughter sent a shock of fear down my spine. "You think you're so smart," someone whispered. The sound crawled between the doors, around the frame, and through the darkness. "I know who you are," the voice said. "I know where you go. I know what you do, and I know how to hurt you, Holly White."

I stumbled back. Dropping the box once more, I dug into my coat pockets for my cell phone and dialed Ray.

My tormentor jiggled the doors and laughed. The person pounded on the walls outside, rattling my nerves and shaking my resolve. "Do you hear me?" the voice growled. "I know how to hurt you."

I broke one glass bottle against another, while the phone rang in my ear. I gripped the broken bottle's neck like a baseball bat, prepared to defend myself against whoever came through that door. I refused to die without a fight, and I absolutely would not take my final breath in a shed full of people's trash.

"Griggs," Ray answered the call.

"Help!" I yelled. "I'm trapped in the glass barn behind the recycling center on Vine, and the killer is here. He shut me in, and he says he's going to hurt me.

The creepy chuckle came again. "Call for help. Call for help," it taunted in a distorted whisper-growl. The sound was barely human. Something hard hit the wall at my side, and I screamed again. I jumped away from the noise and tripped on my exhausted, wobbly legs, toppling into a box of cans.

Something covered the space beneath the doors and everything went black.

"Holly!" Ray yelled.

A sob burst from my lips as I forced myself upright and scrambled back, unsure where the killer was now. Unable to get out. Unsure if he could get in without me seeing.

"I'm coming," Ray said. "I'm going to call Evan."

"Don't hang up!" I screamed.

The lunatic slammed his hands against the wall outside again, just inches from my head. I stumbled toward the room's center, knocking into piles of recycles and scraping up my palms as I tried to guide myself along. The thundering blasts of metal on metal kept coming, rattling my nerves and scaring me half to death with every new explosion of sound. I didn't know where or when the next one would come. I was frozen. Unable to go. Unable to hide. My shins were skinned from the fall. My palms stung with cuts from the broken bottle. "Stop!" I screamed, turning in a small circle, horrified, hands over my ears. *"Stop!"*

"Holly?" Ray's voice boomed through my phone speaker. "What's happening?"

'Twas the Knife Before Christmas

The thunderous sound came again, and I cried out, tripping over something behind my feet. My thin, shredded pants tore further. My ankle twisted, and I hit the ground hard. *Just like last year,* I thought. *It's just like last year.*

"Holly!" Ray screamed into the phone. "Answer me!"

My eyes blurred with tears, and my throat ached with a fist-sized ball of fear.

A long, scraping sound began along the wall near my head. The dragging of metal over metal. A butcher knife headed my way, perhaps?

I sucked in a long deep breath and screamed, "Hurry!"

Chapter Thirteen

I patted the ground, in search of whatever I'd tripped over, and came to my feet with what felt like a pipe. I left the broken bottle behind. My arms trembled from fear and exertion, but adrenaline had come to the rescue. I wouldn't make it easy for whoever eventually came through that door for me, and I was tired of being scared and helpless.

My illuminated phone screen made a small cone of light in the darkness, and I turned it toward the entrance. Only one way in or out, and I was gathering up the nerve to bust my way out. Because staying inside the glass barn meant I was prey.

I propped the phone against a box, then marched forward with nothing but determination and hardheadedness. If whoever had shut me in had wanted to hurt me, they would have by now. They hadn't. So they'd just wanted to scare the coffee out of me. Mission Accomplished.

Now I had a goal. I needed to get to my truck without injury or abduction.

I stalked ahead on aching, fatigued legs, dragging the length of the metal behind me until I was close enough to kick the door open and reach anyone in my way with the large, improvised bat.

A wide shaft of light suddenly flooded under the door. The thing that had sealed me into darkness had been removed. It seemed my assailant and I were on the same page. It was time to open the door. I hefted the pipe in my hands and gave myself a silent countdown.

The door opened, and I swung.

"Ah!" The looming figure before me ducked, barely dodging my blow. "Hey, hey, hey." Ray's voice projected from the big silhouette, backlit by the mega-white snow and beautiful sun.

I froze, blinking against the blast of gleaming sunlight.

"It's me," he said, stepping closer as I began to tremble violently. Ray took the pipe from my hands and tossed it aside. "I'm here. You're okay."

He wrapped me in long, strong arms, and I collapsed against him, tears flooding my cheeks and sobs racking my chest. He pulled me in close, letting his cheek rest on the top of my head while I lost my mind. "Someone laid a two-by-four in front of the door," he said. "Why would anyone do that? It wasn't heavy, and the door wasn't locked."

"It blocked out all the light," I said, wiping frantically at my eyes. I hadn't truly been trapped. Someone had just wanted me to think I was. "It was terrifying. Did you see anyone?"

"No."

The bark of a siren startled me, but Ray held me tight.

"Sorry," he said. "I called Evan the minute I got here. You asked me not to hang up, but I had to. I didn't know what I would find . . . if you'd be hurt . . . if the killer would still be here. There were too many what-ifs. Don't be mad."

I squeezed his middle and rolled my head to the side, pressed my hot, wet cheek against his cool, slick coat. "Thank you for saving me." My breath puffed out in white clouds, which changed to ice crystals before my eyes.

"Anytime."

Evan strode into view, one hand on the butt of his sidearm. "What happened?" He scowled at me clinging to Ray, but I couldn't bring myself to let go. "Are you hurt?"

"No," I said. "Just shaken by some lunatic, tired from lack of sleep, and sore from a monster's workout, but only one of those is your fault."

Evan squinted at me, then dragged his gaze to Ray, who shrugged.

An hour later, Evan had asked me a hundred questions about the incident, walked every inch of the exterior of the recycling center, then went in search of the Santa I remembered seeing on the street, my only potential witness. Evan didn't find Santa, and no one else he spoke with had seen anyone follow me through the gate. Including myself.

I drove the Reindeer Games truck home with Ray following in his little green pickup. We parked at the inn and walked to the guesthouse, which didn't have any parking.

Ray had shed his coat and started a fire before I could kick my boots off and take off my coat, scarf, and hat. "I'll wait here while you do whatever you need to do," he said, flipping on the television and coaxing Cindy onto his lap. "Even if you need to nap. Don't worry about me. I'm self-entertaining, and I can work from anywhere with Wi-Fi."

I didn't argue. I went to soak in a tub with my hat on because my aching arms didn't go above my shoulders. I sank into a steaming tub of water treated with my favorite oils, frankincense and myrrh. My muscles responded, warming and unwinding. My head fell back against the little inflatable pillow I kept in place with suction cups, and my hat fell off.

I took my time with each step of the resurrection process, and returned to Ray with soft, blown-out hair, warm, scented skin, and drooping eyelids. He patted the seat beside him, and I curled up against his side. "I'm a mess."

"You don't look like a mess," he said, a touch of admiration in his voice. His strong arm wrapped my shoulder and held me tight.

"Someone tries to kill me every Christmas," I said, "and I'm really out of shape. You should have seen me at the gym."

Ray's chest bounced gently with silent laughter. "Well, you look beautiful, and you smell amazing," he said. "At least you have that."

"At least," I agreed.

My phone applauded from somewhere behind us, and I cringed. I must've left it in my coat pocket.

Ray turned his head in the direction of the sound. "Your phone's been doing that the whole time you've been gone. I considered bringing it to you, but I thought that might get me in trouble."

I laughed. "Correct." I dragged myself up to retrieve the

phone. "Oh my gosh. There are at least twenty-five new orders." I hung my head and fell back against Ray. "And I didn't bring any bottles home from the recycling center." I silently pounded my feet against the floor. "That was the whole reason I ended up in that mess. I need more glass to make the jewelry, and I didn't want to make a second trip into town." I shook my phone in the air. "Now I spent part of my day terrorized by a murderer, and I *still* have to make a second trip into town."

Ray crossed his long legs and stretched back against the cushions. "I'll get the bottles on my way home. Don't worry about it."

"What?" I sat up to look into his face. "Don't do that. You've done enough already. I can handle it."

"Of course you can handle it," he said, "but why should you have to? I go right by the recycling center on my way home, plus, last time I checked, you and I are friends, and that's what friends do. We help each other. So, don't worry about it."

I thought of the way Caroline had paged through twelve binders, flagging products for the inn. The way Cookie always had what anyone needed inside her giant Mary Poppins bag of care. The way Evan tried to keep me safe, even when he was barely talking to me. How Ray had come to my rescue today, no questions asked. And my eyes filled with fresh tears. "Thanks," I said, controlling my voice as well as I could. "Can I do anything to help you? Stalk your mom? Make her a Christmas gift that proves you're the best son ever?" I tipped my head toward the mess of jewelry pieces on the coffee table.

"You do enough," he said. "If you're making offers, I'd like it if you didn't go investigating on your own anymore. Call me. I'll go with you."

I didn't like the implication that I couldn't handle myself, and yet I had a bad habit of winding up in situations that supported the suggestion. "I'm having dinner at Evan's tonight," I said. "I expect to learn some things about what's going on with Caroline, but I won't need protection."

Ray chuckled. "If Evan weren't the sheriff, I'd say you were wrong about that. He yelled at me when I called to say you were scared and in trouble. Apparently, he thinks I'm your keeper or that I have influence over you somehow. Has he met you?"

I laughed.

"I thought his head was going to explode when he got there and saw us together."

I leaned away again. "What do you mean?"

Ray gave me a crazy face. "I mean, I don't do jealousy. It's ugly. And I've never seen Sheriff's pretty face look so red."

I smiled. "You think he's pretty."

Ray laughed. He shoved to his feet and checked his watch. "What time is dinner?"

"Probably now," I said. "He didn't really give me a time."

He reached a hand out. "Let's go. I'll follow you, then hit the recycling center before it closes. Make me a list."

I snagged a pen and paper from the coffee table, mired in relief. "I love you."

"Back at ya."

* * *

I stared up at Evan's respectable little craftsman home on the opposite side of downtown. He'd lined the roof and porch in twinkle lights, set a dusk-to-dawn candle on every windowsill, and wrapped his door to look like a giant present. His tree was proudly displayed in the front window, lit in all-white lights and adorned with red ornaments. Most passersby probably assumed he was patriotic, and he was, but I knew the tree was an homage to his hometown and favorite team: the Red Sox.

The front door opened, jarring me back to the present. Evan stepped onto the porch, propping the door open with his foot. "Are you coming in tonight?"

I wasn't sure if that was a reference to the time I'd only come by to spy or if he'd noticed how long it was taking me to make it up the sidewalk. "Nice to see you too," I said, climbing the steps to his porch.

He stopped me with a hand as I crossed the threshold, then pointed to the mistletoe above his door and smiled. My parents hung mistletoe over their front door every Christmas, though they kissed hello and goodbye whenever the door opened, regardless of the season. Evan brushed a chaste kiss against my lips, then escorted me inside with a palm on the small of my back.

Flames crackled and danced in the fireplace beneath two red felt stockings hanging from the mantle. Glittery letters had been written across the fluffy white top of each. One for Evan. The other for Libby. I did my best to pretend the heat pinking my cheeks and slicking my palms was from the fire, not the kiss.

I breathed in the warm scents of cinnamon and gingerbread as we passed through a small dining room on our way to his kitchen. Christmas music lifted from a phone lying on the counter when we arrived.

"Hello." A petite redhead dusted crumbs from her hands and came to greet me. "I'm Libby," she said. "You must be Holly." Libby's cheeks were freckled, her eyes as green as her brother's, though hers were rimmed with thick black lashes and liner. Her apron had the body of a curvy elf printed on it that stopped at the neckline where Libby's head began.

I offered her my hand. "It's nice to meet you."

"Same here." She shook my hand, then slid her eyes to Evan. "I've heard a lot about you."

"Funny," I said. "he never said a word to me about you until this week."

"Well, Big Brother isn't much of a talker unless the topic is Holly White." She grinned.

I made plans to overthink the meaning behind that later. "Do tell."

"No." Evan crossed and uncrossed his arms in front of him like an umpire. "That's not what we're doing tonight. Tonight, we're going to have dinner and talk about you, Libby."

Her smile twisted into a tight frown. "Right."

Evan ladled hot cider from a Crock-Pot and handed a full mug to me. "I also want to talk about what happened to you today, but I'd like to start by getting myself out of the doghouse. I owe you an explanation about all the secrets I've been keeping."

Libby stripped off her apron, revealing dark washed skinny jeans, a fitted black sweater, and knee-high zip-up boots. "Here we go," she said, filling a wine glass to the brim with chardonnay and leaning against the counter. "I was a senior at Boston College last year."

Libby's accent was thick and easy. Everything about her screamed city girl, and I suddenly felt like a frump.

"You graduated this year?"

"No." She gave her brother a look.

"Libby dropped out," he said. "Almost a year ago. I found out when I went to surprise her on New Year's Day, and her roommate said she'd left town three weeks before."

I did a low whistle.

"Yeah," he said, nodding at Libby.

"I was trying to help a friend," she said, moving toward the empty seat beside me. "My other roommate was missing, and I wanted to find her."

"Did you?" I asked.

Libby gave a stiff nod. "Eventually."

I looked at Evan. I felt as if her story was going somewhere but couldn't quite connect the ends. "What happened?"

"Heather was an art history major from Idaho when we met," Libby said. "She'd never been to Boston or any big city. She was always chasing a thrill—going to the wrong parts of town, hanging with bad people." She made air quotes around the last two words. "She started experimenting with drugs and keeping a blog about it, sharing pictures of everything. She called it life experience. One day she was just gone."

"That's when you went looking for her," I guessed.

Evan leaned his arms on the table and folded his fingers. "All the way to Los Angeles."

I felt my eyes go wide. I'd never been that far west. I'd never been that far in any direction. "How?"

"I drove," she said. "I started by asking our mutual friends when they'd last seen her and where she might be, and I followed the trail." Libby ran the pad of her thumb under each eye, then glanced at Evan. "He found me in California and helped me."

Evan didn't smile. He didn't look proud or angry. He just looked tired. "I worked with the local PD to get a bead on Heather, but LA's a big place, and we didn't have anything to go on except some photos taken in a questionable club. By the time we found her, it was too late. We tried, but . . ." He shook his head.

"She's dead?" I asked, unable to believe Evan had gone through all this, and I'd badgered him about where he went on his days off. "When?"

"April," Libby said. "Overdose. I went back to Boston and read every word of her blog, looking for answers. I wanted to know how she could be gone. And then I found him. A smug little creep from Southie. Now I want him to go to jail for what he did to her."

"A boyfriend?" I guessed.

Libby nodded. "Yeah. She loved him, and he took advantage of her big heart and limited experience. Once she was hooked on whatever he was peddling, he sent her out West to pick up a package for him, probably drugs—I don't know. She never came home." Libby swallowed a mouthful of wine. "So I was going around Boston trying to find this awesome guy, but all I had to go on was a few photos from her camera and the blog posts. I figured out a little too late that she had some incriminating photos on her camera, and her boyfriend got wind of that. Now he's looking for me, and I'm not in a big hurry to meet him anymore."

Evan stretched his neck. "I brought her here to keep her safe until Boston PD can find this guy and pick him up."

"And here I am," Libby said. "Hiding out in the freaking North Pole of Maine. Living with my older brother in some bizarre replica of Santa's workshop village."

"I'm sorry," I said to her. "I'm sorry about your friend, and I'm sorry you had to leave your home because you were trying to do right by her." I turned my eyes to Evan. "And I'm sorry I gave you such a hard time when you were just trying to protect your sister and have a little privacy while you did it. I didn't know."

"That's probably my fault too," Libby said. "I asked him not to tell anyone. The things I was going through were scary and personal, and I didn't know you."

"It wasn't his story to tell," I said, looking warmly at Evan. Now I understood, and despite the awfulness of the story, I was relieved to know Evan hadn't kept me out of it because he didn't trust me.

Once the story portion of our evening had ended, Evan lectured both of us about our dangerous decision-making, from appetizers to dessert. Libby defended herself to the very end. I just observed. I'd never had siblings, and the sight of Evan interacting with his was kind of fun.

I told her about Reindeer Games, Cookie, and my folks. Then I told her about Caroline. Libby understood—friends do anything they can to help one another, even if it means being a little headstrong and hasty.

After dinner, Evan walked me to my truck. He held the door

for me after I beeped the locks open, and waited while I climbed inside and started the engine to warm it up.

He cast me a woeful look. "I'm sorry I didn't tell you about Libby sooner. I knew her roommate, and finding her like that was a hit to my heart. I felt as if I'd failed them. Heather was such a sweet girl. Heck, that could have easily been my sister. A few bad choices can change your life before you know what's happened. Or end it."

"It wasn't your fault," I protested. "You're not even in Boston anymore."

"Still, pushing you away to honor Libby's feelings wasn't easy. I didn't like how it felt."

"Me either," I admitted. I'd hated when Evan had pushed me away. Hated not knowing what was going on in his life.

His searching gray eyes sent shivers across my skin. I looked away, unwilling to get lost in them with a killer on my trail and my best friend in jail.

"I wish I could visit Caroline," I said. "I hate that she's scared and alone."

"She's okay," Evan assured. "She's got her own cell, and she's getting special treatment. Trust me. I know a guy."

I smiled. "You think she'll be out soon?"

"Yeah. Her folks will spring her after her arraignment. We're trying to reach Judge Porter, but he's on a family ski trip. The only other judge in town is the victim's father, and he has to stay out of this case."

I grimaced.

"The minute bail is set, she'll be free."

"She didn't do it," I said.

Evan hooked a swath of flyaway hair behind my ear and brushed his warm fingers across my cheek. "I'm doing my best to prove it," he promised. "I need you to stop trying to help. Between the actions of you and my little sister, I'm aging in dog years. I can't take it. You've got to let this go. Let me handle it."

I nodded, unable to answer with my breath still stolen from his touch.

"You sure you don't want me to follow you home?" he asked. "I'd feel better if I knew you made it safely."

"I'm fine," I promised. "Take care of Libby. Tell her I'm really glad we met, and I'd love to see her at Reindeer Games sometime."

He nodded and stood in the street as I drove away.

Chapter Fourteen

I poked along in traffic toward the square on my way home from Evan's. I'd never imagined him as a big brother, but seeing it in action was sweet and quite heartwarming. He'd told me once that he appreciated my straightforward approach to things, and now I could see why. I probably reminded him of his sister, who held no punches. I liked her style too.

I eased the truck to a stop at the corner where a tour bus loaded up its day-trippers. Locals and overnighters still had a little time left before the stores closed. I considered joining them for some last-minute shopping. I still wanted to register Mom for the wine club, but it was dangerous enough for me to talk with Samantha Moss in the light of day. I'd have to put a pin in that until morning.

The light changed, and I waited patiently as a mass of pedestrians puttered through the crosswalk before me, arms heavy with bags, hands busy with coffees, cocoas, or kettle corn.

Across the street, the Cookie Corner had emerged. Cookie Corner was a pop-up business selling award-winning cookies for two weeks a year, and I had never known a year without a box of their little butter cookies with strawberry jam in the center. Indecision tightened my muscles as I debated buying some to take with me tonight. On the one hand, I'd promised Evan I'd to go straight home. On the other hand, this was *Cookie Corner* I was looking at. The ultimate comfort food. Ray had texted a photo of himself and two big boxes of glass bottles on my porch while I was at dinner. He'd come through as promised, and I'd be able to make twice as much progress on my work tonight if the efforts were fueled by the sweet strawberry heaven of Cookie Corner.

I pulled into a parking spot two blocks down and hopped out. The availability of the space, right when I needed it, felt serendipitous. Who was I to thumb my nose at destiny? I hurried to the back of the line and listened to my tummy getting all worked up at the warm buttery scent of what was in store. My decision had been made. I'd over-buy on my favorite cookies, take them straight home, build a fire, make some warm chai tea, and fill jewelry orders until dawn.

The woman in line ahead of me turned to stare. Her hood had made her unrecognizable, but that young freckled face was etched in my mind. "Nadia Ford?"

She turned away again, wrapping her arms around her middle.

"Hey!" I scooted a few baby steps to the side, careful not to lose my place in line, but hoping to strike up a conversation. "Remember me? I'm Holly White. We met at your husband's shop earlier, and he yelled at me."

"I remember." She scooted forward with the slowly moving line. "What do you want?"

I wasn't sure what to say next, or even if I wanted to say anything given the day I was having, but when would I have another chance to talk with her alone? And the chance encounter, like the available parking space, seemed as if it had been written in the stars.

I smiled. "I always come for cookies when Cookie Corner opens. Their Christmas cannolis melt in your mouth, but I buy the strawberry butter cookies."

"Are you following me?"

Before I could answer, her cheeks slowly darkened. "You are," she answered her own question, tucking flyaway hair beneath the edge of her hood. "You know about Derek and me. That's why you keep coming after me."

"I'm not after you," I said. "But, yes, I know."

Nadia's eyes glossed instantly with tears, and she turned away from me. "Derek used me to hurt my husband. I really liked him, but I was just part of his game. I'm not a cheater. I don't do that." She rolled her eyes briefly skyward and blew out a long breath. "I wasn't looking to wreck my marriage."

"What happened?" I asked

She turned exhausted eyes my way. "Derek approached me last year, wanting to know how Brian's company was doing and if he needed an investor. Derek claimed he was turning over a new leaf. He said he wanted to put any hard feelings behind him." She gave a humorless laugh. "Obviously, that was all lies. I was so naive."

I felt badly for Nadia. She probably had been naive last year. She was barely an adult now, and she'd gotten stuck in the childish game her husband and Derek had played for years.

"Derek was jealous of Brian's success," she said. "He wanted Brian to need his money so he could brag publicly about his affiliation with the company and gloat privately that Brian was in his debt. I'm sure he would've also enjoyed collecting the interest every month. When I told him Brian didn't need the money, Derek weaseled his way into my life by posing as a friend and confident at first, then as something more." She blushed and averted her eyes. "I thought I'd found someone who understood me. Someone who knew how hard Brian can be sometimes." She laughed softly. "All he wanted was something to shove in Brian's face, and he didn't care how he got it."

"I'm sorry," I said. "And Brian found out?"

"Yeah, because Derek told him!"

The force of her admission nearly knocked me off my feet. As if luring her into an affair just to hurt his nemesis wasn't bad enough, he'd told her husband? "That's awful. I'm sorry you went through that. I don't know what to say."

She shrugged and blinked away her tears. "It was my fault. I was the one who cheated." Nadia blew out a long puff of air, visible in the cold. "I know it's completely heinous of me, but I'm glad Derek's gone. Brian was always mean, but hearing I'd been with Derek nearly pushed him over the edge. Maybe now he'll calm down." She moved with the line again, not looking the least bit guilty for the heartless statement. "There's no more visible reminder of my infidelity strutting around town like a jerk."

Except for you, I thought.

I felt my mouth turn down at the corners. "Do you think Brian could have killed Derek?"

She shrugged. "He certainly wanted to, and I don't blame him. Derek was a horrible person."

"Were you with Brian at midnight the night Derek died?"

"No, Brian was out of town that night. I have no idea what he was doing at midnight, and I don't care. Brian's a jerk too. He and Derek both deserve the worst."

Nadia's phone rang, and her husband's face appeared on the screen. "Ugh," she groaned. "Speak of the devil." She said hello, then listened a few seconds before shooting me a dirty look and walking away, abandoning her place in line. Apparently the happy couple act was reserved for time spent publicly or at his shop.

I stuck around, processing all that she'd said and shuffling forward. Could the young, spurned Nadia Ford be a killer? If so, had following her into the line at Cookie Corner been a huge mistake? She'd flat out accused me of coming after her, exactly what all my threats warned me against. Tonight, I'd done the opposite of leave things alone, and Nadia had walked out of sight.

She could be anywhere. Watching me. Preparing a new threat or worse.

By the time it was my turn to order, I was more than a little worked up and no longer in the mood for cookies. I excused myself without buying anything and headed back in the direction of my truck.

A few steps from the crowd, I noticed a Santa staring my way. He stood on the curb across the street from me with a familiar stance and lilt to his head. I wondered idly if he'd been the Santa I'd seen outside the recycling center, but there was no way to be sure. The fur of his hat rode low on his forehead, nearly reaching his eyebrows, and a thick white beard hid most of his face. Something about him didn't set quite right with me, and I kept one eye on him as I careened through clutches of people toward my truck. A small dark spot on the white fur of his coat caused me to lose my step. I'd seen a Santa drip chocolate on himself at Oh! Fudge the day I'd received my first threat-present. Could this be him? I couldn't recall that Santa's face. I'd purposefully looked away before, so he wouldn't be embarrassed by the messy faux pas. Now the shadows, the night, and the crowd made it impossible to see the man behind the mask.

If it *was* a man.

Across the street, this Santa kept pace with me, but made no move to cross. I walked faster, my mind racing as I dodged families and shoppers, in a rush for the safety of my pickup. I fumbled through the pockets of my coat and jeans, searching for my keys and pepper spray. The sounds of cans and bottles thrown against the recycling center's roof gonged in my mind.

My truck came into view, and I gave in to the building panic. I launched into a sprint, forcing my sore and tired limbs to comply. I unlocked the doors, then shot the stalking Santa a look. He stopped when I did and stared from the opposite curb.

Something crunched beneath my boot as I yanked on the door handle.

Crushed peppermints were scattered over the ice and snow beside my truck, and the thick black handle of a hunting knife protruded from my front driver's side tire. Its sharp silver blade had pierced a scrap of happy holiday paper to the rubber.

Another message from the killer.

You were warned.

My breath caught in my throat as I jerked my attention toward the Santa across the street. Was he responsible for this? Was he the killer? A tour bus trundled past, temporarily blocking my view. When it was gone, the Santa was too.

* * *

Evan arrived minutes later. I was locked inside the cab of my truck, pepper spray in one hand, my cell phone in the other. "You can unlock the door," he said, his voice echoing through both the phone's speaker and the window at my side.

I pushed the automatic window button with one finger, lowering the glass an inch but making no move to get out. "Santa did this." I said. "He's following me. He might've been following me all along. And I think he killed Derek."

"You think Santa killed Derek."

I nodded. "He has a chocolate stain on his coat."

"Okay," Evan said, tugging on the door. "Get out."

I unlocked the door and let Evan pull it open. "I'm willing to admit it sounds a little crazy, but I can pick him out of a lineup by his suit."

Evan cocked a hip and rubbed his eyebrow. "You want me to haul in all these Santas in for a lineup?"

I cast my gaze around the square and counted three St. Nicks. There were probably more I couldn't see. "Yes."

"You know I can't do that."

"Then just bring in the ones with the stains," I said, using a hand to indicate the stain's location on my jacket. "There can't be more than one or two with chocolate right here."

"Come on," Evan said, waving me out of the cab.

I slid to my feet at his side. "Okay, but I can't stay. I need to go home."

Evan pointed to my flat tire. "I'm going to have to give you a ride."

My stomach coiled. I couldn't bring myself to look at the recently impaled tire. I never wanted to think about it again, but I didn't have a choice. My parents would probably notice Evan driving me home, and they'd definitely wonder why my truck was missing in the morning. Also, I suspected the knife would star in my nightmares for weeks to come. I flipped my phone over on my palm. "I need to call a tow truck."

"Truck's on its way," Evan said. "Let me drive you home."

My eyes stung, and I nodded, hating the lump of emotion building in my throat.

He pressed a palm to my back and guided me toward his cruiser.

I dragged my feet. "Aren't you going to stay and talk to the Santas?" I asked.

"The deputies will talk to folks, see if anyone saw anything."

"He followed me," I croaked.

Evan rocked his head side to side. "Followed from across the street?"

"Yes! I also saw him outside the recycling center and at the fudge shop." I stumbled as another Santa sighting blinked into my mind. "And at the purse shop! He got into a cool black sports car."

"Holly." Evan's voice was low and patient. "This is Mistletoe in December. There are Santas everywhere." He unlocked the cruiser door and bumped me inside. "Let's talk in the car."

I fell inside without complaint and organized my scrambled thoughts as Evan drove us in the direction of Reindeer Games.

We passed the tow truck on our way out of town.

"How did you end up on a sidewalk near the square tonight?" Evan asked. "I thought you were on your way home when you left my place."

"I was." I fiddled with his heating vents. "I stopped for Cookie Corner. I was going to go home, make jewelry, and eat comfort cookies."

He shook his head and smiled.

"Who do you think somebody stabbed my tire?" I asked. "Who is threatening me?"

"Santa?" he guessed.

"Yeah, but who's behind the beard?" I pepped up as a new train of thought gained speed. "The killer, right?"

Evan flicked his gaze in my direction, wrenching it temporarily from the snow-covered road. "Probably."

"But Caroline's in jail," I said. "If she's in custody, then she didn't follow me. Caroline can't be the killer." I bounced on the seat a little. "Turn around," I said. "Let's go get her out. She's innocent, and this proves it."

"It doesn't prove anything."

"Why not?"

"Because," he snapped, "correlation isn't causation. Anyone could be bothering you for any number of reasons. We have no proof that your harasser is related to Derek Waggoner's murder."

"There are the mints from the murder scene," I said. "Who would use those besides the killer?"

Evan turned the cruiser up the gravel lane to our tree farm. "Someone who wants to scare you? Someone who's jealous of you or mad at you about something. Someone who's just not right in the head. Look," he said, parking in the lot outside the inn and shifting in his seat to face me head on, "I agree that it seems as if the killer is trying to stop your private crusade to save Caroline, but all we know for certain is that someone is threatening you, and based on the hunting knife in your tire tonight, they've escalated that threat." Evan ran his intense gaze over my face and held me in place with a tortured expression. "I don't feel comfortable leaving you alone tonight. Let me take you and Cindy to your folks' house instead."

My heart fluttered. He hadn't forgotten my cat, and he knew I'd never go without her.

He knew me, but I didn't know him at all.

"No thank you," I said. "I think I need some time to process everything and get my head together. Plus, I have a ton of work to do."

"You shouldn't be alone."

"If I remember correctly," I said smartly, "staying with my parents didn't keep the last nut from walking right through their door to get me."

Evan ground his teeth. "That should never have happened."

"But it did." I opened my door and climbed out. "Would you like to come in for a minute? Or do you need to get back?"

"I have a little time." Evan followed me to the front door of the guesthouse.

I smiled at the glass bottles Ray had left on the porch, then hoisted them onto one hip and unlocked the door for Evan.

Cindy Lou Who met us with a list of complaints, mainly that her bowls had been overturned. By her. I left the bottles by the couch and went to refill Cindy's food and water while Evan checked my rooms for a killer.

He returned with his fingers laced on top of his head. "Are you going to be okay tonight?"

"Yeah." I popped the lid off a container of Caroline's mini cupcakes. "I mean, I'm not happy my best friend is in county lockup or that there's a Santa out there who wants to hurt me, but things could be worse." I shoved a cupcake into my mouth and chewed thoughtfully before continuing. "I have faith that Caroline will be freed soon, and you will catch the Santa eventually." I swallowed and looked briefly at the ceiling. "My life is really strange."

Evan laughed. A real belly laugh that reached his eyes. He swiped a cupcake, then started my coffee pot. "This whole town is a little strange. A big adjustment from Boston, for sure."

"You like it," I said, smiling up at him. His love for Mistletoe shone in the way he spoke about our people and their problems. The way he was always willing to get involved in our community games and activities, from caroling to Frisbee. Evan was happy in Mistletoe, and that only made me like him more.

"I do," he said with a lift of his brow. "It's fun here and usually pretty safe. A single annual crime spree is the kind of thing other towns only wish they had. Personally, I'd be a little happier if the one major criminal I have to chase every year wasn't always after you, but there doesn't seem to be much I can do about that."

No. That was all on me. "I'd stop getting involved if the people I loved would quit being killed, accused, or arrested," I said.

Evan hung his head and rolled tired eyes up at me. "Is there anyone in this town you don't love?"

"I'm not real happy with the stained Santa right now."

"Right." Evan poured two cups of coffee, then led the way to the living room. "That's a lot of tiny candy," he said, staring at the piles of jewelry pieces littering the room.

"I have new orders to fill and a bunch of envelopes to stuff and address." I dropped the cupcake container onto the couch, then cleared space on the coffee table for our drinks. "Caroline was going to mail all these orders for me. Now I have to do it, but my truck is broken." I curled onto the couch and stuffed another cupcake into my mouth. "Why is everything so complicated?"

Evan crouched before my fireplace and arranged a pile of logs. "I'll take the finished orders with me when I go. The post office is on my way to work tomorrow."

I opened my mouth to object, but I really needed the help, and I loved that he'd offered. "Okay. Thank you."

* * *

The fire lit slowly, and Evan took a seat beside me while it grew. "I appreciate you letting me off the hook about Libby," he said.

"You honored your sister's request. I would never fault you for that," I said. "Trust is the most important thing in any relationship, and I want you to know that whatever happens, you and I will always be friends. I don't hold grudges, and I never put pride ahead of people. You can count on me. Anytime. For anything. If you ever want to talk or just need someone to listen, you can call me."

Evan nodded, a small smile on his lips. "That means a lot."

The smile slowly faded as we looked into each other's eyes.

"Can you stay for a movie?" I asked, suddenly feeling the warmth of the fire.

Evan's lips drifted closer to mine, sending shockwaves of his signature gingerbread and cologne scent through my senses. "Yeah."

A knock sounded against my door, and my heart stopped.

Evan was on his feet, one hand on his gun, and moving quickly toward the window before I'd managed my next breath.

I pulled Cindy into my arms and cowered until she bit me and left.

"It's Libby," Evan said, pulling the door open and letting his sister inside.

Her eyes were wide as she entered. "Can I stay?" she asked.

I hurried to greet her. "Of course. Come in. We have coffee and cocoa. There's water for tea, and just about every kind of cupcake you're ever heard of."

Evan followed us into the kitchen, where I chose a mug for Libby. "Is anything wrong? Did something happen?"

"No. I was lonely, and his house makes all kinds of weird noises."

"How did you find me?" he asked.

She pulled a keychain from her wallet and wiggled a little square doodad in front of her face. "I put one of these in your glove box."

I recognized the little thing. I had one too. I'd bought mine to help me keep track of the things I lost most: my phone and keys. It used a corresponding app on my phone to see where either item was at any time. Libby must've used the app to track Evan's car. Libby was a smart girl.

"You lo-jacked my cruiser?"

She shrugged. "I was scared. The wind never stops rattling your windows. It sounds like someone is constantly breaking in."

He kept his eyes on her as she helped herself to some coffee. "How'd you get here?"

She rolled her eyes. "I called the only cab service in Mistletoe, and some woman showed up ten minutes later in a VW bus with Christmas lights on the top."

"Jane Anne," Evan and I said together.

Libby blew out a laugh. "This town, right?"

I smiled. "Yeah."

Evan lifted his brows at me, and I nodded in response.

"So, Lib," he asked. "You in the mood for a movie? We were just about to put one on."

Her shoulders sagged with relief. "Yeah."

We returned to the couch and let Libby pick the show. Cindy

Lou Who jumped into Libby's lap and began to purr. Evan slung his arm over my shoulders, and I offered a toast to friends before sharing my container of mini cupcakes.

When my phone applauded, I shifted the volume to silent. There was another long night of work ahead, but first I had a movie to watch with my friends.

Chapter Fifteen

I spent the next day at the Hearth, helping Mom, waiting tables, and having an exceptionally good time considering I'd barely slept. The place was hopping until dinnertime, when tourists often made reservations for fancy meals in town, and the Hearth became more of a game location than a food center.

I wiped the last of the tables clean, then slid into a booth across from my favorite reporter. "Ready for a few rounds of Holiday Bingo?" I asked Ray.

"Always," he said with utter seriousness, but there was mischief in his eyes.

I laughed.

He passed me a bingo card, then dumped a handful of peppermints in front of me and dusted his palms. "You're going to have to be in charge of these markers. I can't be trusted." He opened his mouth, revealing a mostly dissolved mint. "I'm addicted."

I leaned away from the candy. "I bet you wouldn't enjoy them so much if someone was threatening you with them."

"True," he said, crunching the remains of his peppermint. "Wait. Did something else happen?"

"Yep."

Ray leaned forward, worry etched on his brow. "When?"

"Last night. This time a note was stabbed into my truck tire. The mints were crushed and scattered on the ground. The note said I'd been warned. That whole scene is bad, right? The first couple of times, the mints were whole, individually wrapped and delivered in a pretty gift box."

"Ominous," he said. "And two threats in one day feels like serious escalation. That can't be good."

"No kidding," I said, feeling the peace drain from me.

"Where were you parked? Outside Evan's? Or did that happen after you came home? Are you okay?"

"I'm fine. The truck was down by the square. I'd stopped on my way home from Evan's when I saw Cookie Corner."

Ray unwrapped another mint. "I love that place."

"Yeah, and guess who was in line ahead of me? Nadia Ford."

Ray flipped his gaze to mine. "You get anything useful from her this time?"

"Maybe. She says her husband was out of town the night Derek was killed. She seems to think that means he can't be the killer. I say it means she can't vouch for his exact whereabouts, and he can't vouch for hers. Seems a little suspicious to me, and she was really angry."

"Why was Brian out of town? Where did he go? Can we confirm that story's even true?" Ray asked.

I'd asked myself the same thing late last night, and I couldn't think of a way to prove it either way. "Nope."

"Does Evan know about your tire?"

"Yeah. He's taking care of that. He drove me home and watched some holiday movies with me and his sister Libby."

Ray folded the mint's empty wrapper like an accordion, looking sad and a little guilty. "I worried about you all night," he said. "That mess at the recycling center stuck with me. I almost called a dozen times, but I know you hate when I check up on you too much, and I figured you'd call if you needed me."

"I'm okay. Thanks for picking up all those bottles for me," I said. "I got a ton of work done last night thanks to you. You can't imagine how much it helped."

"Don't mention it," he said. "Wait a minute." Ray's eyes went wide. He leaned over the table, an expectant look on his face. "Did you say Evan has a sister?"

"Yep."

"And she's here? In Mistletoe? Tell me more."

"She's nice," I said. "Plucky. I like her. She's a few years younger than me, about eight years younger than Evan."

Ray smiled. "My age."

"Can I tell you something without you thinking I'm crazy?" I asked. The memory of the Santa racing along with me but staying across the street had kept me awake most of the night. It was the creepiest thing I'd ever experienced, and I couldn't shake the fear. It would have been less frightening if he'd just made a run at me instead of staring blatantly, silently, like the disturbed person I assumed him to be.

"Too late," Ray said. "I'm already aware you're nuts."

"Ha ha." I leaned forward and lowered my voice. "I think the killer is openly following me now. In a Santa costume."

Ray frowned. "What?"

I slouched back in my seat. "That's exactly what Evan looked like when I told him," I said, pointing at Ray's face."

Ray stretched his long legs beneath the table, knocking his boots into mine. He laced his fingers on the table and nodded slowly. "Okay." He sucked his mint and contemplated my statements. "A costume is kind of brilliant, actually."

"In a completely horrifying way," I clarified.

"Absolutely."

The Hearth door opened, and Ray's mom walked inside, dusting snow from her coat and smiling up at an older man in a black newsboy cap. An icy burst of wind whipped through the warm room before the door clattered shut behind them.

Ray turned for a look over his shoulder, then froze.

"Speaking of stalkers. How's that going?" I asked. "Get any good pictures? Some dirt on your new daddy?"

He shot me a bitter look.

"Sorry," I said. "Too soon?"

"It will always be too soon."

He pulled his legs back and sat straighter. "I told Mom I'd be here tonight, so what on earth is she doing?"

Ray's mom scanned the room, clapped once, then headed straight for us.

"Coming over to say hello, apparently," I said.

He looked again, and his mom waved, pulling the man along behind her until they reached our table. "Ray," she said, leaning in and kissing his cheek, "I'm so glad you let us know where you'd be. We've been trying to catch up with you for weeks."

I smiled at the man beside her. "I'm Holly White. I don't believe we've met." Though he looked vaguely familiar. I tried to imagine him in various jobs. Cook? Cop? Nurse or doctor?

"Pierce Lakemore," he said. "I believe we met briefly when my firm handled something for your family earlier this year."

I searched my brain for the memory. "Your firm? You're an attorney?"

"I rarely practice these days," he said humbly. "I keep trying to retire, but I can't seem to find someone suitable and willing to replace me as partner."

I smiled, impressed. "Partner," I repeated for Ray's benefit. "Nice." It didn't exactly sound as if Ray's mom had scraped the bottom of the barrel for this guy.

Ray frowned.

"Why don't you join us?" I asked, scooting over to make room.

Pierce accepted the offer easily. Ray's mom took the seat beside her son. Ray scowled. I could practically see daggers shooting from his eyes. I bumped the toe of my boot against his under the table and made my most encouraging face.

The Hearth's speakers gave a sharp screech, and I jumped. "Pardon me," Cookie said in her best British accent. "I do believe it is time for this evening's Reindeer Game. That game is bingo, and I, Delores Evelyn Cutter, shall be your official caller and judge. Is everybody ready?"

Ray's mom smiled at Pierce. "I love when Cookie does her British accent."

I did too. Sure, it was a little silly, but weren't we all? "She says everyone loves a British accent, and she refuses to disappoint a crowd." I pushed my bingo card closer to Pierce. "It's a full house and we're out of cards, but you and I can share, if you'd like."

He smiled back warmly, seeming surprised by the offer. "Well, thank you," he said. "I would love to." He cast a smile to Ray's mom, who blushed in return.

Ray begrudgingly moved his card nearer to his mom.

She patted his hand. "So, what have you been up to?" She looked from me to Ray, then back to me. "Ray has virtually disappeared from our home, and I don't think I've had the pleasure of chatting with you since last Christmas, Holly. What's new?"

I felt my smile falter. Had it really been a whole year? Where had the time gone? "Well," I started, pausing to think of what had been happening lately. A little of everything, it seemed, though not much for me personally. Nothing I wanted to talk about anyway. "Ray helped Cookie make a calendar featuring her goat, Theodore," I said. "She's giving them away but has plans to make more to sell so she can give the proceeds to charity."

"That's nice," Mrs. Griggs said. "Ray is pure genius with a camera. He took all our family photos every year when he was growing up. Took some very good ones of his daddy the year we lost him too."

Ray's expression went flat. His jaw tightened.

Mrs. Riggs reached for Pierce's hands across the table and squeezed them as her eyes misted with tears.

"Doesn't get easier," he told her. "We just learn to deal differently in time."

My heart ached for them. It sounded as if Pierce could

personally identify with what she was going through, and wasn't that kind of beautiful? Had two broken hearts found some peace and joy in each other?

"I'll be sure to buy a calendar," she told Ray.

Pierce smiled. "Put me down for fifty. I'll hand them out to our clients."

Ray forced a smile, but it was a little feral.

His mom released Pierce's hands and put hers on her lap. "How's Caroline?" she asked. "Her cupcake shop has been closed the last two days, and I haven't seen anything more in the newspaper since they announced her butcher knife was linked to the crime."

"She's in jail," I said, sounding blunt even to my own ears. "Her prints were the only ones on the knife, so I'm not sure what happens next." And I'd been too sidetracked last night to get all the answers I'd wanted from Evan.

Mrs. Riggs pressed a palm to her collarbone. "Dear me."

Pierce patted his fingertips on the tabletop. "Caroline will be fine. Her family keeps an incredibly talented attorney on retainer."

"I hope you're right," Mrs. Riggs said. She turned her attention back to me, a world of compassion working in her deep blue eyes. "How are you handling that?"

"Okay, I guess."

Ray grinned, and a look of pride or satisfaction bloomed on his face. Maybe both. "Holly's trying to prove her best friend's innocent, of course."

His mom's expression suddenly matched her son's. "How's that going?"

"Scary," I said. "Lots of threats so far, and I'm no closer to knowing who did it today than I was when I started. But I have a few suspects. One of them doesn't have an alibi, so I'm leaning toward him at the moment."

"Who?" she asked.

"Brian Ford. Do you know him?"

Pierce's bushy eyebrows lifted. "The purse maker?"

"You know a purse maker?" Mrs. Griggs asked.

"Professionally."

She laughed. "Is there anyone you don't know?"

Pierce stroked his neatly manicured mustache. "Tom Selleck."

The older couple giggled.

Ray unwrapped another peppermint and crunched it into smithereens with his teeth.

Four losing rounds of bingo later, Pierce and Mrs. Riggs said their goodbyes and left for their eight o'clock dinner reservations.

Ray's pinched expression eased slightly once they'd gone. "I hate that guy."

"No you don't," I said. "You miss your dad. I don't blame you. No one does. But Pierce seems like a nice man who's financially stable, educated, handsome, and he makes your mom smile. What else could you want given the reality that you have?"

"You think Pierce is handsome?"

I shrugged.

Ray chomped another mint. "Fine. I'm willing to admit he's not the worst guy she could be interested in."

"There, see?" I said. "That was very mature of you. Unlike

the time I found you photographing them from behind a pile of snow."

His lips twitched. "That was too much, huh?"

I shrugged again. "I like that you go the extra mile. It's nice."

Ray laughed, and my heart unfurled. I hated seeing the people I cared about hurting.

A sharp wolf whistle drew my attention toward a redhead striding our way. Libby Gray was dressed to kill in designer jeans, heeled boots, and a fitted leather coat. She stopped at the table's edge and smiled at Ray. "Hello," she said. "I'm Libby." Her long black lashes nearly reached her prefect eyebrows. Reaching red curls hung over her back and shoulders.

Ray's eyes bulged and his tongue nearly rolled out of his mouth like a vintage cartoon character's. "Hi. Hello. Hi," he stammered. "Ray Griggs."

Evan grabbed his sister's shoulders from behind and guided her to my side of the booth. He took the seat beside Ray. "That's my baby sister," he said in a warning tone.

Libby rolled her eyes. "I'm hardly a baby. I'm twenty-three."

"Ray's twenty-four," I said, "but he's a total baby."

Ray laughed.

Libby took a long look around the Hearth. "You grew up here, huh?" she asked, turning back to me with a flip of her hair.

"Yep."

"Must've been tough."

"Sheer misery," I agreed. "All the sugar and endless merriment nearly did me in."

A slow smile spread over Libby's lips.

"All righty." Cookie's high-pitched voice broke through the

soft holiday music once more. She'd returned to the microphone, sans her British accent, and smiled brightly at everyone. "I've been told the horses are bridled and the sleds are being brought around for all you love birds wanting to share a romantic sleigh ride through the countryside. Courtesy blankets are available for snuggling in every sleigh."

Libby jumped up. "That sounds like fun. Let's go." She reached across the table for Ray.

Evan glared up at her. "What are you doing?"

"I'm going for a sleigh ride." She looked at me. "That's what the lady said, right? I've never been in a horse-drawn sleigh. Just the carriages that run back home by Quincy Market."

I climbed out of the booth on a beam of excitement and addressed Evan. "Your sister has never been on a proper sleigh ride. We need to fix that."

Evan scooted out to join us, but he didn't look very happy about it.

Ray followed. He circled around my side and looped an arm over my shoulder. "I love sleigh rides. I can ride with Holly if you'd prefer to ride with Libby, Sheriff."

Evan's eyes narrowed.

Ray took one of my hands in his and pressed it to his chest.

I tipped my head back for a better look at his face. "What are you doing?" A hot young redhead wanted to ride with him. Had he misunderstood her somehow?

He smiled down at me, then winked.

"All right," Evan said, letting the full weight of his Boston accent drip from the words. "You two can take the sleigh ahead of us."

Libby gleefully hooked her arm with Ray's. "So, tell me about yourself," she said as they moseyed toward the door.

Evan ground his teeth.

I grabbed my coat and scarf and hurried after Ray and Libby. Evan stuck close to my side. "Your friend is in big trouble," he mumbled, tugging a black knit cap over his ears.

"Why? Are you going to defend your sister's honor if he sits too closely on the sleigh?" I teased.

Evan hooted with laughter. "Oh, that's funny. I was thinking more along the lines of that big marshmallow had better run or my little sister will eat him alive."

I watched carefully as Libby and Ray climbed into the next open sleigh and covered their legs with a blanket. Evan had given me an unsettling visual to think about, and now that I was really looking, Ray did seem unsure of where to put his long arms in the confined space of the curved sleigh seat. Libby, on the other hand, looked as if she had a few ideas and was willing to share. "Poor Ray," I said.

Evan zipped his black sheriff's coat to his chin. "That's for sure."

People streamed forward from multiple directions, gathering in twos to catch the next sleigh. Evan and I brought up the rear. Waiting had never been my favorite thing, and I especially hated it now. It forced me to stop and live in the moment. For the first time all day, I wasn't rushing through one task or rushing toward another. I was trapped in that minute of time. Standing close to Evan with a thundering heart.

My mind raced, and I realized with a start that I was nervous. My cheeks flamed hot against the chilly night air.

"Everything okay?" Evan asked, probably seeing the change I would absolutely blame on the cold if asked.

"Yep." I scanned the pretty horizon. Our property always looked like a Norman Rockwell painting come to life this time of year. A clear, star-filled sky overhead. Rows of evergreens lined in twinkle lights all around. The air was crisp and clean, scented with pine and new fallen snow. It was impossible to lack clarity with those oxygen levels.

Something red flashed in the distance near the barns. I held my breath, waiting for it to come again, but it was gone. Was it a coat? A Santa costume? The Santa hired by my dad to entertain guests tonight? Or someone more sinister? And how did I know the man Dad hired wasn't the same one stalking me?

Evan grabbed my sleeve and tugged me along as the line moved forward. "You sure you're okay? Cause you're acting a little squirrely."

"I'm fine." Besides, even if a killer was at the farm tonight, he'd see I was with the sheriff and go home. Evan wouldn't let anyone hurt me—I was certain of that.

Evan puffed breath into his bare hands. "I think they ran out of sleighs. That last one left awhile ago. We might have to wait for the first one to finish the trip and return."

I squinted into the shadows, searching for the previous sleigh. Evan was right. It was completely out of sight. "That's strange," I said turning on my tiptoes in search of another sleigh. "We have ten, and I only counted eight ahead of us."

A few moments later, our sleigh arrived. I waved to the driver, then climbed aboard, towing Evan behind me.

"Having some trouble tonight?" Evan asked the driver.

"No sir." He snapped the reins, and we took off.

Evan and I snuggled low in our seat beneath the heavy wool blanket, prepared for a beautiful but chilly ride over the Reindeer Games grounds. Dad's horses had made the journey hundreds of times in their lives here. They knew the route as well as I did. Along the length of the white fence at the property's edge, between the reaching groves of dormant deciduous trees. Around the lake. Over the rolling hills, then back to the Hearth for a warm cup of tea, cider, or cocoa.

Wind raced over our skin as the horse picked up speed along the fence, forcing Evan and me to sit a little closer. We buried our hands beneath the blanket. Our bodies aligned from shoulder to knee, and a horde of butterflies flying kamikaze in my tummy. "What does Libby really think of Mistletoe?" I asked, desperate for something to think about besides Evan's nearness, his warmth, and the perfect winter night all around us.

"She misses Boston," he said. "A lot. But she can't go back. Not yet. Not until Boston PD brings the guy in who's looking for her."

"She's lucky to have you," I said. "She'll be okay in the end."

He watched the forest dance by, averting his eyes, lost in thought.

I'd have given anything to know what that thought was. "Do you miss Boston?"

He shifted beside me, turning warm green eyes to meet my gaze. "Not at the moment." His fingers found mine beneath the blanket, and he curled one strong hand around my smaller one.

Icy air washed over my teeth, and I had to force my giant smile closed.

A flash of something red whipped by as we neared the lake.

"Did you see that?" I asked. "At the tree line?"

The sharp sound of a snapping branch or flying rock erupted as Evan turned to look, and our horse reared back, jostling the sleigh and tossing the driver from his seat into the snow.

I jumped to my feet and leaned out for a look at the lost driver when the sleigh stilled. "Are you okay?"

Crack! The sound returned, and a blotch of red appeared on the horse's hindquarters. She whinnied and reared once more, throwing me backward.

The sleigh jerked forward before I could regain my footing and took off through the snow. We rocketed ahead as I floundered, having fallen onto Evan in a graceless heap. The sleigh darted and rocked as our horse left the well-trodden path, terrified of whatever had happened to her and whatever had left that mark on her.

I pushed off Evan as we raced closer to the lake. "Whoa!" I called, scrambling to catch the reins. "Whoa!" The leather snapped against my palms as I strained to regain control. I gave a strong, confident pull, but the harness broke free, setting our sleigh on a direct path with the frozen lake.

Evan swore behind me.

We were on a collision course. "Jump!" I said, my mind snapping into action. "Jump!" Whatever happened, we did *not* want to end up in that lake.

Evan pushed onto his feet and reached for my waist. "You first. Ready?"

The sleigh hit a lip of packed snow, and we no longer needed to jump—Evan and I were airborne.

We'd been launched onto the fast-cracking, ice-covered water.

Chapter Sixteen

We hit the frozen lake in a tangle of limbs and panicked screams. The horrendous crash of our bodies against the ice sent cracks cascading in every direction. Pain reverberated through my bones as my teeth rattled. I scurried onto my knees, wincing with each movement of my head, hip, and wrist. "Evan!"

He was on his side near the bank, not moving.

"Evan!" I slid toward him on my hands and knees, wincing against the pain in my head.

A burst of snow erupted from the bank above us, stopping me short as sheer panic clenched my heart, muscles, and mind. The runaway sleigh shot into the air at the lake's edge and plummeted headlong onto the frozen water with us. The blades hit first, sharp and loud as an earthquake. The ice beneath me began to splinter.

Evan raised onto his forearms, probably jarred awake by the newest catastrophe.

"Run!" I told him, unable to force my own limbs into cooperation. Evan was only a few feet from solid ground. He could make it.

I visually trailed the largest fissure as it sprinted across the ice in my direction.

"Holly!" Evan shouted. He dove toward me, drawing my attention away from my eminent doom. Blood streamed over his face from a gash near his eye.

"Get back!" I shouted. "Get away! Off the ice! Get my dad!"

I was underwater in the next second, breath stolen, skin and lungs screaming in protest of the deadly temperature. My clothes, coat, and boots tripled instantly in weight. My muscles were weak from yesterday's unwanted workout. My mind was paralyzed with fear.

I fought against the darkness, kicked against the ache in my legs, against everything literal and figurative that worked to pull me down. I wouldn't die like this. Wouldn't give up. Wouldn't be the victim of some lunatic psycho Santa Claus.

I kicked again. And again. Longer. Harder with each effort, using the burn of my limbs as a reminder I was still alive and this fight wasn't over. I broke the water's surface with a ragged, painful gasp. Frigid gulps of oxygen poured into my burning lungs.

Two massive hands clutched onto the soaking fabric of my coat and towed me toward the broken ice. Evan's terrified face swam into view. He was on his belly, arms extended, blood streaming around his left eye. His face was red and swollen. While I'd landed on my side after being thrown from the sleigh, it looked as if Evan had landed on his head. "I've got you, White," he croaked.

The creak and groan of bending metal pulled my blurry eyes toward the sleigh, ten feet away and now at a ninety-degree tilt, going down like the Titanic on its maiden voyage.

My body bobbed in the icy water, being tugged and hoisted as Evan reared back, careful not to be pulled in with me.

"Take my hand," he said, teeth gritted, no doubt from the pain of his injuries.

I reached for him, clasping my weak hand in his strong one. "Don't let go," I whispered.

"Never."

"Holly!" My dad's voice boomed in the distance. He was on the ice a moment later, paying no attention to the growing cracks.

With one combined heave from Dad and Evan, I was sliding like a seal toward land.

The sound of breaking bones reverberated in my skull as the ice-covered lake behind us broke completely, no longer a sheet of shattered ice, just deadly frigid water and a whole lot of tiny icebergs. The sleigh was upside down and sinking.

"Baby," Dad cooed, wrapping me in his big arms.

Blankets were arranged over my shoulders in stacks as other riders emerged from their sleighs. Horses and sleighs had stopped and rerouted so people could look at the show.

The telltale cry of an ambulance echoed in the distance, and a rush of hot tears melted my frozen eyeballs.

Ray broke through the crowd, running over the hill toward us, breaking Dad's grip on me and nearly tackling us both in the process. "Are you okay?" he panted, his cheeks red from exertion, breath coming in wild puffs of steam. "I heard you screaming, but we were almost back to the Hearth. I jumped out and told Libby to call 9-1-1." He stopped to catch his breath and look around. "Holy—what happened?"

Evan's chest rose and fell in enormous gasps. "Libby's okay?"

"Yeah," Ray said. "She's with Mrs. White and Cookie. What can I do?"

"Stay with her?" Evan asked, brushing a hand down my arm. "Always."

Evan nodded and moved into sheriff mode.

A sob wrenched free from my trembling lips, and I tightened my grip on Ray's middle.

"You could've died," he said, tremendous fear and sadness in his voice. He tipped his cheek against the top of my frozen head. "This is horrible, Holly. What if you hadn't been with Evan?"

"I'm-m-m ok-k-kay," I said, unable to control the violent chattering of my teeth.

"I don't understand how this happened. It was a peaceful sleigh ride. How did this happen?" he repeated.

"I s-saw someone in the tr-tr-trees," I said, working hard to get the words out. "They sh-o-t-t the horse."

"They shot your horse?" Ray squeaked. "Who does that? How is she?"

"Sh-sh-she r-r-r-an." The tremors spread over my limbs until my entire body vibrated in his grip.

"Find that horse," Dad barked.

Evan tucked his phone into his pocket. "Whoever did this might still be on the farm." His eyes were hard as steel as he turned them to meet Dad's waiting stare.

"On it." Dad pressed the button on his long-range walkie-talkie. His unit was linked to every member of our farm staff. "Lock this place down," he said. "Someone tried to kill my daughter and the sheriff. They're not walking free on my watch."

"Yes, sir," a number of voices reported back.

"I'm coming!" My mother's frantic voice pealed through the speaker. "What do you need? What can I do?"

Dad turned and walked a few feet away, presumably to calm my mother and provide her with some answers.

Ray turned us toward the path where our sled had diverted. "Come on. The ambulance is almost here."

Evan hung back, phone pressed to his ear. "Sheriff Gray," he said. "I need some deputies at Reindeer Games immediately." He listened, then raised his gaze to my Dad. "How many Santas do you have on the payroll tonight, Mr. White?" he called.

"One."

"Can you get him over here? I'd like to talk to him and anyone else on this property wearing a Santa costume as soon as possible."

Dad lifted a thumb to indicate his agreement. His expression said he hadn't quite calmed my mom yet.

When the deputies arrived, Evan assigned one to search the tree line and the other to round up anyone in so much as a red coat or hat.

The EMTs worked me over thoroughly, insisting I change from my wet clothes into a set of dry scrubs kept in the ambulance. They bundled me up in heated blankets and checked my vitals. I was thoroughly bruised and shaken—and I might call a therapist in the morning—but I was physically fine.

It was past closing time when Evan and his men finished speaking with everyone on the premises. The only Santa they'd found was Mr. Miller, a retired schoolteacher Dad had hired for the weekend. Mom and Cookie were able to vouch for him.

Apparently, Mr. Miller had come into the Hearth for his break shortly after I'd left for my sleigh ride. A line of kids began to form at the sight of him, and the poor Santa had never gotten that break. His beard was nearly dragging on the ground from fatigue by the time Evan released him.

I watched the remaining staff and guests trickle through the gates from my place inside the Hearth. I'd had a hot shower and redressed in my warmest clothes before returning to the café.

"Are you sure I can't get you anything else?" Mom asked, rubbing my shoulders and still fretting at maximum capacity.

"Where would you put it?" I asked with a warm smile. The table before me was crammed with enough sweets, treats, and hot drinks to end hunger in six countries. She'd even made grilled cheese and ladled out a cup of her homemade chicken noodle soup.

Mom fell onto the bench across from me, exhaustion replacing fear on her tired face. "I can't believe you fell through the ice," she said. "That was always my biggest fear when you were growing up. I couldn't keep you off the ponds in your little red skates."

"Really?" I'd spent a lot of time alone as a child, exploring the land, reading in the trees, or drawing the landscape. "I was always more afraid of falling off a limb than through the ice."

She snorted. "Well, the fall wouldn't have killed you from where you sat. Never so high that I couldn't hand deliver snacks without a boost."

"A win–win."

She smiled. "I never gave it much thought, but you really don't like heights, do you? You love to ski, but look how long it took us to talk you into going every year. Was it the size of the hills as you got better at it?"

"No. I didn't mind the hills. Those were solid under my feet. It was the ride to the top on that deathtrap of a swing-thing that made me want to lose my cookies."

Mom laughed softly. "I believe folks call that a lift, sweetie."

I helped myself to a slice of cashew caramel fudge and sighed. "Funny how even the worst nights come back around to peaceful eventually," I said.

Dad, Evan, Libby, and Ray interrupted my peace a heartbeat later. They moved toward our booth like a mismatched squad of some sort, all wearing bleak expressions. They pulled out chairs from a nearby table and took their seats, clearly frustrated and tired.

"Something sweet?" I asked, waving a hand over my table's bounty.

Mom hopped back into action, distributing the wealth.

"You okay?" Evan asked.

"Yeah. You?"

He gave a humorless chuckle and touched his swollen cheekbone with careful fingers. A butterfly bandage covered the formerly bloody real estate near his brow. "I'm about as mad as I've ever been, but I'll get that sorted soon." He accepted a mug of hot cider from Mom and lifted the steam to warm his face. "Your dad found the horse and got her situated for the night. Wasn't blood on her hindquarters—it was paint."

"Paint?" Mom voiced the question before I could. "How did paint get on Luna? I'm sure she wouldn't have gone out like that."

"I'm thinking she was shot with a paintball gun," Evan said.

"We heard the crack of the gun, I but didn't recognize the sound then. Now that I've seen the paint, I'm sure that's what it was."

"Mean," I whispered.

Libby stirred her steaming cider with a cinnamon stick. "That's what I said. Tell her the rest, E."

Evan made a sour face, probably over being called "E" in front of the rest of us. Definitely a new one for me. "My deputy checked the tree line along the sleigh's path."

"I saw someone there," I said. "Did you find him?" My chest constricted. He hadn't, or he would've led with that information. Which meant whoever did this was still out there.

"No." Evan set his mug aside, "but we found about a hundred of those little red and white mints."

Dad pulled Mom against his side and leaned his head on hers. She was almost taller than him when he was seated. "I think Holly needs to stay with us until this is over," he told her. "We can trade shifts looking after her. I can finish up whatever chores the farmhands don't get to after you've closed up here each night."

I formed a *T* with my hands. "Time out," I said. "I don't need a security detail."

The group began to murmur their united disagreement on that point.

"I can assign a deputy to help out," Evan offered my parents, who nodded urgently.

"Hey," I interrupted. "What if we focus on the problem instead of the symptoms? How's the investigation into Derek's murder going?" I asked Evan. "Are you planning to keep Caroline in jail for Christmas?"

"No," he said. "Judge Porter will be back from his ski trip

tonight. He'll hold Caroline's arraignment first thing tomorrow, and once bond is set, she can go home."

"Okay, but are you any closer to finding the actual killer? I won't be safe again until you do, and it seems like whoever it is has moved from threats to actions."

Evan's jaw locked and popped. "I'm aware. I'm working every lead, and I'd feel better if I left a deputy with you for now."

"You need your deputies to look help you for the killer," I said, suddenly remembering everything I'd forgotten to tell him. "Did you know Derek had an affair with Nadia Ford?" I asked.

Evan dipped his chin. "Yes."

"And you know she is the wife of a man Derek called his archnemesis?"

Another nod.

"Nadia told me Derek was the one who exposed their relationship to her husband, and she felt as if Derek had used her. She also said Brian was out of town on the night of the murder, so she can't account for his whereabouts, and he can't account for hers," I added. "Also, Derek's maid said he fought regularly with his business partner Greg Pressey. I'm not sure Greg had any reason to kill Derek, because their business is obviously thriving, but he was unreasonably coy when I tried to ask him about Derek, and I don't know why."

My dad's face moved from red to eggplant. "How do you know all this?" he asked. "Tell me you aren't getting involved with a murder investigation again. Tell me you haven't forgotten how that ended for you last year?"

Mom rubbed his back.

"What else am I supposed to do?" I asked. "Caroline is not a killer, and she's stuck in jail at Christmas. It's horrifying and ridiculous, and someone needs to prove she didn't do it. Also, I think the sooner we stop the person trying to kill me, the better."

Dad's eyes bulged and Evan's eye twitched. He pressed a finger to it.

"You need to stop this," Dad barked. The deep color in his cheeks had spread into his thinning hairline while I'd watched Evan.

"Fine," I snapped.

Dad pulled in a breath, his facial features relaxing infinitesimally.

I locked my attention on Evan. "If you can't prove someone else killed Derek, then at least try to prove Caroline wasn't with him when he died. Check her cell phone bill and local security camera feeds. Find *something*."

Evan widened his eyes. His chair scraped over the floor, and he was on his feet moving toward me.

I held my breath for whatever came next.

He stooped, and cupping my cheeks in his palms, he pressed his lips to mine for a long beat of gusto before jogging out the front door and leaving us all to stare after him.

"Did he just kiss you?" Libby asked.

"He does that sometimes," I said.

Too bad he kept running away afterward.

Chapter Seventeen

Cindy Lou Who and I slept at my parents' house. Much as I'd wanted to make a point that I was fine, when it was time to go home alone, I let my mom talk me into spending the night in my old room without a fight. Dad had tucked me beneath his arm as we made the trip home, and Mom had hurried around the house, stripping my old bed and making it up again with soft flannel sheets from the dryer. She even delivered a hot toddy to my nightstand and kissed me goodnight. My eyes brimmed with tears at the gesture. At my innumerable blessings. And at the toll my week had taken so far.

I didn't care that I was twenty-seven years old and being treated like a child. I was thankful to the tips of my toes for another night in my creaky daybed. I knew that one day, far too soon, a night like this would be impossible to repeat. One day, Christmas would be missing the two things that made it so special. I hugged Mom and Dad tight and told them I loved them before they made their way back downstairs to watch their favorite holiday movie. I pulled the warm fleece blankets up to my chin and drifted slowly to sleep, surrounded by the sights and sounds of my childhood.

I woke to the mouth-watering scent of homemade Belgium waffles and fresh-brewed coffee. I could almost taste them as I dragged my tired body out of bed and tied a robe over my pajamas.

I padded to the kitchen on slippered feet, eyelids at half-mast, in search of caffeine and sustenance.

Mom delivered a plate of bacon, waffles, and fruit to my seat at the table.

"Bless you." I pulled the chair out and dropped onto the red gingham-print cushion.

She patted my head. "How did you sleep?"

"Like a log." My body felt five hundred pounds too heavy. I probably could've slept forever if my nose and tummy hadn't dragged me down the steps.

A mug of coffee arrived next, followed by a portable turn-table with different choices of syrups and whipped cream. Mom stepped back to smile once she'd thoroughly surrounded me with food. "I hope you're hungry."

I was always hungry.

I grabbed the syrup and soaked my waffle. How had I eaten cold cereal for so long before moving home again? How had I been happy with that when I'd grown up with this?

I pushed a long crispy strip of bacon between my teeth and devoured it like a ticket machine at an arcade. "Yum." Slowly, I felt my limbs twitch back to life.

Mom filled a second mug with coffee and took the seat across from me. "I'm so glad you and Cindy decided to stay with us last night. It gave your father and me such peace of mind. To think we came so close to losing you." She sniffed, then looked at the ceiling, combating tears.

"Stop." I waved a strip of bacon at her. "If you cry, I'll cry, and I just woke up. I don't want to cry."

The doorbell rang, and Mom wiped her hands on her apron. "You're right. This is a perfectly wonderful morning. I won't ruin it with tears." She hurried away to answer the door with a smile.

A moment later, she gasped, then started to bawl.

"Mom?" I ran for the front room, grabbing a heavy silver heirloom on my way to save her. Images of a lunatic holding Mom hostage and threatening her life ran through my mind. That guy was going to meet the business end of Great-nana's candlestick.

Mom stood in the open doorway, rocking side to side in a long embrace with Caroline.

"Care!" I set Great-nana's candlestick aside and ran to join them in a group hug. "You're free!" I cried, tears flowing in a hot deluge over both cheeks. "I can't believe it. Judge Porter set your bail?"

Caroline pushed back from us with a beaming smile. "No. Better. All charges have been dropped!"

"What?"

"My name has been cleared," she said, "and I believe I have you to thank for it." She looked over her shoulder and waved someone in from the porch.

Evan strode into view, big sheriff's hat in hands and wearing his official uniform. "You suggested I come at this from another angle, so I did. I remembered Caroline's statement from the night you brought her in. She said she'd been alone at her shop, eating whipped cream and watching Cupcake Wars. But I've been to Caroline's Cupcakes dozens of times. She doesn't have a television anywhere in that place. What she does have is a smart refrigerator. Turns out she was watching via the screen on her new fridge."

"I love that new fridge," she said.

Evan spun his hat on his fingers. "She also loves chatting with fellow bakers about the episode while she watches, and her fridge logged every minute she was online. It kept a timestamped record of every message sent or received, and it proved she was there at the time of Derek's murder." Evan grinned. "They were having a heated debate over the merits and drawbacks of fondant."

"I'm a fan," Caroline said. "I can't help it if GimmeSugar74 doesn't know how to use it properly."

"Thank you," I told Evan, a lump rising in my throat. "This is the best Christmas gift ever." I threw myself at him and held on until he hugged me back.

After breakfast, Evan went to work, and so did Mom. Caroline stayed to help me clean the kitchen.

She passed me a stack of dirty plates and took up space beside me with a dish towel. "You wash. I'll dry."

"We can just load the dishwasher," I suggested.

"I think better if I'm moving."

"What are you thinking about?"

"I'm thinking now that our babysitters are gone, you'll let me help you with your investigation."

I smiled. "I'm not supposed to keep doing that," I said. "I almost died last night."

Caroline hugged me. "I heard. How do you feel today?"

I tipped my head briefly over each shoulder. "Okay."

"Good. Then let's get this killer caught before he takes another run at you."

"This go-getter attitude is one of my favorite things about you," I said. "You know that, right?"

"I thought it was because I never poo-poo on your hare-brained plans."

"That too."

Caroline waited patiently as I washed a syrup-covered plate and passed it her way. "I'm not sure what to do next," I admitted, "or if I want to do anything after taking that impromptu swim in Lake Ice Cube."

"But?"

"I guess there is something niggling in the back of my mind. Nothing big, just a little needle of curiosity."

Caroline stacked the dried plates together and hoisted them into the cupboard. "Go on."

"When he got here, Evan thanked me for helping him think outside the box, and it's got me wondering if I need to take my own advice and try looking at things from a different perspective."

"Like?" Caroline asked.

"I don't know," I admitted, "but I can't stop wondering how your knife wound up at a murder scene. Maybe figuring out who might've had access to the knife will help us figure out who used it that night."

She pointed at me. "I like it," she said, "but I can't remember the last time I saw the knife at my shop. We've been so busy lately that at least one of the dishwashers is full all the time. If I'd even noticed it was missing, I would have assumed it was being washed before I would have assumed it was stolen. Who steals knives? Especially ones that are part of a custom set."

"Murderers who plan ahead and wear gloves so they don't leave prints." I wiped a forearm across my brow, then checked the clock over the stove. "Okay. I don't want to be a sitting duck. Whoever is after me knows what I drive and where I live. Staying with my folks is nice, but it puts them in danger, and honestly, it didn't keep me safe last year."

Caroline put the last mixing bowl on the shelf. "What do you want to do?"

"I visited Derek's business partner a couple days ago," I said. "I didn't get any information from him, and I don't know why he wouldn't just answer me. It seems like he should have at least tried to help."

"Is he any nicer than Derek?" she asked.

"Gina from Merry Maids thinks so," I said, "but I never met Derek."

Caroline shrugged. "Well, let's go ask him again."

I stepped away from the sink, loving the idea of taking backup to the gym with me in case of another ambush workout ploy. "Okay, but be careful or he'll make you work out, and then he'll withhold information anyway."

Caroline popped a hip and tossed a mile of blonde hair over her shoulder. "I work out four days a week, and I don't need a man to help me do it."

"Good luck telling him that," I said.

She narrowed her eyes and her glossy lips quirked up on one side. "Would you consider bringing your gym bag and gear just in case?"

"I guess."

"Excellent," she said. "Because I have an idea."

We parked in the crowded lot at Ironman Training Center, and I led her along the cobblestone path to our destination.

She looked longingly at the building marked Wellness Center. "I was just here last week with my mom," she said. "The spa is beautiful, elegant, and smells like heaven."

"Cinnamon rolls?" I asked.

"No. More like a spring morning after the rain. Clean. Green. A hint of blooming flowers and something sweet and rich like honey. Very peaceful. We spent the entire day getting massages and facials. I had a seaweed wrap and mud bath too." Caroline dropped her head back and groaned. "It was amazing. Mom reaches her stress limit sometimes, and she just cancels everything to rejuvenate. As much as that woman makes me crazy, she knows how to unwind."

I gave the spa a wistful look. "I want a seaweed wrap."

"Miss White." Greg Pressey strode in our direction, a smug look on his face. He balanced a disposable tray of steaming cups in one hand and lifted the other in welcome. "I knew you'd be back, though I'm a little surprised to see you so soon. Are you ready for another workout?"

Caroline's leather-gloved hand shot out to greet him. "Hello, I'm Caroline West, Mayor West's daughter. It's lovely to meet you."

Greg's congenial smile wilted. "You're the woman from that news clip. You fought with Derek the night he died. Weren't you arrested?"

"I was released when the sheriff verified my whereabouts at

the time of the murder, thanks to my sweet friend here." She wrapped an arm around my back. "Friends help one another like that. Now, I'm here to help her figure out who killed Derek and put the criminal behind bars in time for Christmas. Do you think you can help me with that?"

Greg smiled, clearly entertained by the thought of Caroline and me solving the crime.

I suspected he had a few antiquated ideas about what women were capable of.

"All right," Greg said, a sly grin crossing his face as he turned his eyes back on Caroline. "We can talk while you work out."

Caroline gave him a stiff nod. "That seems fair, but I'm afraid I have work to do. You made a similar deal with Holly a couple days ago. You broke it."

"I'm ready to talk today," he said, flashing his eyes back to me. "Are you ready to work?"

"No."

Caroline nodded. "We'll give you one last chance to make this right. Holly will work out and you'll answer her questions. Deal?"

"What?" I gasped. "No!"

Greg's smile turned predatory. "What do you think Holly? Are you up to it?"

"Not even a little." I looked to Caroline for help. She needed to recant the offer. I was in no shape to deal with Greg and his insanity workout again. "You said this gym stuff was for you."

"No," she said. "I said you should bring it in case we needed it. Now we need it." She smiled at me. "Fitness is the best gift anyone can give you," she said, leaning in close for a hug. Her cheek brushed mine, and she whispered, "Keep him busy while I go through Derek's office. If he won't tell us anything about Derek, maybe I can find something worth knowing in his office."

My head hung forward as Caroline released me. I raised my chin slowly, unable to refuse. My bottom lip jutted and trembled. My muscles wept. "Sure," I said. "Let's go."

Thirty minutes later I was slapping the mat like a defeated wrestler. "Uncle," I cried.

Greg offered me his hand and hoisted me upright. "Good work today." He clapped me on the back and I pitched forward. "Bet you never sweated like that at yoga," he said with a prideful grin. "This is the only real way to get in shape. This grunting, sweating, dig-in-deep, Ironman training is the only way to true full-body fitness. All that cardio and stretching, yoga and spin class nonsense is for pansies and the elderly. You keep coming here, and you'll be bench pressing me in a year."

I struggled to steady myself from his pat on the back and clear the spots from my vision. "If I keep coming here, I'll be dead by Easter."

Greg chuckled, obviously mistaking my point of fact for an attempt at humor, and walked away. "See you in a few days, Miss White. Alternate heat and ice if anything's tender in the morning."

In the morning? I could barely walk *now*. I stumbled to the locker room, like a drunkard, on numb and wobbly legs. Caroline was on her phone on a bench near the locker where I'd left my clothes. "Yikes," she said at the sight of me. "What happened?"

"I don't want to talk about it," I said.

219

"Okay, then let's get out of here." She hiked her purse onto one shoulder and looked at me expectantly. "What?"

"I can't move." I slid down my locker to the floor. "Go on without me."

She rolled her eyes. "I don't know what you did out there, but it's only been thirty minutes. Whatever it was can't be that bad."

"You don't know." I shook my head. "You don't know," I whispered a second time for impact.

Caroline hoisted me onto my feet but refused to help me change clothes, and she wouldn't call me an ambulance. She helped me into my coat, however, and I appreciated it. "I hate this place," I grouched, shuffling along behind her as we headed for the exit. "I'm not even going to drive past it again. I'll go out of my way never to see it. My pain was all for nothing. Greg barely spoke to me," I rambled on. "He just tried to kill me with that big tire and assigned an inhumane amount of squats and box jumps."

"Really?" Caroline held the locker room door for me to pass. "Nothing?"

I reconsidered the complaint. "He said Derek has made plenty of investments and that surely at least one of them has tanked, and then he suggested we talk to whoever that theoretical business owner is."

"Did he give you a clue about what other businesses Derek invested in?" Caroline asked.

"No. He said he was just the gym manager, not Derek's best friend, and it was common sense that not everything Derek touched turned to gold." I couldn't help thinking of Nadia Ford. He'd touched her and her marriage nearly failed. "He also said that if finding Derek's killer is so important to me, I should leave him alone and figure it out. Then he tried to sell me a membership package." I laughed, but it hurt.

Caroline rolled her eyes. "Well, I had time to go through what was left in Derek's desk drawers," she whispered. "Either Derek was a minimalist, or someone beat me to the job. The computer was gone. Evan probably has that. I took photos of everything else and made sure it all went back into its place before I slipped out of there. None of it felt overly important, but maybe you'll see something I didn't when you look through the pictures."

I waved to the woman at the desk when we rounded the corner. "See you soon," she said.

I shivered at the bowl of mints on the countertop and picked up my pace getting out of there.

Caroline's little black BMW cruised up and down the hills outside of town. The interior smelled like leather, new carpet, and a mix of Caroline's perfumes and hair products. If a car could smell sophisticated, hers did. My truck smelled like Big Red chewing gum and black coffee.

"What do you think?" she asked as I flipped through the images she'd captured on her phone.

"I think Greg was right. It looks like Derek invested in quite a few businesses. I guess I can research them all and see if any of them went belly up. I also think it's interesting that the only picture in his entire office is this one." I turned the screen to face her. He'd kept a framed photo of himself with Samantha Moss at the edge of his desk. They were dressed for skiing and surrounded by white mountains. "Think of all those bikini-clad women from his social media feeds. He could have put any of those on display, but he chose this one. She was important to him."

"I hadn't given that photo a second thought," she said. "You're good at this."

"Even if I'm right, I'm not sure the insight actually helps." I rolled my head to face her. "And if I was any good at snooping, the killer wouldn't be after me right now."

"You're not snooping," Caroline said. "You're sleuthing. And you *are* good at it." She smiled. "You inspired Evan to prove my innocence instead of focusing on someone else's guilt."

I had done that. He'd said so himself. "I wish I could take my own advice and have a huge epiphany, but I don't know any other way to look at things."

Caroline stretched her neck and rolled her shoulders. "I wonder if Derek's family was the reason he and Samantha broke up."

"Maybe," I said, "but let's not forget she's totally bananas."

"True, but I had a lot of time to think about things while I was waiting for Judge Porter to come back, and I think Derek and I could've been friends if he wasn't so rude and inappropriate. Our families run in the same circles. I'm sure his parents are just as obsessed with appearances as mine. Samantha owns a wine shop, but maybe that wasn't good enough. Maybe, like me, he was supposed to marry someone pre-vetted by his family's attorneys and public relations staff."

"Is that what your parents do to you?" I knew they'd set her up on awful dates with pompous, entitled brats, but I didn't know they were arranging alliances to determine who she could or couldn't marry.

"Every day," she said, "and Derek would probably have understood that if he'd talked to me instead of grabbing me every chance he got." She slowed and hit her turn signal as Reindeer Games came up on the right. "I'll bet his folks wanted him to follow in his father's footsteps too. I'll bet they hated that he hadn't gotten a law degree and wasn't interested in a judgeship. My parents lose their minds every time I mention my shop. They hate that I want to serve people cupcakes for a living. I guess now that Derek's dead, I can see the missed opportunity we had for camaraderie, and it makes me sad. Why couldn't Derek have just talked to me like a normal person instead of being such a punk?"

I didn't know what to say. "We can't control people," I said.

"I should've tried harder to connect with him instead of just yelling at him."

"No. Caroline," I said, drawing her attention from the bumpy gravel road to our new inn, "Derek chose to be awful, and you chose to take a stand. You did the right thing, and it had nothing to do with his death. Nothing," I repeated. "Got it?"

She wiped a tear from her cheek and nodded.

"We can't change what's already happened, but we can still set things right." And if we got the job done fast enough, *I* might live to see Christmas.

Chapter Eighteen

We found Mom's bridge club members running the floor and kitchen at the Hearth. Apparently Mom was preparing for the Christmas Tree Ball, so Caroline and I bundled back up and headed across the property to the large barn my folks rented as a reception hall most of the year. In December, it was home to our annual fundraiser.

"What are you wearing to the ball this year?" Caroline asked.

"I don't know," I said. "Mom hasn't told me what the theme is." Last year the ball had featured Victorian-era decor, and I'd worn the most uncomfortable dress known to man, complete with a corset and bustle. The pointy boots weren't much better. I'd found the whole ensemble in a trunk in the attic, and Cookie had worked some seamstress magic to flash it up a bit. This year, I just hoped I could choose something with shoes I could walk in.

Another set of Mom's friends, clearly assigned to keep tree farm visitors from wandering in to where the magic was being made, greeted us at the barn door. Folks had to buy a ticket to the Christmas Tree Ball, and no one was allowed to look behind the curtain until everything was ready, which wouldn't be for another few days.

Caroline and I exchanged hugs with the happy women that we'd known all our lives and slipped into the enormous barn to see what had been done so far. I did an immediate double take. Unlike the usual, fancier balls, where Mom turned the entire space into a real-life Norman Rockwell painting or dressed everything in hoity shades of silver and mauve, this year's barn was fast becoming an explosion of color. It was like Christmas in Candy Land, complete with a winding multicolored path around the perimeter and peppy, animated decor. Life-sized gingerbread people and their homes polka-dotted faux mountains and landscape. Mounds of fiberfill stuffed with white twinkle lights gave the impression of snow on everything. Candy cane posts held swinging signs, directing people to Christmas Concessions, Merry Melody Mountain, or the Angelic Tree Auction.

The sound of a small motor drew my attention to Mom, who was being lowered from the rafters in a bucket like the ones power company employees used to repair outdoor lines. Above her, large silver and white snowflakes hung from nearly invisible strands of wire, and more faux snow with white lights stretched across every exposed beam. Dad stood at the base, keeping an eye on her in case of emergency. "Do you like it?" Mom called, maneuvering the bucket in our direction.

"I love this," I said, hurrying to hug her when she stepped out. "Quite a departure from your usual, isn't it?"

"It is." She smiled. "Your jewelry inspired me to replace classic with whimsical this year. I think we all need a little whimsy in our lives sometimes, don't you?"

"I do."

"All these years," she said, "I've tried to impress our guests with an upscale gala, but maybe what we really need is a break so we can let loose. Folks can't get enough of your jewelry, and I realized it's because your pieces are so much fun. A whole month of choosing the perfect gifts and hosting guests while worrying about the budget is a drag, and we try so hard to make things special for everyone else that it stops being fun for us. Your jewelry gives us grown-ups a chance to be silly. I want to do that too."

Dad smiled. "Best part is the changes are saving us a fortune, and since the proceeds go to charity, the food bank and shelters are going to get a whole lot more from us this year. We don't even have to pay out the nose for a string quartet or harpist this year. I got my buddies from the lodge to bring their polka band. *No* charge." Dad hooked his thumbs in his suspenders and arched his back with pride.

"Wow." I shot Caroline a broad smile. "Christmas polka? That sounds amazing."

"It really is," Mom said. "Tickets to the ball sold out weeks ago, and we've been given more trees and raffle donations to auction than ever."

The pure delight in her eyes made my heart soar.

Caroline clapped her hands. "I want to help! Maybe I can give away my cupcakes?"

"Hey there, Caroline. Holly." Scooter arrived in a tangle of tinsel garland and multicolored lights. His smile was broad and genuine.

What he was doing here? Had my parents let him in? Did

they know him somehow? I checked their faces for answers but found none.

"I can help with deliveries," Scooter said. "I've even got a great Santa costume I can wear."

My heart froze over at that.

Caroline looked less than enthused but smiled politely. "That's a very kind offer. Anything to make someone's Christmas brighter, right?"

He beamed.

I sized him up. Could Scooter be my Santa stalker? The thought had crossed my mind before but had fallen aside with everything else that had happened. Not to mention, I hadn't seen Scooter since I'd last seen Caroline. "How did you get roped into all this?" I asked Scooter, lifting my arms to indicate the work around us.

"I came to buy my Christmas tree and ran into your dad," he said. "We started talking, and it turns out that he was in the Coast Guard with my uncle. Isn't that crazy?"

"Unbelievable," I said.

Scooter's cheerful expression wavered a bit. "Well, I'd better get this garland to Cookie before she comes looking for me. It was nice seeing you." He nodded and stepped away.

"I'll come with you," I said, waving goodbye to my folks. "Keep up the magic while I'm gone."

Dad playfully swatted Mom's backside, and she laughed.

"Not what I meant," I called, matching my pace with Scooter's and Caroline's.

The auction trees were arranged together in a section marked "The Enchanted Forest." Spruces, firs, and pines lined both sides of a wide walkway, carefully separated by red velvet ropes. Dad had cut and donated the trees for auction, and local companies sponsored and decorated them. Then Mom would auction the completed packages to the highest bidder at the ball. Normally, I'd go crazy trying to create the tree that everyone wanted most, but this year I was consumed with other things.

Next year, however, I'd have to make a comeback.

Scooter stopped at Cookie's tree, and she went for the garland like she was thirsty for it. "Thank you," she crooned, bundling the mess into her arms and starting around the tree in circles. Caroline followed, hooking and draping the colorful strand in calculated flips and swoops.

I watched Scooter watching Caroline. "Did my dad tell you about what happened during the sleigh ride last night?" I asked him.

"No." He pulled his gaze from Caroline and gave me a regretful look. "I heard a couple of EMTs talking about it at the pie shop this morning, though. I didn't want to bring it up in case you weren't ready to talk about it. How are you feeling?"

"I probably won't be the first one in line for another sleigh ride this year," I admitted. "Did you hear that the person who scared the horse was dressed as Santa?"

Scooter clucked his tongue. "That's awful. The sheriff arrested him, I hope."

"No. He got away." I tried to gauge his response but couldn't. We looked into each other's eyes for a long beat.

"Are you sure you're feeling okay?" Scooter asked. "You don't look so good."

I broke the stare. "I'm a little sore from a terrible workout, but I blame Greg Pressey for that," I said. I looked down at myself, suddenly remembering how badly I needed a long hot shower and change of clothes.

Scooter's face puckered. "You worked out at the Ironman Training Center?"

"It wasn't my intention. I'd just wanted to ask him a few questions," I said. "But yeah." Heat rolled up my neck and fanned over cheeks. I bit my tongue. If Scooter was the killer, I definitely shouldn't be telling him that I hadn't stopped snooping.

"What kind of questions?" Scooter asked.

I begged my brain to be quick and lie reasonably, then silently requested my face to cooperate. "Derek ordered a Christmas tree for the gym earlier this month," I said. "I needed to know when and where he wanted it delivered and set up."

Caroline caught my eye as she wound around the tree again, after Cookie. She knew I was lying, but she didn't say a word.

Scooter crossed his arms. "And instead of answering those questions, Greg made you work out?"

"Yes." I nodded in support of the fib. "And I had to buy workout gear from their shop to do it in," I said. "It was ridiculous."

"Unbelievable," he agreed.

I bit the insides of my cheeks.

Caroline moved back to my side, having finished the garland. "Do you know Greg Pressey?" she asked Scooter.

Scooter shook his head. "No."

"But you knew he owned the gym," she said.

"I came across his name when I looked Derek up online."

"When did you do that?" she asked.

Scooter lifted his chin by a fraction, cheeks darkening

beneath his simple round glasses. "After I saw you two arguing at the dinner. He wouldn't stop touching you, and you kept pushing him away. Then you yelled at him, and he took off. I followed him outside to tell him to keep his hands to himself, but he was already driving away when I got to the lot. I went back in to offer you a ride home, but by the time I made it to your table, you were gone. I was worried and frustrated, so I went home and looked him up. I wanted to know who he was and why he thought he could treat someone like that. Greg's gym was mentioned in one of the articles about Derek." He shrugged. "It was probably rude to go digging online, but I like to have all the information possible on topics that interest me."

I couldn't help wondering if Scooter really went back inside after following Derek into the parking lot.

"What do you think?" Cookie asked, her chipper voice drawing my attention away from the flash of goosebumps racing over my skin.

"I'm calling this year's creation Tree-odore." The pine behind her was covered in tiny golden picture frames with a little photo of Theodore in each one.

"Nice," I said. "He looks great."

She beamed. "Doesn't he? Ray is a genius, and this tree is going to be a great preview for our calendar."

My phone buzzed with a text from Christopher, thanking me for returning the binders and for making all the decisions he'd requested for the inn. Mom must've taken the binders to him after I'd left them with her at the Hearth. Now it was time to choose spindles and railings.

"Everything okay?" Cookie asked.

"I have to go look at railings for the steps and balconies at the inn."

Cookie tugged a knit cap over the crown of silver hair on her head. "I'll go with you. I've been dying to get a look inside that place. Everyone asks about it, and I never have any answers. Will there be fireplaces in the guest rooms?"

"Every single one," I said. "If you like what you see, thank Caroline. She helped me make all the detail decisions."

Caroline flipped her scarf over one shoulder and bumped her hip into mine. "It was the least I could do. Thanks for letting me freeload while I waited for my arrest."

I laughed. "Anytime."

Scooter stepped back as we walked past him. "Mind if I come along?"

"Of course," I said, though it was a bit of a Freudian slip. I really did mind. I wasn't sure what I thought of him yet, and spending less time with him seemed like a solid idea, but he took the words as approval and fell in step.

Christopher was outside the inn when we arrived, pounding a large wooden "Opening Soon" sign into the frozen lawn. Reindeer Games' website and contact information was written across the bottom. I had to admit, the home looked utterly enchanting from the outside, and Mom had great plans to make every guest feel like royalty. Inn guests would be entertained, fed, and catered to in the extreme. Plus, they would have access to special before and after-hours tours, games, and events on the Reindeer Games property. "Merry Christmas!" Christopher called as we made our way up the walk.

"Merry Christmas," I answered. "I got your text and didn't

want to make you wait. Hope you don't mind that I brought a few friends along."

"The more, the merrier." He smiled at each of us. "It's nice to see you again, Delores," he said with a wink.

A blush rose on Cookie's cheeks in return.

Christopher nodded at Caroline, "Miss West. Merry Christmas."

He shook Scooter's hand. "How are you, Scott?"

"Good, sir, thank you." Scooter furrowed his brow. "I'm sorry. Have we met?"

"No, no," Christopher said, "not officially, but I try to know everyone I can. Makes small town living a little more special."

"You live in Mistletoe?" I asked. That would explain how he seemed to get here so early each morning and stay so late these last few nights.

"Nooo," he dragged the word out in a chuckle, then ushered us inside with a rumbling laugh.

Caroline raised her eyebrows and mouthed "Santa Claus" as she passed me.

I rolled my eyes and took up the caboose position until our little gang was huddled in the foyer.

Stacks of woodwork were set around the perimeters of each room. Rolls of uninstalled carpet and padding covered the floor. Holes in the walls and ceiling were lined in something metal, presumably for the installation of lights, chandeliers, and sconces. Everywhere I looked, things were incomplete, and I couldn't help wondering if we were going to run into another situation like Mom had at the Hearth with her half-finished kitchen, especially if Christopher was really leaving for another job on Christmas Day.

Christopher opened the coat closet in the front hall and carried out a pile of spindles. Some were wooden, others iron. Straight. Curvy. Twisted. Enough choices to make my head spin. "This is a two-step process," he said. "First you choose your favorite spindles for each location, then you select the handrail you want to go with them. We'll need both for the main staircase and each balcony and veranda upstairs." He displayed the spindles in a row, leaning them gently against an unhung sheet of drywall. "And we can't forget the widow's walk," he added. "I recommend wrought iron for that, but it's your choice."

"Sounds good," I said, thankful Caroline was here to help with the rest of the night's choices.

She squatted before the samples, running her fingertips over the wood and metal spindles. "These are nice." She tapped a crimson nail against a deeply detailed rod.

"Bring it with you," Christopher suggested. "I've got the handrails laid out upstairs. You can see what they'll look like together. Matter of fact, let's bring them all. I probably should have done that already."

Scooter piled the spindles in his arm like firewood. "No problem."

We took a curving staircase to the second floor, sans handrails.

"Do you still think you can get all this finished in time for Christmas?" I asked. "It seems like a lot of work to be completed in one week."

"My crew and I keep a tight schedule," Christopher said, "and we're giving this project all we've got as a gift to your father. He's a man who has dedicated himself to maintaining and spreading the spirit of Christmas all his life, and I'd love to give a little of that back."

"Me too," I said, liking Christopher even more for saying such a nice thing about my dad. "Thank you."

"We can take a look at the balconies and veranda first," Christopher said. "Then we'll head up and look at the widow's walk."

"No," I waved a hand. "That's okay. I don't need to see it. You're right about the iron. I'll just choose the spindles and we'll be all set." Helpful as I wanted to be, I couldn't bring myself to walk on a roof that didn't have guardrails.

Six lengths of railing lay on the plywood subfloor of the unfinished master bedroom, and Scooter set the sample spindles alongside them. Christopher opened a set of French doors and walked onto a ledge overlooking the patio twelve feet below. "It might help you to walk out here and take a look in," he said, waving me to him. "Try to imagine how the balcony railing will look from here, then from the inside with the patio railing in view below."

Cookie went to stand with him, and my muscles went rigid. "Be careful," I told her. "Don't go near the edge."

She frowned at me. "Why would I go near the edge? I'm just taking in the view. I can see all the way to town from up here. I'll bet I could see the tree on the square if it was lit right now."

Caroline went next to join them, then Scooter.

I inched closer, concentrating on breathing and not passing

out. "Okay. Sounds good. Come back inside," I urged. *Before you slide over the unguarded edge. Before the whole patio breaks off in a freak accident and takes you with it. Before a sudden wind blows you to your deaths.* "It's cold." I hugged myself. "I'm freezing, and look! I like this one." I pointed to the floor. I pick this one. Now, come back inside."

Christopher's bushy gray brows jumped upward as he led the group to me. "You're pointing at my level and measuring tape."

I looked down. "Oh." I'd missed the sample handrails by a foot. "I meant this one." I pointed to a bulbous number stained in four different shades, light to dark. "I love the dark cherry stain." What I didn't love was heights. I headed back downstairs and hurried away from the staircase while the rest of my party locked up the French doors and took their time getting back down.

Caroline helped me mark my spindle and handrail choices on a notepad for Christopher before we said goodbye. I handed the list to Christopher with a sudden question on my lips. All his talk of my father's dedication to Christmas had reminded me of how much my mother did for everyone as well. "The contractor my mom hired to remodel her kitchen at the Hearth has made a big mess of everything," I said. "He bypassed his estimated completion date by a month, then took the next two weeks off for Christmas. She finally fired him, but it's been a lot for her to deal with. Is there any chance that you might be able to help her or maybe know someone who can?"

Christopher stroked his gray beard. "Let me see what I can do."

"Okay," I said. "Thank you."

We waved our goodbyes and headed back through the snow toward the barn, where a festive polka version of "Jingle Bells" was going strong.

Cookie looked over her shoulder every few seconds. "I sure do like that Christopher," she said. "He's a good guy, and not too hard on the eyes either. You know I love a nice beard.

Caroline laughed until her eyes watered and she began to cough.

I giggled along with her until Scooter pulled a red and white swirled mint from his pocket and passed it her way.

Chapter Nineteen

I woke late at my parents' house the next morning, rested but stiff from my second run-in with Greg Pressey and still mulling over how I could approach my investigation from a new angle. More specifically how I could track the knife's role in the crime. Who could have gotten possession of it and how?

I dressed in my softest jeans, favorite boots, and a cozy tunic sweater, then went in search of breakfast.

Mom was already gone, but she'd left a ham and cheese casserole warming in the oven and a note to have a wonderful day. She would be at the Hearth and didn't need me until lunch. I filled my tummy with casserole and coffee, then grabbed the keys to my truck. Dad had taken me to pick it up after dinner last night. I'd driven it home on four healthy tires, but with some bitterness over whoever had caused me to repair it. I also wasn't happy with whoever set the price of truck tires at two hundred dollars apiece, but that beef had to get in line.

I rolled into a very crowded downtown Mistletoe thirty minutes later. With just six days until Christmas, the streets were overflowing with tourists and locals grabbing last-minute deals for their loved ones. The number of street vendors and charity collectors seemed to have doubled overnight, and every parking space in sight was taken.

I headed away from the square and parked near the dumpster behind Caroline's Cupcakes, then made a circle around her shop on foot, checking the door and window locks. Either someone had nicked Caroline's knife from under her nose during regular business hours, or the killer had slid inside undetected and taken it while no one was looking. *If only her fancy smart refrigerator doubled as a security camera.*

All the windows I could reach were secure, but the one in her kitchen was too high for me to test from the ground. I considered leaving, but it was the last one in need of checking. I looked around the alley for something I could work with to make me a little taller, then stacked an overturned bucket on an empty wooden pallet I found leaning against the shop next door and climbed on top of the combination to rattle the window frame.

A splinter of wood rammed itself under my skin, and I said an unladylike thing. I shoved my thumb into my mouth to ease the sting.

Beside me, a pair of women carrying cleaning supplies stood motionless on the back steps to the shop next door. I had no idea how long they'd been watching me or how much they'd heard, but one had a cell phone in her free hand.

"Oh no. No. No." I smiled. "I'm not a burglar. I'm a friend. Just checking to be sure the place is secure."

The woman with the phone raised it and snapped a photo of me on the bucket.

"Please don't send that to the sheriff," I said, lifting my palms in surrender. "I promise you, I'm just here to check on things for Caroline. We're friends." I stepped down slowly.

The lady closest to the steps walked away. She climbed inside a parked minivan and shut the door.

The van had the same logo as the one that had been in Derek's driveway: Merry Maids.

"Hey," I called to the woman still staring from the steps. "Did you know Derek Waggoner?"

My phone buzzed, and Caroline's face appeared on the screen. "That's Caroline now," I told the stranger. "She'll clear this up for you."

The second woman walked away with her head high.

I answered the call, then covered the speaker with one palm to say goodbye to the maid. "Merry Christmas," I called. "I'm not a criminal."

"Are you breaking into my shop?" Caroline's voice echoed in my ear.

"No. Of course not."

"Are you sure, because it kind of looks like it."

My phone beeped with an incoming text. "Hang on," I told her, pulling the phone from my ear to check the message. A photo of me centered the screen. I had both hands on the window above my head in the shot, and it looked admittedly sketchy. "That's misleading," I told her. "It's not like that at all."

"What are you doing?" she asked. "I want to come and help, but my mom has me hostage today. We're preparing statements for the press conference Dad's giving tomorrow morning about my arrest and release."

"Good times," I said. "I'm not doing anything grand, anyway.

I'm just checking to see if someone could've slipped in and out of your shop to steal the knife."

"But why would anyone go to my business to get something to kill Derek? Unless they wanted to frame me. Oh my goodness," she squeaked. "Does someone want to frame me? Why would someone do that?" Her voice climbed the octaves with each word.

"I don't know," I said. "I'm just trying to look at what I know from a different angle."

Caroline yelled at someone in the background, then sighed. "I have to go."

"Okay. And no worries. Your shop is locked up tight."

We disconnected, and I took a seat on her rear steps to think.

"Holly?" Pierce Lakemore approached slowly from the direction of my truck. His fancy black sedan now sat parked at its side. "I thought you might be the one driving that truck," he said. "Do you have a minute?"

"Sure." Though I couldn't imagine what Ray's mom's new boyfriend would want from me. We'd only met once, and the experience had been nice but underwhelming. "What's up?"

"You and Ray seemed close the other night."

"Yeah." I wasn't sure I liked where this was going. "We aren't dating," I clarified, in an attempt to redirect whatever he was thinking. "We're good friends. Nothing more."

"I know." He looked around, then moved swiftly closer.

I leaned away. "What are you doing?"

"I need a favor," he whispered, his voice low and urgent. "Can we make a trade?"

"What kind of trade?" I asked, inching back on my step.

Pierce hung his head and lowered onto the step at my side. "I've fallen head over heels in love with Fay, and I can't stop thinking about her. I want to marry her."

"Congratulations?"

"Not yet," he said. "Everything's a no-go with her unless she has her son's approval, and he doesn't approve of me."

"Oh." I looked away, suddenly sorry for Pierce and Mrs. Griggs. It was nice that she cared so much about what Ray thought, but ultimately, the person she loved was her decision, and Ray should want her to be happy, no matter what.

Pierce gave me a desperate look. "How can I get Ray to like me?"

"I'm not sure I can help," I said. "This is really between Ray and his mom."

"Please?" he begged. "She makes me laugh, and when I'm with her I feel like I'm in college instead of looking at retirement. I'm a better man with her than I've ever been without her, and I don't want to know what will become of me if I can't love her for the rest of my life. You've got to help me."

I tried not to wonder if I would ever be loved that much, and sighed. "That's the sweetest thing I've ever heard anyone say about another person."

"It's all true."

I lifted my palms, then dropped them on my lap. "I'll talk to Ray," I said.

"Thank you." Pierce handed me a business card with his contact information. "If you think of anything I can do, just let me know, and I'll do it."

I tucked the card into my coat pocket. "Okay."

"There's something else," he said. "I didn't want to bring it up the other night because we'd just met, and butting into your investigation seemed rude."

My brows rose. "Hit me."

Pierce looked both ways down the empty alley. "Brian Ford really was out of town on the night of Derek Waggoner's death. A friend from law school is handling a case that involves Brian, and he is willing to testify that Brian was in Phoenix giving testimony in opposition to allegations of stolen handbag designs all weekend."

"He couldn't have killed Derek," I said, feeling the flutter of excitement in my chest. I could mark a suspect off my list.

Pierce nodded, then was gone.

I walked to the church, whose parking lot bordered the alley, and checked for security cameras. Nothing.

I went back to the alley behind Caroline's shop and walked in each direction for a full block, looking for any surveillance camera that might've caught an intruder coming or going while she and Derek had been at dinner. I still couldn't imagine who would go out of their way to get Caroline's knife to kill Derek. She didn't have enemies. Caroline hated the thought of offending anyone. Ever.

Samantha Moss opened the back door at Wine Around, and I slid behind the nearest dumpster, waiting for her to leave. She hauled a bag of trash in each hand, and I wasn't convinced she wouldn't throw them at me if she saw me. She glanced my way but kept her course. Samantha wore head-to-toe black again. She hated Caroline for being perfect, and she loved Derek obsessively. Add that to her quick temper, and I got a little nervous. Maybe I'd been wrong to discount her.

I tried imagining her in a fake beard and Santa suit.

She went back inside, and I jumped away from the icky dumpster.

Evan's cruiser pulled into the alley and rolled to a stop beside me. "What are you doing, White?"

I wiggled my fingers in greeting. "Hello. How are you?"

He leaned across the seats and popped the passenger door open. "Get in. It's cold."

I obeyed, avoiding eye contact. "Funny meeting you here," I said. "What brings you out this way, Sheriff?"

He drove on. "The usual," he said. "Got a call about a tall, skinny, brown-haired woman peeping into shop windows. Thought I should check it out."

"I haven't seen anyone fitting that description," I said.

"No? What are you doing behind a dumpster?"

"I was making sure Caroline's shop was locked up tight."

Evan kept his keen eyes on me. "Her shop isn't on this block."

I considered lying but assumed the woman who'd tattled on me to Caroline had also sent that photo to the authorities. "I was walking the alley, checking for surveillance cameras that might've caught someone breaking into Caroline's shop while she and Derek were at dinner."

"Holly," Evan groaned. "What is it that you think I do all day? Because you don't seem to think I do any investigating."

"All I know is that my threats are coming closer together, and they're becoming actions. I want to find the killer before I end up like Derek."

"You've got to stop this."

"I marked Brian Ford off my list today," I said. "He was in Phoenix the night of the murder."

"I know."

"Did you know Scooter has a Santa costume? And he keeps those red and white peppermints in his pocket?"

Evan ground his teeth. "You need to stop following these people before you get charged with stalking or hurt—or worse."

"I'm not following Scooter. He keeps showing up where Caroline is. He admitted to being at the benefit dinner when Caroline yelled at Derek, and he followed Derek outside when he walked off. He says he came back in to offer Caroline a ride home, but since she was already gone, I can't say if he really went back inside at all."

Evan accelerated, and the cruiser rolled forward, creeping back down the alley.

"Where are we going?" I asked, hoping the answer wasn't jail for attempted burglary or interfering with an ongoing investigation.

"Back to your truck. I saw it behind the cupcake shop. How's the new tire?"

"Expensive," I said.

My phone applauded, and I frowned at the new order. "How's Libby?"

Evan puffed out his cheeks. "She's a little too interested in Ray Griggs for my taste, but at least he has a clean record, and a respectable job and reputation."

"Ray's a good guy," I said. "And Libby seems like the kind of girl who can handle herself. She's sassy."

"She's stupid," he retorted. "Chasing after a Boston drug dealer to get justice for her friend. That's what the police are for. And despite the fact he's actively hunting her now, she still claims it was worth the risk—that Heather deserved to be vindicated and that the police weren't moving fast enough. It's borderline insanity." He slid narrowed eyes my way. "It's like all the women in my life have a death wish."

"I don't have a death wish," I said. "I'm trying to figure out the killer before . . ." I drew a hand across my throat, closed my eyes, and stuck out my tongue.

"Stop that. "Evan swatted my hand away from my throat. "Open your eyes—you're creeping me out."

I smiled. "She'll be safe here. You're invisible online, so even if the bad guy discovers she has a brother, it will be pretty tough to figure out where you went when you left Boston. Maybe he'll even see you work in law enforcement and just let it go."

"I doubt that."

"Do you think Mistletoe is growing on her? Will she stay for a while?"

"She'll stay long enough for Boston PD to catch the man who's after her," he said. "It's not her first choice, but it's her only one."

"What are you going to do?" I asked. "Hold her captive if she refuses to stay?"

"Yes." His voice was low and even. "Whatever it takes. I promised our dad I'd protect and look out for her. Always. That's what I intend to do."

"Okay," I said. "Maybe we can spend more time together. Help her fall in love with our little town."

Evan shifted into "Park" behind my truck and fixed me with a broad grin. "How about this afternoon?"

"I'm working at the Hearth from lunch until dinner."

"See you then."

The happiness in Evan's eyes bordered on mischief, and it occurred to me that I might've just agreed to babysit.

Chapter Twenty

B usiness at the Hearth was out of control all afternoon. I spun through the tables like a lunatic delivering Santa's cinnamon tea, every kind of cocoa under the sun, and a rainbow of cookies in every shape and size. I couldn't help wondering if Evan had really meant he'd see me this afternoon. So far, there hasn't been any sign of him.

The bell on the counter rang, and I grabbed my next piping hot order for a table of couples in coordinated tops. One man's sweater featured Santa in a sleigh, and everyone else at the table had a reindeer. All together, they were a few reindeer short, but they didn't seem to mind.

"I have three holiday ciders, two peppermint twist hot chocolates, and a cinnamon tea, with one order of saint snickerdoodles and a tray of reindeer gingerbread cookies," I said, placing the treats on the table. I tucked the empty tray beneath one arm and smiled. "If you'd like anything else, just give me a jingle." I wiggled my wrist in the air, then turned to walk away.

"Oh!" The lady on my right caught my wrist in her hands. "How lovely," she said, looking appreciatively at my new bracelet.

"Do you sell these here?" She twisted in her seat for a look at the counter and cash register.

"No, this is mine. I made it," I explained. I'd put the bracelet together on a whim, inspired by a pack of leftover mini-jingle bells in my craft box. I couldn't remember the project I'd originally intended the bells for, but they looked adorable on a wide red leather strap with alternating glass gumdrops.

"Look Priscilla," the woman pushed my arm across the table in her friend's direction.

Everyone at the table leaned in for a gander.

Priscilla pulled glasses from her purse and slid them up the short length of her nose, then took hold of my arm, turning my body to face her. "Fun! I want one too. Where can we get them?"

"I made this," I repeated. "I make holiday jewelry, but I don't have another like this one. This is more of a prototype."

"We love it," the first woman said. "We'll take four." She looked at her husband, who'd been silently watching our exchange, and he produced a wallet.

She began counting out his cash. "We need one for Priscilla and for me, then another one for each of our daughters." She looked to the third woman seated opposite her husband. "Do you want one?"

The woman shook her head. "She just told you she doesn't have any more."

"What?" The woman with the money looked as if this was brand-new information. "But you can make them," she told me. "We can order them."

I pulled my wrist free and hid it behind my back. "I can, and I would be happy to, but I don't know how soon I can get to it, and I don't want to take your money." I dug a business card from my back pocket and offered it to her. "I have an online store, but I can't guarantee anything in time for Christmas. I'm under an avalanche of orders already."

"Shame," Priscilla said, pulling my attention back in her direction. She caught her friend's eye across the table. "Reminds me of the strap of sleigh bells your mama hung on the door every year for the holidays. She was such an amazing woman."

The woman holding her husband's wallet seemed to sag at those words. Her eyes misted. "Yes, she was. I think I miss her more every year. Is that even possible?"

Mom hit the order bell, and my heart gave a tug. I never wanted to think of life without my mom and dad in it.

I unfastened the bracelet and handed it to the woman with the wallet, now dabbing tears from her eyes. "Merry Christmas."

Her mouth popped open, whether to thank me or protest, I wasn't sure.

I hustled to the counter for my next delicious delivery.

Mom winked when I got there and patted my hand before I left. She'd apparently caught me giving away the bracelet, and she approved.

Pride drew a smile over my face as I hurried to my next stop with a load of whoopie pies and wedding cookies.

When I turned to check for signs of guests with needs, I found Evan and Libby at a two-seater by the window.

"Hey!" I rushed to their sides. "What can I get you guys?"

Evan's jaw was tight, and Libby's eyes were cold. "A babysitter," she said.

"A what?"

"I have a lead I need to chase," Evan said, "and I can't trust her on her own."

"What kind of lead?" I asked.

Mom hit the bell again, and Libby stood. "I'll get it."

Libby was gone before I could argue, winding through the crowded room to the front on heeled, knee-high leather boots. A cropped leather jacket began where her dark skinny jeans stopped and red curls draped over her shoulders. She spoke briefly to my mother, who looked mildly alarmed, then sought me visually in the crowd.

I gave Mom a thumbs-up, and Libby strode away with the tray.

Evan was on his feet then, pushing his chair seat back under the table and stuffing his hat onto his head. "I'll be back for her later. She'll be safe and happy working here until then. She's been waiting tables since seventh grade, when our aunt opened an Irish pub four blocks from our school."

"Where are you going?" I asked. "Is your lead in connection to Derek's death? Do you know something?"

Evan looked beyond me to a point over my shoulder. "Be good," he said, his voice deep and firm. Clearly issuing an order, not a request.

"Get outta here already," Libby's thickly accented voice came back immediately.

Evan left without answering my questions.

I went to pick up the next order.

Libby smiled at a pair of elderly men in Mr. Rogers sweaters. She doled out steaming mugs topped with marshmallows, then met me at the counter. "This place is madness," she said. "Do you normally do this on your own?"

"Yep."

"How?"

"People are patient. They come for the experience as much as the sweets, so they're never in a huge hurry."

Libby's face was pure disbelief. "Where I come from, everyone's always in a hurry. I eat meals on the go or standing over the kitchen sink most days, always on my way to work or class or just out. People get cranky if they aren't in motion."

"Welcome to Mistletoe," I said.

Libby and I worked in a companionable rhythm for hours that seemed like minutes instead of the other way around. When the room emptied just before dinner, I went to find her for a high five.

She accepted with a grin. "Where'd everybody go? It's five o'clock."

"Most folks make dinner reservations in town," I said, "which works out well because this is when we set up for the evening Reindeer Game."

Mom appeared with an enormous bakery box of mini gingerbread houses. "Tonight we play Bling That Gingerbread."

Libby looked from Mom to me. "What?"

"Help me set the tables," Mom said, passing little houses to each of us. "I'll explain as we go."

Libby and I set up the houses, one at each seat.

Mom followed with plates of gumdrops, various little candies, licorice chunks, and icing. "Contestants blindfold themselves, then decorate these houses," she told Libby. "When the game ends, we'll set the finished houses across the front counter for judging, and the winner gets free cookies and cocoa. Plus, bragging rights until next year."

Libby laughed.

"You're quite a waitress," Mom said, flattening the emptied box. "This clearly wasn't your first spin around a dining room, and we appreciate your help today."

"Thanks," Libby said. "It was fun. Everyone was happy, and no one yelled when I got behind. That was nice."

Mom gave me a strange look. "How long are you staying in town, Libby?"

"I don't know. I'm ready to go home, but E wants me here. He thinks Boston's not a safe place for me at the moment, but I can't hide out in Mistletoe forever. I'd need a car here, and the rest of my things from back home, plus a job. I definitely can't live with my brother any longer than is absolutely necessary."

"But you might stay?" Mom asked.

"Maybe. For a while."

Mom's smile brightened. "I might be able to help you with one of your problems. I'll need an experienced waitress to replace Holly when she becomes the innkeeper, and we can always use an extra pair of hands until then."

A light blush spread over Libby's freckled cheeks. "That's very nice of you to offer, Mrs. White. If I stay, I'd like that very much."

"Then it's settled. We'll wait to hear what you decide before we go looking for a new waitress."

Libby's normally overconfident expression turned shy and youthful. "Thanks."

The after-dinner crowd trickled in slowly, filling the tables one by one, all ready to Bling That Gingerbread. Libby and I shared a table near the door so we could pop up and explain the game to new arrivals. Despite the fact that Libby knew the rules, she was already working on her house. She'd borrowed powdered sugar and food coloring from the kitchen, then blended it into a thin icing with a little water, and was applying it like paint to the roof.

"That's beautiful," I told her as the careful sweeps of blue and white took on a familiar pattern. "I was an art major for a while. I love to draw, but I could never paint. Evan told me you're an artist. A lot of people say that, but you're really good."

Libby glanced up at me, looking half-startled, as if she'd forgotten I was there. "What's the deal with you and my brother?"

I opened my mouth, but nothing came out, so I shut it.

She waited.

"It's complicated," I said finally, unable to articulate more.

"That's Evan," she said. "You know, he felt awful about arresting your friend. He did what he had to do based on the evidence, but he came home every night saying that none of it made sense because he knew she didn't do it."

"Really?" My heart warmed. "He said that?"

"Yeah, and he hated that you were mad at him. That's how I knew there was something going on between you two. Normally he's all about the job. He says facts don't lie, but this time he refused to believe the facts that added up to the obvious."

"I'm really glad to hear that," I said, "because he's right. The facts we have don't tell the whole story, and that's what I'm still trying to figure out."

"Evan too," she said. "This place has been good for him. He was all rough sides and hard edges in Boston, but your town must put softener in the water because Big Brother is losing a little of that hard exterior. He asks me how I feel sometimes or what I'm thinking. He never did that before." Her cheeks flushed pink again. "I like it. It reminds me that he knows I'm a real human and not just some task Dad charged him with before he died."

"I'm sure he doesn't think that," I said. "You mean the world to him. Maybe he just never knew how to say it before."

She shrugged, a small smile on her lips. "Maybe." Libby ignored the blindfold rule of Bling That Gingerbread and also continued painting her house until several minutes after the buzzer sounded telling everyone to stop. What she'd created was remarkable. A personal rendition of Van Gogh's *Starry Night* swirled over her home's roof and sides. Tiny black and purple silhouettes of a town lined the bottom of each wall.

"That's amazing," I said, marveling over what she'd accomplished with sugar, food coloring, and water.

Libby slid her work of art across the table to me. "Keep it."

"Really? Thank you!" I lifted the house for a closer inspection, partially hiding my face behind the masterpiece. "Did you happen to hear what kind of lead Evan was chasing? He took off in a hurry this afternoon."

"No, but I had a look through the files he brought home after he fell asleep at his desk last night."

My pulse quickened at the mention of Evan's files. "What did you see?"

"A lot of useless details, but after reading the statements, my money is on Nadia Ford as the killer. If some sleaze manipulated me into having an affair just to one-up my husband and then told him about it, I'd want to knock him into next week. No question."

I returned her gingerbread house to the table, a new and powerful sense of camaraderie and appreciation overcoming me. "You were looking into my investigation?"

"You mean my brother's investigation?"

I tipped my head over each shoulder.

She laughed. "Yeah. I have a curious mind. Evan hates it, but he took that guy's statement about the affair."

"Brian Ford's?"

"Yeah. Brian said he beat Derek at cards on a major bet and in front of a bunch of people. Then, while he was riding the high of that public victory, Derek blurted out the thing about Brian's wife. She was there too. Talk about horrifying. Brian said the announcement had everyone jeering at him and Nadia, and Derek came out looking like the winner, even though he'd lost big on the poker game."

I tried hard not to think any more ugly things about the deceased than I already had. "Did anything else stand out to you in those files?"

"Not really. That's why I've been going out to get a look at everyone. Sometimes it helps if I see a person."

"Going out?" I asked.

"Sure. In Boston it would be nearly impossible, but here I

just stop anyone working at a business. I know they're local, so I ask where I can find someone, and the worker always knows."

"And you just go look at them?"

"Sometimes I eavesdrop a little, then I vanish. They never know I'm there. Hopefully I never accidently ask the person I'm looking for where I can find them." She laughed. "I don't have an explanation ready if that happens."

I smiled. "That's how you've been spending your days?"

"It gets me out of the house, and I've got to do something to pass my time, right?"

Mom wiped down the table beside ours, clearly eavesdropping. "You can help out here anytime you want," she said with a grin.

"I'd need a ride out here," Libby said. "This is a little farther than the town square."

I smiled. "Lucky for you, you've got a friend with a truck." I scanned the thinning crowd and let a new idea take form. "When do you think Evan will be back?"

Libby's smile curled over her lips and reached all the way to her eyes. "Not sure."

I tossed my truck keys into the air and caught them. "You want to get out of here?"

She was on her feet in an instant.

Libby and I were going to be great friends. I could feel it.

Chapter
Twenty-One

I parked the big Reindeer Games truck near the pie shop and ran inside to pick up an order. The cashier recognized me and lifted a finger before disappearing below the counter.

Libby followed me in, but split her attention between me and the hordes of people on the street outside. She seemed genuinely mystified by the mass merriment and overall hoopla. "You realize you live at a place producing desserts all day and night, right? Why are you picking up a pie? Your mom probably has ten waiting to be cut."

"Mom doesn't do pies," I said. "The pie shop does pies."

Libby did a dramatic eye roll.

"I came for something else."

The cashier popped back up with a smile and pushed the festive green certificate across the counter for my inspection.

Libby read over my shoulder. "You're getting that for my brother?"

"Yep," I said, slipping the paper into a fancy golden envelope. I fished my credit card out of my wallet and swiped it through the machine. "He loves this place."

"Our mom used to waitress," Libby said softly. "I barely remember that, but I know she did. She worked in offices most of my life. Filling in as a temp through one of those services."

"Well, Evan has fond memories of the diner, plus this place serves pie for breakfast and keeps hot, delicious coffee flowing eighteen hours a day. What's not to love?" I signed for my purchase, then followed Libby outside. "Let It Snow" was rocking merrily through speakers on rooftops. Street vendors shook sleigh bells as they called out their offerings. Chatter and laughter enhanced the sounds of horses' hooves on the pavement as carriages rolled past. I bee-bopped to the magically blended soundtrack of my childhood.

Libby pressed a palm to her middle. "I'm going to gain fifty pounds living here," she said. "Does it always smell like this? I want to eat everything."

I inhaled the scents of warm buttered popcorn, the spicy tang of hot cider, and the sweet cinnamon of sugar-dusted pecans. The square was a collision of the senses, and my smile widened.

"What do you think I should get Evan?" Libby asked, sidestepping a couple pushing two conked-out kids in a double stroller.

"I don't know. You must know him better than I do."

"Not really," she said. "Evan's eight years older than me. He was driving when I was in second grade, and I was only ten when he left home. To be honest, we never had much of a relationship until Heather went missing. We had nothing in common and no reason to talk outside of holidays, weddings, and funerals. He showed up at college periodically out of some misguided obligation to look after me, but that was it."

"I'd never guess that," I said. "You seem close. Like two

people who grew up together. Like siblings." And it was true. They bickered and challenged one another in all the same ways I'd watched my friends interact with their brothers and sisters all my life. Maybe it was natural for people who shared DNA. Maybe Libby and Evan were making up for lost time. Either way, they didn't seem like the virtual strangers Libby described.

Libby took a strong interest in the street, keeping her gaze low as we talked. "Evan and I have spent more time together this year than we ever have. I've gotten more comfortable around him, but I don't *know* him. For example, if someone had told me he'd leave Boston, I would've called them a liar, and if they'd given me one hundred possible locations where he might move, I never would've guessed this one in a million years."

I tried not to feel the sting of that jab. What was wrong with Mistletoe? Nothing that I could think of. "Evan said he came here because there was no crime, and he'd seen enough awful things to last a lifetime," I told her.

"Boston's gangs and homicide division got too bloody, so he moved to Mistletoe, Maine." She raised her eyes to scan the street with its ambitious holiday decor and busloads of tourists in reindeer antler headbands and elf hats. "Talk about one extreme to another. Your town is like some kind of out of control amusement park without the rides."

"We have near-death sleigh rides."

She puffed out a humorless laugh. "No joke."

I slowed as we passed the square, enchanted by the blinking lights on the giant town tree.

It was hard to believe a ten-foot candy dish with a corpse had stood there last week.

"What happened to the weird memorial?" Libby asked. "I saw that lady roasting marshmallows on a stick over a fire in a trash bin. Talk about creepy."

"That was Samantha Moss," I said. "Apparently Derek Waggoner was her soul mate. She's angry about the loss but wouldn't say anything more."

"I heard she chased you down with a box of Christmas ornaments."

So Evan does *discuss things related to the case; he just doesn't discuss them with me.* "She hates me," I said. "I'm not even sure why. She runs that shop over there. Wine Around."

Libby smiled. "She hates you, but she doesn't know *me*." Libby stepped off the curb and marched across the road in wide purposeful strides.

I raced along after her. "Where are you going? You're jaywalking. There's a crosswalk like ten feet away."

"That's Wine Around on the corner, right?" she asked, stepping onto the curb and out of the street. "I'm going to go take a look."

"Bad idea," I said. "She's bananas, and she likes to throw things. Her shop is filled with bottles of wine. Those could kill us. Plus, she hates my face. I can't go in there."

"So wait outside."

I shook my head. "Can't. I told Evan I'd look after you."

Libby stopped at the door to Wine Around and struck a hands-on-hips pose.

I rubbed a mitten over my mouth. "Fine. I'll go inside and hide behind something."

"Atta girl."

The Wine Around store was beautiful. Classical music lifted softly from a speaker behind the counter. Murals of vineyards from around the world covered the walls. Each aisle and section was labeled by country, region, and wine type. The shelving units, display stands, and tables were painted in rich earthy tones and accented with punches of silver and gold. The whole place was very well organized, professional looking, and sophisticated. One hundred percent opposite of what I knew about Samantha Moss.

Libby pulled a bottle from the first display she came to and made a show of examining it.

Three men immediately offered their assistance.

I ducked behind a bookcase and found a comfortable position where I could watch without looking insane.

Samantha took quick notice of the little crowd and hurried to Libby's rescue. "Hello. Can I answer any questions for you?"

Libby frowned. "I hope so. My ex-boyfriend is seeing someone else, and I'm so mad." She twisted her face into something angry and weird. "I thought I'd take home a bottle of wine and plot revenge."

The gathering men dispersed.

A glimmer in Samantha's eye said she understood boyfriend troubles. "Men are the worst. I know. Believe me. My ex was my soul mate, but he kept leaving me to date other women." She inhaled deeply, then blew the air out for so many beats I thought she'd collapse. "You know what they say. You can't live with them." She gave a soft laugh.

"Can't kill them?" Libby asked.

Samantha cut her laughter short and stared. "What did you say?"

Libby hiked a perfectly manicured brow in silent challenge.

Samantha's stunned face turned defiant. "Who are you? What do you want?"

"I'm a girl with a broken heart," Libby snipped. "What do you know about it? At least your boyfriend keeps coming back. Mine's gone for good."

Samantha's body trembled visibly. She made a strangled sound and clutched her hands into fists at her sides. "You don't know anything about me."

The store went still as other shoppers took notice of the uncomfortable exchange.

The temperature inside seemed to drop as I awaited what would come next.

Samantha twisted at the waist and grabbed something from the display beside her.

I strained for a better vantage, but couldn't see what she had without giving up my hiding spot. I imagined her cracking a full bottle of wine over Libby's head, an ambulance racing to save her life, and Evan's face when I tried to explain why I couldn't keep his little sister safe for one evening. "Wait!" I called, jumping out with my hands up. "Please don't do whatever it is you're about to do."

Samantha's jaw dropped. "You!" She had a stack of cork coasters in her grip and raised one behind her like a baseball pitcher.

A thread of relief wound through me. She couldn't kill us with cork.

Zip! The coaster buzzed past my head like a ninja throwing star and stuck in the drywall behind me.

"Whoa!" I covered my head. Maybe she *could* kill us with cork.

Shoppers scattered.

I ducked, hands still on my head. "Let's go, Libby!"

"You tattled to the sheriff," Samantha yelled. "He forced me to remove Derek's memorial from the square." A coaster hit my shoulder and bounced off, knocking a line of books over like dominoes.

"Ow!" I moved a hand away from my head on instinct and covered the throbbing pain at my shoulder. "Stop! That hurt."

"Tattletale!" she screamed. "Memorial ruiner!"

"You were throwing glass bulbs at my truck," I said. "You could've caused an accident. I had to tell."

Samantha stalked forward, throwing arm back.

Libby caught Samantha mid-step and pulled her arms tight behind her. "Calm down, lady."

Samantha thrashed, but Libby was shockingly strong for someone so small and precariously balanced on spike-heeled boots.

"Look," I said. "I know you and I got off on the wrong foot, but it's Christmas, and you've just lost someone very important to you. Can we please call a truce?"

Samantha struggled a moment longer, then gave up the fight. "Yeah, all right, fine."

Libby relented her grip, but stayed close.

"I'm sorry Sheriff Gray took down your memorial," I said. "But you don't belong out there in the cold at Christmas."

"I belong with Derek," she said.

I considered asking if that was because they were soul mates like she said or because she felt guilty for stabbing him with Caroline's butcher knife, but I couldn't bring myself to say the words. The pain in her eyes was too much, and all the things that Caroline had said to me about her life and Derek's came crashing back.

Samantha shook out her arms where they'd been pinned behind her. Her eyes dripped fresh tears.

I gave her my most sincere look. "If you want someplace to hang out when you aren't working, you could come to Reindeer Games," I suggested. "There's always lots of people and things to do. You won't be alone, and being there could help take your mind off all that you've lost, at least temporarily."

Samantha cocked her head like a puppy trying to interpret a new sound. "Why are you being nice to me?"

"I've always been nice to you," I said.

She seemed to think that over, dragging her suspicious gaze from the puffy ball on top of my knit cap to the chunky white snow boots on my feet.

"Do you remember my friend Caroline West?" I asked. "You threw her cupcakes at me."

Libby coughed into her fist to cover a laugh.

Samantha wet her lips. "Yeah. What about her?"

"She got a look inside Derek's office recently, and he only had one picture in the whole room. It was of you and him skiing. He had it framed and sitting on the corner of his desk, where he could look at it all day if he wanted."

Samantha covered her heart with her hands. "Really?"

"Yeah. Caroline didn't like Derek. They didn't get along, but they went to that dinner together to please their families. She didn't try to take him away from you, and she's not the reason he's gone."

I took a leap of faith and moved closer to her. It felt strange, discussing something so personal across a room. "Caroline believes Derek loved you, but his family might have been what was keeping you apart. She knows all about what it's like to have family control her love life."

Samantha's expression softened. "It's true."

I dug through my purse for a travel pack of tissues and handed it to Samantha.

She tugged a few loose from the rest and wiped her nose and eyes. "I was a waitress at a winery when Derek and I met," she explained. "I was happy. I liked my job. Loved learning about the wines. Then I fell in love with Derek, but his family wouldn't allow him to date a server. They thought I was 'beneath him.'" She formed air quotes on the last two words with her shaky fingers. "We dated in secret for a while, and I saved all my money to open this shop. Derek helped get me started. He was an amazing businessman," she said, her voice thick with appreciation and pride. "Running my own successful business is so much more than I ever thought I was capable of, and it still wasn't enough for his family. I will always be that waitress from a winery."

My heart broke for her, but the story begged a big question. "Please don't get mad and start throwing stuff again," I said, "but I have to ask. Could you have been so sick of the unfair treatment that you lashed out at Derek and did something you couldn't take back?"

"No." She shook her head vehemently. "I would never have hurt him. Not ever."

"Okay," I said. Samantha Moss was intense, just like Cookie had said, but she also seemed sincere. "I believe you."

"Yeah?" A small smile curled her lips.

I nodded. "I'm sorry we came here under false pretenses."

She bobbed her head, eyes bright with unshed tears. "S'okay."

I chewed my lip, hating to miss another opportunity. "Can I sign my mom up for your wine club? As a Christmas gift?"

"Of course." She handed me to flyer. "You can register her online."

"Thanks."

A brave shopper placed a basket of wine on the counter near the register, looking slightly confused and more than a little afraid.

"I have to take care of that," Samantha said, turning reluctantly toward the register. "Thank you for telling me about the picture. I have that same photo on my nightstand. Derek made me a copy of it a long time ago."

Libby lifted a hand waist high in goodbye to Samantha and the handful of gawking shoppers. "Merry Christmas. Sorry about your loss, Miss Moss."

I held the door for her. "Hey, Samantha?" I gave the broken-hearted woman one last look. "The offer to visit us at Reindeer Games still stands. It's always a good time, and I'd be glad to see you if you decide to come."

She nodded, and I let the door close.

Libby's expression was flat when we reached the sidewalk.

"Now *that's* what I'm used to dealing with. You accuse someone of murder; they hit you with stuff."

I laughed and shoved her shoulder toward the crosswalk. "Come on. We'd better get back before your brother finds out we left."

"You think she did it?" Libby asked. "She definitely has a temper. I know she said it wasn't her, but it's not like she's going to confess to murder in front of a room full of witnesses."

"She used to be my main suspect," I said. "Now I think she would've forgiven Derek for anything. I don't think she'd have lashed out at him. She feared losing him too badly."

"So we're back to Nadia Ford," Libby said as we crossed the street to my truck.

"And Scooter, Caroline's schmoopy stalker," I added. His Santa suit and pocket mints had given me nightmares.

"Who?" Libby asked.

I beeped the truck doors unlocked as we drew near. "Get in. I'll tell you on the way."

Chapter Twenty-Two

L ibby called Evan on our way back to the farm. Not only had he not gotten back yet, he was caught up in following a lead and was going to be awhile longer. Libby and I exchanged silent high fives and promised to meet him at the guesthouse whenever he finished.

I made the fire and put on a Christmas movie when we got there. Libby made a pot of tea and got comfy on the couch until it was ready.

I felt marginally guilty for not picking Cindy Lou Who up from my folks' house, but then I remembered she was with my mom, probably being catered to and fawned over like the grandchild Mom didn't have, and Cindy would be crazy to want to leave.

I rocked back on my heels in front of the stoked fire and admired the view. My tree was up. The room was heaving with twinkle lights, and my tiny Christmas village looked great in front of my frosty, snow-lined window. I added Evan's gift certificate to the pile of presents beneath my tree, then unpacked a few tubs of cookies and muffins from the kitchen.

"What do you think Evan's doing?" Libby asked. "He's been gone a long time. What could he be up to?"

"Who knows," I said, making my way back to the living room with snacks. "I've been racking my brain since you told me he'd be late, and I can't think of anything." I eased onto the opposite end of the couch and sighed at the warmth radiating from my little fire.

Libby pulled my grandma's afghan over her legs and propped her socked feet on the coffee table. She watched the movie in bits, her attention more focused on her phone than my television. "Sometimes I think I'd make a good cop," she said out of nowhere. "I love art, but the need to cuff bad guys runs deep in our family blood."

"I've heard," I said. "Your dad was a cop, right?" I remembered Evan telling me how much his dad had wanted him to become a teacher and how hard Evan had tried to be happy doing that, but the crime-fighting gene couldn't be ignored.

"I didn't know Dad as well as Evan did," Libby said. "I was young, and I was a girl. Our personalities didn't mesh, but I admired him. What he did. What Evan does."

"It's dangerous work," I said. "Have you thought of fighting crime another way? Maybe by becoming a lawyer or getting involved in politics? You could help make and shape the laws that protect us."

She shrugged. "Maybe. I like research."

"Me too," I admitted. "I've always been naturally curious. Growing up here made being an only child less boring and lonely. I could observe folks from all over the country anytime I wanted, listen to their conversation, watch their interactions."

"Spy," she corrected. "You're actually really nosy, and you like to spy."

I laughed. "I like answers, and I usually have a lot of questions."

"Evan said you nearly got yourself killed last year." She peeked sideways at me. "Is that true, or is he just trying to scare me into doing what he says?"

I pursed my lips, deciding how to answer. "Last year I got caught up in another murder case like Derek's, and I got hurt, but it was worth it. A murderer went to jail."

Libby nodded, attention back on her phone, thumbs sliding against the screen. "I'm not seeing much about Nadia Ford online. It's like she didn't exist before she married Brian. Now she's in lots of articles and interviews, but never as Nadia Ford. Always as Brian Ford's wife."

I got my phone out too and settled in beside her. I had a few things I wanted to look up, beginning with Derek Waggoner's life as an investor. We'd scoped out his personal profiles on social media, but I hadn't looked at who he was as a businessman. Samantha Moss had brought the point up again tonight when she said he'd invested in Wine Around. Both the businesses I knew Derek had invested in seem to be doing stellar, as far as I could tell.

Several articles later, I'd read nothing but good things about Derek's investments, though he did seem to sell most of them, and some rather quickly. I supposed that was the nature of the business. One person couldn't be everywhere.

I opened another article and read much of the same sentiment. *Everything Derek Waggoner touches turns to gold.*

If that were true, I thought wryly, *every female who'd passed within his reach lately should look like an Oscar statue.* I rubbed my tired eyes and refocused. "Derek kept an office at the Ironman Training Center," I told Libby. "He must've cared about that business, but Greg took offense when I called Derek his partner. It's weird because they were. Everything I've read tonight says Greg founded the place, and Derek grew it into the complex it is now. So why the bitterness from Greg?"

Libby dragged her eyes from whatever she was reading. "I don't know. Did Greg have a wife for Derek to move in on?"

I frowned. "Jeez. I hadn't thought of that." I opened another window and looked up Greg Pressey. No wife, but he was impressive: a fitness expert and former medal-winning body builder. "Maybe he begrudged the way Derek had grown his business into a spa and café when he'd wanted it to be more manly," I hypothesized. He'd made it abundantly clear that his way was the only way to get in shape. Still, it hardly seemed like motive for murder.

Libby shifted in her seat, getting comfortable. "Did Greg seem like a misogynistic pig?"

"He seemed sadistic. Does that count? I think he liked hearing me beg to quit during those awful workouts."

Libby's head jerked in my direction. "Why ask? Why didn't you just quit?"

"I naively believed he'd answer my questions if I did what he wanted first. Turns out, he's a liar."

"Did he say anything we can look up? Something that could become a springboard and point us in the right direction?"

"No. He was tight-lipped and cranky. He said Derek wasn't

perfect, and he had to have made a bad move somewhere. He said I should be looking for those instead of bothering him."

"I'll see if I can find one of his tanked investments," she said. "Could be that we haven't even found the right suspect yet."

Someone knocked on my door, and I jumped.

Libby smiled. "Relax. It's Ray. When I told him I was hanging out here until Evan finished up, he offered to bring a pizza and his *Die Hard* collection."

I checked the window before dragging Ray inside. "You brought pizza and chips. Bless you." I hadn't had proper junk food in ages. Just endless desserts and Mom's home cooking. I set the food on the coffee table and went to fetch plates and napkins from the kitchen. When I came back, Ray had made himself at home on the middle cushion of my couch.

He winked, patting the cushion beside him. "I have a few more photos of Mom and Pierce for you to look at and tell me what you think."

I slapped his shoulder. "You've got to stop doing that," I scolded. "You can't keep following your mom around. It's intrusive and a little nuts. She's fine. She's happy. Leave her alone."

Ray turned on the cushion to face me, hooking an elbow over the back of my couch. "Oh no, you don't," he said.

"What?"

"You're the biggest stalker in town. You don't get to tell me I can't follow my mom while you're out there following anyone you want."

"Hypocrisy," Libby said. Her voice carried around the wall of Ray twisted between us. "Are you the goose or gander in this scenario, Ray?" she asked.

Ray poked a finger against his chest. "I'm the goose."

"Well, goose," I said, remembering something I needed to tell him, "this town might be the place for creepers because your mom's boyfriend found me in the alley behind Caroline's Cupcakes and asked me to put in a good word with you for him. He's in love with her, and he thinks she's holding out for your approval. I told him I'd pass the message along."

Ray had been pretending to choke himself since the word *boyfriend.*

"Did you hear me?" I asked. "Stop that."

"I heard you." He turned on the cushion to face forward again. "Mom really likes him too. It's all I hear about day and night. Pierce does this and Pierce says that."

I rubbed my palm on his shirtsleeve. "You know what I'm going to say now, right?"

He let his head fall forward. "If he makes her happy, I should get out of the way because I love her, and therefore I should want her to be happy."

"Yes."

Ray lifted his head and dropped it against the seatback. "What if he doesn't treat her right? What if it's all smoke and mirrors to woo her and nothing more?"

"What if she has a second chance at happiness?"

He looked at Libby. "She's such a pain."

Libby smiled. "She's not wrong."

I dished up some pizza and passed two plates down the row. "Let's eat and plan our fifty questions for Evan when he gets here."

"I love fifty questions," Ray said, biting into a stringy slice of double cheese. "It's literally my job."

My phone buzzed on the table, where I'd set it down to trade it for a plate of pizza. "It's Christopher," I said, reading the message. "He wants to see me. Hopefully this has nothing to do with the railings because I'm not going anywhere near that veranda again without them."

Ray set his plate aside and dusted his palms. "You didn't go anywhere near it the last time."

I felt my tongue swell at the memory.

"His truck was still there on my way over. It's kind of late for him to be working, isn't it?"

I put my pizza down and went to get my coat. "He says he's going to finish the inn by Christmas. That's only about five days away, so I guess he'll be there a lot between now and then."

"You want us to go with you?" Ray asked.

I took one look at Libby's shy smile, and I shook my head. "No, I'm fine. I'll try to be quick, but if I'm not back in half an hour, call Caroline. Christopher might be forcing me to choose grout colors for every backsplash and shower in the place."

Ray smiled. "Deal. Keep your phone in your hand for the walk over. It's dark out there."

Libby tucked her feet underneath her and hooked a perfect strawberry curl behind her ear. "Call if you need anything, even if you get there and decide you'd rather not walk back alone."

"Okay, but you can literally see the inn from my kitchen window. I'll never be out of sight if you want to watch."

Ray turned to Libby as I opened the door. "Want to watch?"

They headed for the kitchen.

"Will you look at those pictures of my mom with me?" Ray asked.

I stepped into the snow without hearing Libby's answer and followed the path I'd created on my last trip to the inn. My previous footprints were only partially filled with new snow, making my path only half as deep as the rest of the field.

The lights were on at the inn, and Christopher had placed a faux candle in every window, their electric dusk-to-dawn flames flickering as if they were truly made of fire.

Christopher's truck was in the drive just as Ray had said, and a mass of cleaning supplies cluttered the front porch. Apparently Christopher was the only business in town not using Merry Maids.

I slowed on the porch and called Caroline, a curious thought poking into my mind.

"Hey!" she answered on the first ring. "What are you doing?"

"I'm at the inn. Christopher needs me."

"Do you want me to meet you there?"

"I don't think so. I'm not sure what he wants yet, but I have a quick question for you. When was the last time Merry Maids cleaned Caroline's Cupcakes?"

"Hmm. I'd have to think about that." Her voice grew softer with each word. "Why?"

"I think I know how someone could have stolen the butcher knife without you seeing them."

"You think the maid took my knife?"

"She hated Derek," I said. "I saw the note she left you, and I spoke with her. She loathed him. Maybe she was his victim before he became hers."

Caroline was silent. "I don't think so," she said after a while. "Let me call her and see if anything unusual happened that day. I'll call you back."

"Okay. Thanks, Care." I put my phone in my pocket and let myself into the foyer. "Christopher?" I stomped snow off my boots and admired the progress. The inn was shaping up, slowly but surely.

A power tool growled upstairs, so I headed that way. The spindles and handrail had been installed, and they looked amazing. I ran my palm over the shiny polished wood. A tool belt and cell phone lay on the bottom step, both Christmas red. Both Christopher's.

"Christopher?" I called again, jogging up the steps toward the sound of power tools and busy hands.

My phone buzzed with an incoming text, and I pulled it out of my pocket, hoping Caroline had the answer I needed.

The message was from Ray. I slowed in the upstairs hallway, fear beating through my heart at the possibility that the killer could've attacked my home, aiming for me, but getting my friends instead.

I opened the text and stared at a picture of Pierce Lakemore kissing Ray's mom as they walked along a towpath outside of town. "Good grief," I muttered. I sent a message back, telling Ray to knock it off.

"Christopher?" I went to check the master bedroom where handrail and spindle samples had been set out on my last visit.

Ray sent an immediate response text.

Look at the men in the background.

I took another look at the photo, and beads of sweat broke across my forehead.

Beyond Pierce and Mrs. Griggs, a trio of men carrying rifles on their backs and covered in paint splatter, strutted into the parking lot outside The Gunslinger, a local paintball arena.

Our horse was shot with a paintball. And the face looking toward Ray's camera was Greg Pressey's.

A painful knot of panic twisted in my gut as I forwarded the photo to Evan.

"I'm sorry, Christopher," I called, shoving my phone back into my pocket. "I have to go."

Instinct raised the hairs on my arms and neck.

The home was still around me. No power tools. No sounds. No jolly contractor answering my calls. I had the sudden sensation that whoever was alone in the house with me *wasn't* a contractor.

My heart thundered painfully as a series of slow footfalls moved toward the bedroom.

I pressed my back to the far wall and prayed I was wrong.

A moment later, Greg Pressey appeared in the doorway, wearing a Santa suit minus the beard, and pointing a nail gun at my head.

Somewhere in the distance, an air compressor kicked on.

And I screamed.

Chapter
Twenty-Three

"Greg," I stammered. "What are you doing here?"

"Looking for you," he said casually, as if the nail gun in his hand was nothing more than a cup of tea. "Thank you for responding to my text so quickly."

"*Your* text?" My mind raced backward over the night. Christopher's phone and tool belt on the steps. His van in the driveway. "You used Christopher's phone to trick me," I whispered, throwing my gaze frantically around the room. "Where is he? How did you get his phone?"

"Is that really what you want to worry about right now?" Greg asked, taking a step toward me.

"Where is he?" I repeated, the seething anger in my words coming naturally as I imagined this lunatic hurting a nice old man. "What are you doing here? Do you even have a plan? My friends know where I am. They'll come looking if I'm not back soon. You can't get away with this."

"I don't plan to hang out and braid your hair, Miss White. In case the giant power tool in my hand is new to you, let me tell you about it. It shoots nails, and I'm going to put one through your skull. Quick and easy—then I can get out of town as planned."

I thrust my hands in front of me like a crossing guard. "Why don't we talk about this?"

My phone vibrated in my pocket, probably Caroline returning my call. The maid service had no doubt informed her that Greg Pressey stopped by Caroline's Cupcakes the last time they were in to clean. Gina from Merry Maids liked Greg. She'd told me he was charming. Gina would have let him in to say hello, and she would have been too distracted by her interest in him to see through the visit. He'd been there to pick up a murder weapon that couldn't be traced back to him.

And it almost wasn't.

"You framed my best friend for Derek's murder." I stuffed one hand into my pocket and swiped the screen before it stopped vibrating. I could only hope I'd accepted and not rejected the call. There was no way to tell.

"Smart, right?" he said. "I'd been dreaming of killing that jerk for months, and then I heard him fighting with that crazy ex of his on the phone. Instead of waiting around to catch him alone sometime, I had all the details I needed delivered right through his closed office door. I knew who he was taking to dinner, where they were going, how long they'd be gone. It was perfect. Then, I saw Gina's van outside that cupcake shop that blondie owns, and the stars aligned. Not only did I know everything I needed to ambush Derek when he dropped his date off, but suddenly I had a way to get my hands on something that belonged to her that I could use to kill him."

My stomach rolled. *Now who's the opportunistic jerk?* I

wondered. *Greg was willing to frame Caroline to get what he wanted*, and he was so proud of himself he couldn't even see the irony of becoming the kind of man he'd wanted so badly to kill.

"Gina loves me," he went on, as I tried to think of a way to avoid the railingless balcony. "She was thrilled I'd stopped by to ask her out. Once she was distracted, I grabbed a plastic service glove from beside the cupcake display and dropped the perfect murder weapon into one of those white pastry to-go bags. The knife even had the murderer's initials carved right into the handle." A wild Grinchy grin spread over his lips. "When I saw that clip of their fight air on the news the next morning, I thought I'd committed the perfect crime" His smile vanished. "Then, you showed up."

I slid my back along the wall, moving away from Greg in sync with every step he took forward, until my back hit the cool glass of the French doors. I had nowhere else to go.

Greg stopped moving. His gaze swept the large glass doors behind me, and his fierce expression curled into a venomous smile. "Even better. Why open another murder investigation that could lead back to me when a clumsy lady who knows too much could just take an accidental fall?"

I took a fast look over my shoulder on instinct and nearly collapsed. My gut fisted, and my cheeks flamed hot. The railing wasn't up yet. "No." I shook my head hard, and my teeth began to chatter. Fear and adrenaline flooded my system.

"Open the doors."

My vision blurred. I clamped a hand over my mouth to keep from being sick.

Greg shot a nail into the glass and it rained over the patio. Icy air whipped through the room. "This is your fault, you know," he said. "I tried to scare you away, but you kept coming back."

"I'm sorry," I told him. "I can't help myself. You don't have to kill me. I don't know anything. I have no idea why you killed Derek Waggoner. Your business is booming."

"I didn't want all that mess!" he snarled. "I wanted what I had, a top-of-the-line gym where people could get strong, feel good, and reach their full potential. I accepted his money for an expansion of the Ironman Training Center, not for some pansy spa and café. I never asked for that, and he never asked before he did it. He didn't ask before he did *anything*. He moved in on *my* dream, calling himself my partner and telling me he was the brains and I was the brawn, but he was ruining everything I'd worked for! I've spent my entire life training, saving, and planning to own and operate a place like Ironman. Then, Derek came along promising to help. Lies!" he snarled. "Derek was just looking for another way to be in the spotlight, to be featured in another article on how brilliant an investor he was, another way to get his face plastered everywhere. It was *my* gym, and suddenly I wasn't allowed an opinion. I hated it. I hated him!"

"Don't you think you're overreacting?" I asked. "You're making more money, drawing in more people. Why does it matter if there's a café and a spa?"

"Because," he said, a sudden look of fear in his eyes, "Derek sold his part of the business to Rick, and Rick's a pansy! I have no idea what will become of my training center. All I know is that he lost half of my business on a bad hand of poker, and I'm supposed to just get on board with that. He gambled, lost, and paid with my dream."

Gambling. I thought of all the other businesses Derek invested in, then sold quickly. Had he possibly lost those at poker too? Hadn't a big loss to Brian Ford become the catalyst for Derek announcing his affair with Nadia? "Derek had a gambling problem."

"No kidding," Greg said, moving into my personal space and forcing me through the gaping hole in my broken glass door.

"You don't have to do this," I begged again, sliding on shards of glass and the icy balcony floor. Hot tears spilled over my freshly frozen cheeks. "You should be running. You could be halfway to Florida by now. You're wasting precious time." I blinked pleading eyes at him, trying to sound sensible, hoping to reason with a lunatic.

"I'm tying up loose ends. You think the sheriff is just going to let this go because I leave town? No way. You'll tell him everything, and he'll put out a warrant for my arrest. He's dogged, like you." Greg's eyes stretched wide. "Are you working with him on this? Is that why you both kept coming back all week? First him. Then you. Him. You. Him." He tipped his head back and forth, nearly singing the last few words. "I haven't had time to get myself together. You guys are relentless. He's been on my back all week, digging through company financials and examining gym records. Anything he can get his hands on legally. He's there now. Been there all day, so I've been hiding out."

"He has?"

"Yeah, which is why I'm here. I've altered as many records as I can, covered the paper trail. The only thread left hanging is you."

"I'm not a thread," I said, wagging my head left and right. "I won't say a word. You can run." I pretended to lock my lips up and toss away the invisible key.

Greg frowned. "I was waiting for your redheaded friend to leave before I texted you, but instead another guy arrived. I don't have all night. I've gotta get this done now."

"Wait!" My frantic mind snapped into clarity. I just needed to buy some time. Ray and Libby would come looking for me once I'd been gone half an hour. "Why'd you put Derek in the candy dish?" I asked. "Seems like a lot of work for nothing."

Greg puckered his brow. "I did it to humiliate him," he said in a tone of disbelief, as if the detail should have been crystal clear. "He always wanted to be the envied rich guy, soaking up the spotlight. Well, I wonder how he feels knowing his last public appearance was in a big bowl of candy, beside a giant blinking Christmas tree, gawked at by hundreds of people?"

My hope sank. Greg was farther past the insanity line than I'd imagined. I glanced toward the open bedroom door at his back, praying Ray and Libby would soon appear.

Greg turned to look quickly in that direction as well. "No more talking. I've got things to figure out," he said. "It takes time to uproot a life, you know, and I don't even want to go. I want to stay and keep my gym. Maybe buy Rick out or find a way to work with him and keep things the way I want them. If not that, then I could sell my part to him, take the cash and open a new gym without a punk investor this time." He dug the fingers of his free hand into his hair and pulled. "I needed more time!"

I inched carefully back, staying out of his reach, hoping he wouldn't use the nail gun again. Searing winds threw my hair into my eyes and across my tear-stained cheeks.

He raised the gun again, and my limbs went rigid with fear. "Don't!"

A nail shot through my coat, tearing the tender skin of my arm beneath. "No!" The bolt of pain buckled my knees, forcing me to double over and slide on the glass and ice underfoot. "Please." I worked my body upright, arms flailing wide for balance.

Greg shot again, and the next nail ripped through my side, eliciting a deep scream of agony from my core.

I crumpled, landing on my backside with a sound thump. My hands reached helplessly for purchase on anything that would keep me on the exposed ledge, but there was no railing. Just hard-blowing wind and a psychopath with a nail gun stalking toward me in the night.

The compressor shut off inside, leaving us again in silence.

A groan rolled low and deep from within the home and sent my heart into a wild skitter. "Christopher!" I called.

Greg waved the nail gun at me. "Get up."

I turned onto my hands and knees and peered into the darkness below. Thanks to the slope of the land and our new rear patio, the near twenty-foot drop would end abruptly when I hit the concrete patio. A dumpster, much too far away, was the only other thing in sight, and it was filled with cast-off construction materials. Hope drained from my heart as the truth of the moment sank painfully in. My death would ruin the inn for my parents. Dad had waited decades for this place to become a reality, and my bullheaded behavior was about to steal it all away. The loss of their only child five days before Christmas would probably ruin the entire holiday for them. Maybe forever.

Fat tears fell from my burning eyes, freezing as they hit the icy floor beneath my palms.

"Up!" Greg screamed, stomping closer.

Something dark moved through the haze of twinkle lights along the patio. I squinted, trying to make sense of the strange, hunched shadow. Light glimmered off a familiar silver star, and a puff of renewed hope lit my night.

My sheriff's here.

Pain shot through my torso as Greg's boot connected with my ribs, throwing me off my hands and knees and onto my back. He loomed over me, nail gun aimed at my head. "Weak!"

The groan came again, and I thought of Caroline and how she'd hoped Christopher was really Santa Claus.

What a stupid way to waste my final thoughts.

Caroline had been so sure he was the real deal that she'd asked him for her freedom from this mess, and she'd told me I should've asked him for something too, but I hadn't.

Tears came hard and fast as Greg stepped back, preparing to kick me over the edge this time. "I want my parents to have a merry Christmas!" I screamed suddenly, desperate for the wish to come true, needing the words to be heard, even if it was just by an old carpenter that a friend thought looked like Kris Kringle.

"Shut up and die already." Greg swung his huge booted foot forward, connecting again with my battered torso.

I didn't scream this time. Instead, I held tight to my Christmas wish as I launched into a freefall over the balcony's edge.

Greg's fiery gaze would be the last thing I saw. And I hated him for it.

Chapter
Twenty-Four

"Holly!"

I woke to the frantic sound of my name exploding in the night, and the familiar, comforting scents of cologne and gingerbread pouring over me.

For one terrifying moment, I feared Evan had died too. I'd seen him in the shadows, running toward the inn. Had he lost his life trying to save mine? Had Greg Pressey turned the nail gun on him when he'd arrived?

"Evan?" I asked, not quite finding my voice.

"Please open your eyes," he whispered, his breath warm against my cheek.

I peeled my lids open, and Evan's handsome face hovered just above mine.

"She's awake!" He jerked upright and waved a hand into the air.

The earth began to move around me, shifting and crunching as other men and women in emergency medical uniforms came into view, working a spinal board beneath my back.

I strained to put my thoughts together as strangers tied me

to the board. A broad stream of light poured from the open French doors above us. "I fell," I said, half-unsure it was true.

"I know," Evan said.

The word *fell* wiggled in my head, not wrong, but not true. My fingers dug into the sleeve of Evan's coat as my final moments on the balcony returned in one powerful jolt. "Greg Pressey killed Derek," I said. "He told me. He tried to kill me too, and I think he hurt Christopher."

"Shh." Evan pried my fingers from his coat, then squeezed my hand gently. "We got him."

I fell back against the board in unparalleled relief. *Evan got him.*

"One, two, three," an unfamiliar voice counted.

The EMTs gave a tremendous heave, and I was floating up and out of the giant metal trash bin where I had apparently landed. Evan climbed over the edge behind me, and I gaped. "I was in the dumpster?"

Evan brushed himself off as he returned to my side. "Yeah."

Confusion prodded my addled mind as the reality before me clashed with what I'd seen from above.

The EMTs transferred me seamlessly to a waiting gurney. One shined a pen light into my eyes while another checked my vitals.

"You were lucky," Evan said, his voice low and gravelly. "If that dumpster hadn't been there to catch you . . ." He shook his head. "I don't want to think about what I'd be dealing with right now."

"It wasn't there," I said softly, working through the fuzzy memories in my mind. I'd seen the dumpster, too far away and filled with dangerous materials. "It wasn't on the patio. It was over there." I pointed to the edge of the inn. "It was filled with broken boards, discarded tiles, and pieces of railing. I couldn't have landed there. It's impossible." And even if I'd misjudged the distance in my fear and panic, I'd never have survived a fall onto all those things. Not from that height.

Evan stroked hair from my forehead. "It was just empty bags and boxes, some extra carpet padding and remnants. They saved your life."

"Impossible," I whispered. "It couldn't be." I turned my gaze to the platform where I'd been shoved to my death. Where I'd begged for my life. *And asked that my parents have a merry Christmas.*

"Vitals are good," A female voice said from somewhere behind me. "Looks like she's bleeding. I need to take a look at that. Better get her inside."

Evan popped the collar on his sheriff's coat and nodded. "Load her up."

I grabbed his hand as the gurney moved away. "Don't leave."

Evan turned his palm against mine and laced our fingers as he climbed smoothly into the ambulance behind me. "Never."

A line ran from the IV I hadn't felt being inserted to a bag swinging near Evan's face as the ambulance rolled away. Whatever had been put into my medicinal cocktail was already removing the sting of my side and arm where nails had pierced my skin. The female medic cut my jacket up the side and began to work on the bloody cut.

"Where's Christopher?" I asked. "I thought for sure Greg

had killed him, but he was alive when I fell. I heard him moaning in another room."

Evan raised his eyes to the woman dressing my wound.

She shrugged.

"Christopher?" he asked.

"The contractor. His van was in the driveway. He's got thin white hair and a beard, looks like Santa Claus."

Evan smiled. "I think you should rest. We'll sort everything else when you wake up."

My eyelids were too heavy to argue, and my mind too fatigued to fight.

*   *   *

I woke on the couch at my parents' house the next morning. I was stiff and sore, but alive and thrilled beyond measure for that. I winced at the tenderness of my side as I pushed myself upright. My injured arm gave out, refusing to hold my weight.

"Good morning, sweet baby girl," my mom cooed. She put a finger to her lips and cast her gaze around the room. "You're the first one up," she whispered.

I followed her line of sight to the sleeping faces before me. Every seat was full and a stretch of the carpet too. Cookie snored in Dad's recliner. Libby and Ray were out cold on the loveseat. Caroline was curled on an inflatable mattress beneath the window, and Evan was at my feet. Seated on the floor at the end of the couch, he'd rested one bent arm on the last cushion and tipped his head against it like a pillow.

He stirred, and I froze.

Mom tiptoed toward the kitchen. "I'll put on the coffee."

Dad moseyed in to kiss my head over the back of the couch. "How are you feeling, darling?"

"Amazing. I thought I died."

Guilt and regret colored his cheeks. "I'm so sorry I wasn't there for you," he said. "You were hurt and scared, being forced off a balcony right under our noses, and I'd had no idea. I could have stopped it."

"Dad." I twisted for a better look at him. "This wasn't your fault. I was the reason Greg came here. He said so."

Dad let out a ragged breath and pressed his palms against his eyes. His cheeks were damp with tears when he looked my way again. "I just keep thinking about how awful that was for you and what you must've been thinking out there on that ledge like that."

"I was thinking of you," I said, suddenly overcome with emotion. "I wanted you to have a merry Christmas."

Dad barked a humorless laugh, then bent over the couch back and wrapped me in one of his warm hugs. "I guess your wish came true because I've never been happier. You're safe, and Evan put the bad guy behind bars. I couldn't have asked for a merrier Christmas, except maybe one where you weren't in danger." He looked toward the front door. "Even the inn is finished. Not just *finished*. It's a masterpiece. I didn't believe the crew could finish by Christmas, and they came in ahead of schedule. It's unbelievable." He pulled his attention back to me. "You know, I won't blame you if you don't want to be the innkeeper now. There are a lot of bad memories there, and I'd understand your choice to stay away."

I gripped his big hand in mine and kissed the back of it. "I will do whatever helps you and Mom. Anytime. Anywhere. And for the record, I have no plans of letting a criminal steal all the amazing memories we're going to make at the inn."

A beam of pride opened Dad's smile. "That's my girl."

"Did you say the inn is a masterpiece?"

"Breakfast," Mom called from the kitchen doorway, and all around me, the room began to stir.

"I've got bacon and sausage, pancakes and eggs, plus a whole slew of sweet breads and fruit. Come on when you're ready."

Scents of everything good in the morning wafted over us, rousing the room to its feet. Dad lifted a finger. He'd be back with a full plate to finish our talk.

Mom delivered a cup of black coffee to me and patted my shoulder. "I put a little cinnamon in the grounds the way you like."

"Thank you."

Dad followed the bulk of my crew as they shuffled, yawning and stretching, eyes at half-mast, toward the promise of sustenance.

Cookie stayed in the recliner, clearly immune and never losing a beat with her snoring.

Evan lifted himself onto the couch beside me. "I'm sorry I didn't get there sooner last night. I know what your dad's feeling. I feel it too."

I rolled my eyes. "Yeah. You were out reviewing paperwork while I was cornering the killer for you," I teased.

Evan groaned. "I was in town trying to get a warrant to search Pressey's apartment all day, but finding one specific judge in this town at Christmas is tough. In the spring, I can find Judge Porter flyfishing. In the summer, he's boating. In the fall, he's hunting. I've never had to track him down at Christmas, so it took me awhile. Finally, I caught him at his granddaughter's little theatre performance of Scrooged, and I got to search the apartment. By the time I had everything I needed to arrest Pressey, I couldn't find him. He wasn't at home or at the gym, so I went, street by street, searching for his car. I should've known he'd be here. Trying to kill you."

"It's like you've learned nothing from last year." I laughed, and tears swam in my eyes. "Ah!" I gripped my side and tried not to laugh anymore.

Evan watched me for a long beat, then barked a short laugh of his own. "Imagine my surprise, as I'm trolling the town for Pressey, and I get a text photo from you. Instead of whatever I'd imagined it might be, it's an image of Ray's mom kissing some old guy on the towpath."

I laughed again and bit my lip against the pain. "You didn't like that?"

"I thought it was a prank that I didn't understand. Then I got a call from Caroline."

Caroline returned from the kitchen with a cup of coffee and sat on the floor where Evan had been. Her warm smile tugged at my heart. "I dialed Evan into our call."

The confusion must've been clear on my face because Evan attempted to explain.

"She called you in the middle of your confrontation with Pressey. You answered the call, but wouldn't answer her."

"The phone was in my pocket," I said, having forgotten about that. "I wasn't even sure if I answered it or hung up. What did you mean when you said the photo was Ray's mom instead of whatever you'd thought it could be? What did you think it could be?"

He smiled. "Once Caroline figured out what was going on, she dialed me in on a conference call."

Caroline's blue eyes were round with anxiety, as if she was experiencing the trauma all over again. "I couldn't hang up on you," she said, "but I needed help, so I got in my car and drove as fast as I could in your direction. I dialed Evan on my way so he'd know what I knew, which was that the maid let Greg into my shop the night Derek died. She said Greg came to ask her out, stayed a few minutes, then left and never called to make the plans she'd agreed to."

Mom reappeared with a mug of coffee for Evan.

"Thanks, Mrs. White." He took the cup and turned bright green eyes on me. "I ran every light getting here."

"He passed me," Caroline said. "I slowed down after that, but I kept coming. I knew you'd be okay once Evan got here, and you were."

Evan gave her a fist bump, then turned to watch Ray and Libby as they reentered the room. "Meanwhile, Ray had called dispatch to tell them about the photo you sent me, so I got those details over the radio, and it all made perfect sense."

Ray and Libby returned to the love seat with plates of food and wide smiles. They shared a high five. "Teamwork," Ray said, Libby nodding.

"I didn't need your evidence to arrest Pressey," Evan informed us, "but I will admit that you all did some pretty strong, unwanted, and unnecessary detective work."

"Is that right?" Libby asked.

Evan's eyes narrowed, and he pinned his little sister with a hard stare. "Don't take the compliment as encouragement to do anything like this again. I'm just giving credit where credit's due. You made an impressive effort. Your methods were a little roundabout and cockamamie at times, but you came to the same conclusion I did, and not too far behind me. It was weirdly impressive."

Libby dragged her gaze to meet mine. "I'm hearing *keep up the good work*. What about you?"

I laughed, and I didn't care that it hurt anymore.

Evan snapped a dirty look in my direction. "Don't ever do anything like it again. No more investigating anything. *Ever.* I don't care if you lose something, don't go looking for it. Just buy a new one."

The room rumbled low and steady with our laughter and Cookie's snores.

"What about Derek's car?" I asked. "Greg told me he'd tossed Derek into the candy bowl as a final humiliation, but I'm still not sure how Derek's car got to Caroline's house."

"Pressey followed Derek home after dinner," Evan said. "He knocked him out, then shoved him back into the car, leaving a little blood on the interior. He stabbed him at the murder site before dumping him in the candy bowl."

"I saw the smear on the glass," I said, recalling the strange mark I'd seen on the night of the tree-lighting ceremony.

"Afterward, he drove the car to Caroline's place and planted it as additional evidence against her," Evan said. "It was a solid plan."

Libby leaned forward on the loveseat. "What was with the Santa suit?" she said. "Is there some bylaw proclaiming that even the killers in this town have to be festive?"

Ray laughed.

I cringed, a memory flashing in my mind. "There's a promotional poster of Greg in the Santa coat and pants on the doors to his gym. He's wearing an Ironman Training Center T-shirt under the coat and promising to make everybody's holiday fitness wishes come true."

"Gross," Caroline said.

Everyone nodded.

"I saw it on my first trip to the gym," I said.

"The same day he followed you to the recycle center," Evan added.

My stomach rolled. "Greg was on to me before I'd even heard his name," I said. "How is that possible?"

"Easy," Evan said. "He was in town on reconnaissance the morning after Derek's body was removed from the peppermints. He was hoping to get a feel for public opinion on Caroline as a suspect when he overheard you asking the ladies at Oh! Fudge about Derek and his ex-girlfriend. By lunchtime, he'd heard you profess your intentions to prove the innocence of the woman he'd tried to frame for his crime, saw you hugging a local reporter and having coffee with the sheriff. Your connections and intentions didn't bode well."

I let my eyelids slide shut. "You told me someone was always listening."

"Pressey certainly was," Evan said. "He got all wound up about you during questioning. I was literally waiting to arrest him last night, and he still sees you as the one who foiled his perfect murder. He's not very happy you survived that fall."

"No kidding," I said, opening my eyes once more. "It was the third time he tried to kill me this week if you count the times I worked out in his gym."

Evan wrapped one strong arm around my shoulders and tucked me against the hard angle of his side.

I relaxed into the gesture and absorbed the beautiful scene around me. Our family tree twinkled brightly with decades of handmade ornaments and memories. The mantel was lined in boughs of holly and family stockings. The faces of everyone I loved most were all in one place. It really was a merry Christmas, even if Christmas was technically still a few days away.

Mom moved to my side, with a mug of hot cocoa, taking a seat on the arm of the couch.

I sat straighter, seeking her face. "Did Dad say Christopher finished the inn? What did he mean by that?"

She furrowed her narrow brows. "It means the inn is finished. That's all." Her eyes widened and sparkled. "The Hearth's kitchen is done too. The note said it was a Christmas gift from you." She lowered onto the cushion at my side, wiggling into the narrow space. "Honey, it's amazing. Wait until you see. I never could've planned something so beautiful. I can't understand how he did it in one night, but things were a mess at closing yesterday, then magnificent at dawn when I went to let my bridge club inside. They're going to handle things today so I can be here with you."

I shook her words around in my head, certain she was wrong. "The inn isn't finished. It's come a long way, but it's not finished."

Mom looked at Dad.

He angled his back to me. "She fell a long way," he whispered.

"I'm right here," I said, fast filling with a new kind of energy. "I did fall a long way, and for the record, I don't know how I landed in that dumpster because it wasn't underneath the balcony when I fell. It was at the edge of the inn, and it was filled with hard, scary-looking materials. I think the fact I'm sitting here is a real-life Christmas miracle. Think about it. The inn. The Hearth's kitchen. Two impossible missions accomplished in one night."

Everyone in the room traded wary glances and looked a little uncomfortable.

"You should rest," Mom said. "Or eat. What can I bring you to eat?"

I ignored her and turned back to Evan. "What happened to Christopher? Was he badly hurt when you found him?" Could he have been well enough to work through the night on both the inn and the Hearth?

Evan didn't answer. "I don't know Christopher."

Mom rubbed my arm. "He's gone now. It's what contractors do. He finished the job and left. I'm sure we'll get a final bill in the next thirty days."

"He was at the inn," I said. "Pressey used his phone to trick me into coming. I heard Christopher moaning in another room."

Evan's gaze sharpened on mine. "Did you see him?"

"No. I heard him." Hadn't I? I thought I'd heard someone.

"I saw his truck, tool belt, and phone." I paused. "I assumed they were his tool belt and phone." I checked the space around me for my phone. "I can show you the text Greg sent me from Christopher's number. Where's my phone?"

Evan gave a humorless laugh. "In about a thousand pieces on the patio behind the inn."

I raked frustrated fingers through my wild, unkempt hair. "There was no one else at the inn when you got there?" I asked. "No one? Did you check every room?"

Evan nodded. "Just Pressey inside and you out."

Mom handed me a snickerdoodle, and I bit into it hard, trying to think.

Had I imagined it all? The unfinished inn, the faraway dumpster and its contents, the moans from another room? My head began to thrum, and Mom tucked a pillow behind it. "Rest," she said. "We'll all be here when you wake up."

I tipped over, allowing her to guide my head onto the cushion where she'd been seated a moment before. She dragged a quilt over my body and tucked it in around me.

My lids drooped and my mind drifted, but I wasn't wrong or crazy. I'd made a wish in my final moment on that balcony, and I'd wanted it with all my heart. Then it had come true.

I knew exactly what had happened last night.

Greg Pressey had beaten up Santa Claus.

Chapter
Twenty-Five

A lot can change in a short period of time. That was the thought circling my mind all day on Christmas Eve as I worked with my mom and Cookie to get the new inn ready for a party. Normally, my folks had an open house policy for their home on Christmas Day, and locals would filter in and out as their schedules allowed. This year, the inn's completion had prompted a new tradition: Christmas Eve at the Inn. I'd sent digital invitations to everyone on our Reindeer Games mailing list once I'd felt a little better, and Mom had kept flyers on the counter at the Hearth for the last three days. Needless to say, we were expecting hordes of friendly faces.

"Do we need anything else?" Mom asked, fidgeting with the overflowing buffet tables.

Cookie guffawed. "If you put anything else on there, it's going to collapse from the weight."

Mom clucked her tongue, then headed to the kitchen, probably looking for something else to add to the buffet.

I made a slow circle around the lower level of the most

beautiful inn I'd ever entered, and tried to imagine how it could possibly be my new home. Every detail had been chosen specifically for this place and our farm, by me, by my best friend, and possibly by Santa. I smiled at the silliness and warmed at the possibilities of that.

However it had come to pass, my new reality was beyond perfection, and it was more than I'd ever dreamed of having. Only a few days ago, this place had been unfinished, and I was facing certain death. Now the inn looked like something off a holiday card, and I was thrilled to enjoy it.

It was strange how much had changed in a year. The things I took for granted now were brand new or nonexistent not so long ago. Evan was new to our town a year ago. Ray was new to me, though he remembered me from years before. I'd just reunited with Caroline last Christmas, but I couldn't imagine life without her today, and Libby had just popped into my life this month but already felt like family.

What a difference a little time could make.

The doorbell began to ring almost thirty minutes before the party was set to start, and it was still ringing regularly four hours later. "Merry Christmas!" I cheered, ushering the next set of guests inside. "Make yourselves at home. There's food and drinks in the kitchen and dining room. A group of carolers came in for cocoa and stayed in the living room if you'd like to join in on that." I giggled. "The rear patio is frozen over if you brought your ice skates, and the self-guided tour is going all night long at your leisure. Welcome to our inn!"

I'd made the speech so many times, it sounded false and rehearsed to my ears, but each set of newcomers looked equally thrilled by the information, and I wasn't joking about the carolers. It was freezing outside and toasty warm by our pretty fire.

I adjusted the material of my fitted red dress and hoped I looked inviting and festive. Not like a cat being forced into a sweater. Which was precisely how I felt anytime I traded casual clothes for fancy ones.

The door opened again, without my help this time, and Libby strode inside, escorted by her brother, the man who made me feel a little like the aforementioned cat. "Merry Christmas," I said. "Come on in. I'm glad you made it. I was starting to worry."

Libby gave her brother a pointed look, then hugged me and walked away.

"Where are you going?" he called after her.

"Wine."

I covered my mouth with one hand and laughed. "Something I should know?"

He looked into my eyes before nodding. "Yeah, but first this was stuck to the door."

Evan passed me a fancy red envelope addressed in impressive golden pen to Miss Holly White, and I opened it immediately.

Dearest Holly,

I hope you've found renewed hope and innumerable reasons to believe this Christmas.

May all your wishes come true.

Sincerely,
Christopher

I tapped the note from my possible Santa Claus against my palm and smiled. *Maybe my wishes were all coming true.*

I tucked the note back into the envelope and looked at Evan. "Are you going to tell me what's going on with you and your sister?"

"Yeah. But I need a drink first," Evan said.

"Cookie spiked the tea," I offered.

"Sold."

He took my hand in his as we moved through the crowded rooms, every face smiling, familiar, and loved. "You look beautiful tonight," he said, pausing to give me a long careful once-over.

"Thank you. The dress isn't too much?"

"The dress is fantastic." He lifted his gaze back to mine. "Would you rather be in jeans and a hoodie?"

"Yes."

"Another one of my favorite things about you." His smile was contagious, and I felt my cheeks warm as my own smile grew.

"I really like it here," he told me, raising a hand in greeting to guests who were strangers to him a year ago. "I might be a square peg in a town of round holes, but I don't care. It works."

"I think your edges are getting a little less pointy," I said, "but you wouldn't be you without them, so don't worry about that. Besides, I like you."

"I like you too," he said, smiling down at me.

"I wish Libby didn't like *him* quite so much," he added, filling a mug with tea from Cookie's special pot.

I tracked his gaze to Ray, laughing loudly in the corner with his sister. Libby had attached herself to his arm, and Ray looked extremely comfortable with it. Beside them, his mom and Pierce chatted animatedly.

"I guess Ray finally got on board with his mom's new boyfriend," I said.

"Fiancé," Evan corrected. "Apparently there's going to be a wedding at the covered bridge next Christmas."

"Oh really?" I let the shock open my mouth and widen my eyes.

Ray saw me staring and lifted his glass.

"I've always loved Christmas weddings," I told Evan, only partially as a jabbing reference to my own cancelled plans last year.

Evan gave a soft snicker, but the laugh didn't reach his eyes. "Ray invited Libby to be his guest. To a wedding. *Next year.*"

My jaw dropped impossibly lower. "She's staying?"

"Seems that way. Apparently a good Samaritan offered her a waitressing job at the Hearth."

I beamed. "She's accepting? This is amazing!"

Libby took notice of my expression and dragged Ray across the room to join us. "Did Evan tell you?"

"That you're staying? Yes!" I hugged her, then turned to Ray. "And your mom's getting married!" I hugged him. "The wedding party can stay at the inn. It will be perfect. Anything you need."

Ray looked less than enthused by talk of his mother's impending nuptials, but he offered me a one-armed hug anyway. "I just want her to be happy."

"You're a good man," I said. "Oh!" I dug into the pocket of

my white knit cardigan and fished out a gift for Libby. "I made this for you."

She unwrapped the little box slowly, looking as if no one had ever given her anything before. I made a mental note to talk to Evan about that later. Her face lit when she saw it. "Goodness!" She lifted the bracelet from the box, and Ray helped her put it on.

I'd strung a series of perfect glass beads, frosted to look like ice, and instead of adding the usual replica candy charm, I'd hung a tiny paintbrush from the center. "Even if you decide to become a cop," I said, "please don't give up your art. You're way too good to ever stop creating."

"A *what*?" Evan asked, his eyebrows reaching for his hairline "Did you say a cop?"

Libby laughed and threw her arms around me. "Thank you," she whispered, sounding more than a little choked up. "You think it's okay if I stay in Mistletoe? It feels really weird walking into a town where everyone is already friends. It's like I'm crashing a party."

"I know another guy who felt that way not long ago." I nudged Evan playfully. "I'll bet he can show you around if you'd like."

"She's not becoming a cop," he growled.

Libby smiled.

"Holly?" Caroline's voice carried over the crowd to my ears.

I spun toward the front door, where she was knocking snow from her boots and pulling a wagon of bakery boxes behind her. "Sorry, I got caught up at the shop taking cupcake orders. Business is booming," she said with a wide smile. "Thank you all for believing in me."

Guests moved to her side with heartfelt words of support and encouragement, and relieved her of her delicious burdens.

Caroline motioned me to come closer and reached for something still outside on the porch. "Guess what I found when I was locking up downtown?"

"Please don't say a box of peppermints."

"No, silly." She cocked her head. "Come on," she whispered.

Samantha Moss crept into view, carrying a card and a bottle of wine. "Merry Christmas."

I dashed to her side and pulled her into a hug. "Merry Christmas! I'm so glad you came."

"Thank you for the invitation," she said.

Samantha handed me the wine.

I gave Samantha another hug. "It's perfect. Thank you. I can't wait for you to give it to her."

A pleasant blush crossed her cheeks.

Locals and guests shuffled closer, recognizing Samantha from her shop and striking up conversations. Her fretful expression eased visibly with each new well-wisher, until I was sure she was truly glad she'd come.

"Excuse me. Pardon me." Cookie threaded her way through the crowd, dragging a big box full of calendars along at her heels. "My turn. My turn," she said, climbing onto a footstool in the parlor near Caroline. "I have something for everyone too," she said. "It's a gift from Theodore and myself to each of you. You can't eat it like those cupcakes, but he could." She climbed off the stool and filled her arms with copies of her Goat for All Seasons calendars, then handed them out to an eager crowd. "This one is free," she said, distributing the merchandise as quickly as her little arms could manage. "Next one's gonna cost ya!"

Evan tipped his head toward the back patio. "Let's get some air," he said. "We should talk before I change my mind."

My tummy flipped stupidly as I grabbed my coat and followed him into the night. "Is it the reason you and Libby were late?"

He gave a stiff nod and kept moving for several more paces.

A shiver rocked down my spine at the realization that whatever he was about to share wasn't good news. The look on his face said it was quite the opposite, and maybe there were more reasons for Libby's decision to stay in Mistletoe than a wedding invitation and a promise of employment.

Libby and Ray had beaten us outside. They walked the patio's perimeter, illuminated only by the starry sky and thousands of twinkle lights along the fence.

Evan slowed to a stop and turned his searching eyes on me. "Do you remember me telling you that Libby and Heather had a third roommate back in Boston? The one who told me Libby had taken off to look for Heather?"

"Yeah?"

"I got a call from Boston PD this afternoon. The roommate was found dead in the apartment. Preliminary evidence suggests it was an overdose, but my buddy on homicide says it was more likely murder. Her connection to Heather's death and Libby's renegade investigation of that death has made the third girl's overdose more than a little suspicious." He stuffed his hands into his pockets and blew out a long breath.

"Is there more?"

"The most recent searches on the roommate's computer were about my sister, and they were made *after* the girl's estimated time of death."

My gaze jumped to Libby and Ray in the distance. Despite the great outdoors around me, I couldn't seem to find enough oxygen. "They're coming here for her?" I asked, praying I was jumping to conclusions.

"Nah," Evan said. "Not yet anyway. I had her social media accounts scrubbed months ago, and there's no record of her coming here. I brought her in my car. She pays with cash. I got her a new phone, on my plan, in my name. I was careful not to leave a trail. It's hard for her, though. Not just the scary stuff, but leaving Boston. She loves Boston, and she barely brought any of her things when she came to town. She had no idea when she left how long she'd be gone, and we'd both assumed she'd be going home by now."

"She can't go back," I said, the sting of fear pinching my chest. "It's not worth the risk." She could get new things. Borrow my things. Keep my things. Whatever will keep her safe."

"That's what I said," Evan agreed. "Her old place, old friends, old hangouts are being watched. Everything she left behind is gone. She has to let it all go, at least until Boston PD gets this guy. Until then," he said, "my job will be to keep her safe. You understand?"

"Yes."

Evan watched his sister carefully as he spoke, and I could tell the words cost him something as he said them. "I might not be around as much for a while. I might go back and forth to Boston on my days off again, and I might not be able to open up about this case the way you want me to, but that doesn't mean I'm shutting you out. It only means I'm doing everything I know how to do to protect the people I care about."

"I understand."

"Good."

"I have one question," I said.

He groaned out a laugh. "Yeah?"

"How is it that you know where to find judges in every season?" I cast him a teasing look, and he smiled. "I mean, that's pretty impressive and exactly the kind of thing that would've made you nuts a year ago."

"I guess a lot can change in a year."

"No doubt," I agreed, leaning my weight into the long length of his side.

"Makes a guy wonder what next year will bring," he said.

"I know what you mean, but tonight's going to be hard to top."

Evan gave me a mischievous look, then dug into the deep pockets of his big coat. He brought out a small green bakery box with the Cookie Corner logo and a little plastic window.

"My favorite butter cookies," I said, opening the box immediately to choose two of the strawberry-filled delights. "You remembered." I set the box aside and handed him a cookie.

"What's important to you is important to me, White," he said. "You haven't figured that out yet?"

I turned my face away, smiling like a goofball into the

perfect cloudless night until the sound of sleigh bells rang in my ears. "Do you hear that?" I asked.

"What?" Evan stared down at me, a curious expression on his brow.

Behind him, a shooting star flew across the sky.